DEATH BLOWS

Screaming panic exploded around Sha'uri. She was buffeted by people frantically attempting to escape while she tried to bring her blast-lance around, to find some trace of the alien to aim for.

A flash of gleaming gold was the only warning Sha'uri received.

The cat-alien used his blast-lance as if it were a mere wooden staff, smashing it with numbing force against the weapon in her hands. The length of the golden quartz was torn from her grasp. Then her legs were scythed out from beneath her by another blow.

A sniper on the wall would have an excellent shot at this fellow right now, Sha'uri thought as the cat brought around his blast-lance to aim the simple, unadorned tip at her. *In fact, that's my only hope of surviving. . . .*

STARGATE™

RECONNAISSANCE

BILL McCAY

A ROC BOOK

ROC
Published by the Penguin Group
Penguin Putnam Inc., 375 Hudson Street,
New York, New York 10014, U.S.A.
Penguin Books Ltd, 27 Wrights Lane,
London W8 5TZ, England
Penguin Books Australia Ltd, Ringwood,
Victoria, Australia
Penguin Books Canada Ltd, 10 Alcorn Avenue,
Toronto, Ontario, Canada M4V 3B2
Penguin Books (N.Z.) Ltd, 182–190 Wairau Road,
Auckland 10, New Zealand

Penguin Books Ltd, Registered Offices:
Harmondsworth, Middlesex, England

First published by Roc, an imprint of Dutton NAL,
a member of Penguin Putnam Inc.

First Printing, May, 1998
10 9 8 7 6 5 4 3 2 1

CHAPTER 1
NEW BEGINNINGS

"I appreciate your taking the time to see me, Mrs. Jackson," the young historian said, setting up his cassette recorder on the desk.

"Sha'uri, Dr. Harris," the young woman replied. Her fine-boned features displayed an ideal of beauty that was old before Greek classicism had even been invented. For a second young Harris saw Nefertiti in jeans, a blouse, and a blue blazer.

He blinked, and Sha-uri smiled. She had more than enough experience with academic vagaries. "I've been reading about oral histories, and I think it's a good idea. Of course, my people had to live on oral traditions for millennia. You should be glad to be able to record and fix the tales in their original form."

She frowned in introspection. "Perhaps then you'd have known that the god Ra was history and not myth."

Harris knew that Sha'uri came from another world, one where the whole population served as slaves of the god-king Ra, her ancestors forced to emigrate to

Abydos more than eight thousand years ago. But he didn't care about ancient history. Sha'uri had married one of the original StarGate explorers, Dr. Daniel Jackson, who had been at the forefront of the major events of recent times. It was Sha'uri's story Harris wanted to hear.

"Have you met any of the Setim?" Sha'uri asked.

Harris shook his head. Like most people on Earth, he'd seen video footage of the bizarre aliens who had also come from that much larger universe opened by the StarGate. With their humanoid bodies and vaguely canine heads, they had probably been Ra's inspiration for the beast-headed gods he had foisted on humanity. Certainly, they had been the original model for the enigmatic Egyptian god Set.

Sha'uri sighed. "Then it's hard to explain to you what it was like to meet your people. It's prosaic enough now to speak of Colonel O'Neil, Daniel, and the others, just as I seem a rather prosaic translator here in this office. But when I first met them, they were literally outside of my frame of reference. Abydos was sealed off in a—a cultural vacuum—a vacuum that allowed only one worldview to exist."

She leaned toward Harris, spreading her hands. "It's very difficult to express. You talk of sports figures and well-known entertainers being as gods. We had the utter certainty that gods walked among us, that they ruled us. We had the stories of Ra's visits over thousands of years. When Ra's vicars came on inspection tours, they literally wielded divine powers.

"We had no conception of technology, much less what your people call high tech. When your explorers arrived, they found us quite comfortable with such things as matter-transmitters, starships, and energy weapons. But we had never seen the smaller, more mundane things you take for granted."

She laughed. "I've watched a couple of—I guess you'd call them 'jungle movies'—where the brave hero convinces the simple savages that he's a great wizard with his trusty lighter. It wasn't quite as ludicrous as that. But the fact is, Daniel and the others *were* aliens, because they did not fit the preconceptions which formed my culture. They were not more powerful—merely incomprehensible. Visitors from the StarGate wore linen kilts and golden jewelry that could change shape, turning into helmets that completely transformed the wearer's aspect. The Earthmen came in olive marine utilities and bearing weapons that, while they were impressive, were as nothing compared to the blast-lances carried by Ra's Horus guards."

Sha'uri paused. "Then there was the greatest difference. Unlike Ra's emissaries, your people treated mine like human beings. That was what caused all the other changes."

Harris let the tape run as Sha'uri described how circumstances had put her in the position of one of the leaders of humanity's second rebellion against Ra. How she'd almost died for her temerity, to be brought back to life by high technology stolen by

Daniel Jackson. How her rebellion had succeeded far beyond the revolt on Earth millennia ago, managing at last to kill Ra the Eternal.

Freedom did not rest easily on the former slaves of Abydos. Cultural problems had arisen even before the planet was attacked by the goddess Hathor, the would-be successor to the throne of Ra's empire. Although she'd been defeated and even lost a starship wrecked on Abydos, she wasn't finished with that world. Infiltrating through the StarGate, Hathor had orchestrated tensions between the various Abydan factions so that their fledgling government shattered when she counterattacked with a ground army through the cosmic portal.

"We'll never know whether the factions could have come to some sort of compromise for the sake of our people," Sha'uri said. "By the end of this battle Abydos had been destroyed."

Using the ancient amulet of Ra, ripped from Daniel Jackson's neck, Hathor had triggered the StarGate to take her to a hidden destination—the *Boat of a Million Years,* an enormous starship built by the predecessor alien race which had spawned Ra.

With this titanic weapon supporting her army, Hathor had driven back the expeditionary force from Earth to a defense perimeter around the pyramid that housed the Abydos StarGate. Sha'uri and several thousand refugees had joined the retreating Earthmen. Then the connection with Abydos had abruptly been snapped.

"The StarGate was constructed to constrain energies sufficient to spew people across a hundred thousand light-years," Sha'uri said. "Those energies were active at the moment the Abydos gateway was destroyed. Your physicists estimate that the resulting catastrophe would be enough to reshape the face of the planet." Her voice trembled slightly. "Humans couldn't survive."

Hathor had then turned her planet-killing starship on a year-long voyage toward Earth. Even with space-borne installations and with the help of an ancient planetary-defense network built by the Setim, the fight had gone against the Earth alliance—until Daniel Jackson had suggested using an experimental fine-tuning program to board the enemy vessel through its StarGate.

Hathor and her killer-ship had both been destroyed. Earth received a new batch of refugees— several hundred Setim—and gained the coordinates for thousands of StarGates located across the universe, downloaded from computers aboard the *Boat of a Million Years.*

"In the months since the orbital battle, your people won the right to establish the first extraterrestrial colony—" Harris began.

"The Ballas settlement will not be the first extraterrestrial colony," Sha'uri gently interrupted.

As the young historian looked at her, flustered, she asked, "What about Abydos, and the other worlds of Ra's empire? He seeded them with humans. Abydos may be gone, but the others still live out there. Ballas will be the first *free* colony established through the StarGate."

"I take your point," the red-faced Harris admitted. "But I was hoping you could explain why the Abydan people would take such a risk."

Sha-uri sighed. "I think it comes down to the fact that we Abydans grew up in what sociologists would call a traditional culture. Trying to adjust to your norms—especially American suburban culture, where most of us landed—has been a jarring experience."

"Culture shock," Harris said.

"Cultural survival," Sha'uri corrected. "Perhaps I can explain it best by referring to part of America's traditional culture—the Thanksgiving myth, a piece of your history I found . . . enlightening. Your Pilgrims originally tried exile in Europe—they moved to Holland. But they didn't like to see their children speaking Dutch, losing their identity. In the end they found it preferable to colonize the wilderness that became New England."

Sha'uri gave Harris an innocent smile. "Of course, the comparison isn't exact. The Pilgrims could always return to England, a choice we don't have with Abydos. And, of course, I don't believe the Dutch ever referred to the Pilgrims as 'rag-head refugees eating up all our welfare money.' "

The historian coughed in embarrassment. If his last

question had roused his subject to sarcasm, what could he expect with the next one?

"About your husband, Dr. Jackson. I understand there had been—er, trouble—between you, although several of the people I've interviewed suggested that a reconciliation might have taken place during the invasion crisis—"

Sha'uri's eyes grew decidedly hard. "Our troubles, as you euphemistically put it, stem from several sources, none of which are any of your concern."

Harris did not meet her eyes as she coldly went on. "As for our reconciliation, well, I overreacted when he volunteered for what appeared to be a suicide mission. After the emotion of the moment passed, we found ourselves at the same old impasse."

"So, ah, you can't tell me if Dr. Jackson will be going along to Ballas?" Harris asked, his face a bright pink.

"I might almost think you're from the *National Enquirer* instead of the Oral History Foundation," Sha'uri snapped. She forced herself to calmness. "I won't give you a 'no comment.' But I will say that you should ask Daniel himself."

"Useless, old-fashioned goddamn piece of crap!" Daniel Jackson muttered, staring at the somewhat grainy video image being relayed back from the planet Ballas.

Less than two years ago, he'd been deeply impressed

by the Mobile Analytical Laboratory Probe, nick-named the Maple Unit, when it became the first Earth-based StarGate explorer in eight thousand years or so.

But in the intervening time he'd been exposed to the technological wonders of Ra's empire. Compared to that yardstick, Maple's technology seemed like old-fashioned crap indeed.

Given the opportunity, Barbara Shore and her colleagues could have rigged up a probe that moved on antigravity, observed in several sections of the spectrum using scanners about the size of a pack of cards, and recorded the results on biomorphic golden quartz memory circuits. Excluding the power pack, the whole shebang would have been about the size of a basketball.

But no, they were stuck using this slow, obsolete behemoth, chugging and swaying on its miniature tank treads, unable to transmit a really clear picture. Because like everything else connected with the Ballas project, they had to do it on the cheap.

When he'd been asked to help pick out some worlds to be evaluated as possible colonies, Daniel had faced the list of thousands of coordinates and shrugged. There were just names and the enigmatic set of six settings. Astronomers had been unable to link them up to any known locations. Barbara Shore was just beginning to figure the cosmic directions. There was no way to rationally choose between any of them.

In the end, Daniel had been struck by a familiar name—Ballas. It was also the name of an extremely ancient site in Egypt—like Abydos and Nagada. Maybe Ra had named locations in his Earthly kingdom after planets of his race's domain.

Ballas had become first choice, and the Maple unit had been sent through, reporting back that the air was breathable, that the temperature wouldn't freeze or fry humans—and that things were pretty dark and fuzzy in the chamber of the Ballas StarGate.

"Sorta get used to anything, don't you?" Barbara Shore said in her West Texas drawl. "There was a time I'd have been peeing in my pants to see pictures from another world. They'd have been all over the Internet, and people'd be jamming phone lines to download 'em. Now?" She whistled a couple of bars from "Another Opening, Another Show."

Daniel stood aside to let her look at the monitor. Her stance as she bent forward did interesting things to the jade green coverall she wore.

"Yeah," Barbara said, "about as interesting as my Aunt Tillie's family videos. Although they usually get a bit more lighting . . ."

Suddenly, her eyes grew sharp, and she shouted a request to the technician operating the Maple. "Hey, Mitch! Swing it back a couple of degrees."

Daniel saw only a vague whitish heap. "What did you find?" he asked.

"That Aunt Tillie's family had better table manners, too—just barely," Barbara replied. "Can you try and focus in on that area?" she asked Mitch Storey.

The image improved—minutely.

"Guess it will need computer enhancement," Barbara muttered. "Or a little poking around when the scout team goes through."

"You still haven't told me what you're seeing," Daniel complained.

"Well, it's too small to be an elephant's graveyard, so I'd say it was a pile of bones in the corner there. Looks like some animal is denning in the StarGate chamber."

"Too bad the damned thing didn't attack the Maple," Daniel growled. "At least then we'd get a more interesting picture."

"I expect whatever it was skedaddled when the StarGate began to cycle," Barbara said. "I guess that settles one thing. Looks like Ra's empire never got around to settling here."

Daniel nodded. "Kasuf told me that his people were expected to make periodic visits just to sweep the place out. I don't think Ra's empire would have gone that far down on its housekeeping." He shrugged. "Well, we weren't really expecting inhabitants. When we got our hands on the StarGate list, we checked it with the old Setim computer in the Arabian desert. As of the Earth rebellion, Ra's people hadn't visited Ballas. That was one of the reasons it made the preliminary list."

Barbara glanced at him. "So when are you going?

They're sure to okay a scouting expedition if this old box of bolts doesn't blow up."

But Daniel only shook his head. "I'm not so sure I even want to go. It's not as though I'm irreplaceable. If they find any hieroglyphic inscriptions, there are hundreds of people who can translate the dialect now."

"I thought maybe you'd jump at the opportunity to give Sha'uri the advance preview."

He gave Barbara a dubious look, knowing she was a friend of Sha'uri's. "I'm sure there'll be lots of Abydan representation on the scouting party. She'll hear whatever she needs to know," he said, striving for coolness. "As for me—" He shrugged. "It just strikes me that there's not much point in my going if she doesn't want me there."

General West was still in his same Pentagon office, an unobtrusive location he'd chosen years before. Colonel Jack O'Neil shook his head as he walked down the long hallway. Some might think it an insult that the man who had saved the Earth should work in such obscurity.

Certainly, West's shadowy responsibilities hardly compared to running the machinery of Space Command, the former NORAD facilities inside Cheyenne Mountain, his former command. Everyone who ever had a score to settle with W. O. West had expected a piece of his hide after the Abydos debacle. There had even been congressional committees. Only Daniel Jackson's drum beating about an alien invasion had saved both West and O'Neil.

But the military establishment had been convinced that both men's careers were over. They'd been shunted into the preparedness program more as punishment than as a vote of confidence. If the rumored invasion didn't take place, they could be ridiculed and cashiered. In the extremely unlikely event that an alien spaceship did turn up, there would only be brief military embarrassment—because they'd all be dead.

West and O'Neil had beaten the odds—the invasion had come, and after great losses and considerable luck, they'd managed a victory. West didn't mind the status quo—or his cramped offices—but O'Neil was getting sick and tired of his new assignment.

The colonel was shown into West's office, saluted, and was offered a seat. "Now I know why Daniel Jackson has such a jaundiced view of talk shows." O'Neil shook his head as if trying to get a bad taste out of his mouth. "If that's really where Americans develop their opinions, we're turning into a nation of idiots."

"I don't watch the damned things," West admitted. "Is it really that bad?"

"The national chat fests were bad enough—being displayed like a prize pig late at night and early in the morning." O'Neil scowled. "Now they're booking me for the local programs. I'd rather face Hathor with a blast-lance than some of those microphone-armed harpies from 'Rise and Shine, Podunk!'"

Behind his desk, West spread his hands in a placating gesture. "You're this war's Schwarzkopf," he said. "Enjoy it while you can."

"Does that make you the new incarnation of Colin Powell?" O'Neil asked. "I know exactly what I am. I'm the generals' poster boy, out there to plaster over people's feelings that with the amount of warning we'd had, the military could have done much more."

"The Joint Chiefs approved all our strategy proposals," West said in a neutral voice.

"Yes, and Congress and the White House went along with all the expense, for just one reason. If they did nothing and Hathor and her spaceship appeared, they'd have probably been lynched before she got in range to kill them." The colonel looked at his superior. "Can you say that anyone in the high command gave unreserved support to what we were doing?"

"No," West admitted. "For the same reason why SDI never sparked that kind of backing. It was Star Wars stuff, science fiction. Fire a rifle, and you can see the result. A man is shot. Artillery and carpet bombing—they leave holes in the ground. Things start to get hazy once you get to ICBMs and nukes. Intellectually, the generals may comprehend the destructive forces involved, but it's not in the gut. We're losing the generation of officers who actually saw above-ground atomic tests, who felt the heat of the explosions from miles away."

The general gave O'Neil a mirthless smile. "It would be very instructive for some of the younger

17

generals to set off a bomb in front of them. Of course, the environmental lobby would scream. And the generals would probably complain that it was a cancer hazard."

"With respect, sir, but that sounds like the long way around to 'Yes, the military could have done more.' "

West's eyes were hooded as he regarded O'Neil. "Perhaps it is. I'd certainly admit that there's a perception of negative public opinion, and a need for rehabilitation of our image."

"So I'm the point man for our media blitz, sent out there to wave the flag and make it all better."

"You're the war hero, Colonel. It came down to you or Jackson—and you know what a loose cannon he can be."

"The longer I'm stuck with this duty, the more I sympathize with him," O'Neil said. He leaned forward. "Isn't there anything else I can be doing, sir?"

West chuckled. "Meaning, 'With your connections, can't you get me out of this shit job?' You don't know what you're asking, Colonel. Right now you're only in the shallow end of the pool. You might end up in the deep shit."

O'Neil simply looked at the general, who finally shrugged and spoke bluntly. "If you want to get out in the field, there's only one assignment available—and you'll do it with TV cameras up your wazoo. You can lead the recon team to Ballas. Take it or leave it."

CHAPTER 2
THROUGH THE
LOOKING-GLASS

The conference room was a familiar locale for Jack O'Neil. Neutral walls, a large table, and one of those plastic white boards where you can write with erasable color markers.

The board would also rise on tracks to reveal a window and the echoing chamber that housed Earth's StarGate. They were deep in the bowels of Creek Mountain, Colorado, at the foot of a silo which had once held the enormous bulk of a nuclear missile.

Once upon a time the place had been designated Ultimate Top Secret. Now it was worse than open school day. O'Neil had withdrawn his scouting team to the conference room not because there was any need for a last-minute briefing, but to escape the noise and confusion of a media circus in the making.

O'Neil had no intention of raising the board to see what was going on around the StarGate. Even through the shatterproof Plexiglas and the shielding bulk of the board itself, they could hear the clatter of media preparations under way.

He looked over the four men who'd accompany him through the StarGate and onto Ballas. All wore woodland camouflage BDUs. Three were recon marines. One was Abydan.

O'Neil glanced at his number two. Lieutenant Feretti always seemed as if his skin had been stretched just a shade too tight for the comfort of his frame or face. But he had held steady against some of the most bizarre enemies the U.S. Marines had ever encountered. And he was a survivor, one of the charmed fifty-seven percent who had first visited Abydos and returned.

Three of the seven members of that original expedition had been buried there—Freeman, Porro, and Roberts. O'Neil hoped for better odds on Ballas.

He didn't know the other two marines, Halloran and Fuentes. They were supposed to be newly minted experts in the art and science of exploring unknown worlds—graduates of the first class in that specialty.

Looking at the fresh-faced pair, sitting at attention, extra-heavy field packs full of instrumentation at their feet, O'Neil wondered what gaps they'd discover in the training curriculum. If for some reason they were stranded on Ballas, the team would have to depend on these two even for finding edible food. It wasn't a comforting thought.

The colonel hadn't spent much time with Halloran

and Fuentes. He now found himself wondering if the newbies had volunteered or been assigned. Had he gotten the reputation of a commander who lost too many troops? O'Neil hoped not. That kind of officer usually wound up with everybody saluting him in sniper territory. Again, not comforting.

He turned his attention to the Abydan who made up the final member of the team, sitting stiffly in even stiffer off-the-shelf BDUs. O'Neil had nothing against Imiseba, although the young man had been the center of considerable friction.

When West had finished reshuffling the deck and O'Neil found himself in command of the recon mission, he had also inherited plans that called for a couple of platoons of marines with a squad of Abydan militiamen. O'Neil had ruthlessly pared the expeditionary force to less than a corporal's guard, arguing that they weren't going there to establish permanent occupation, but just to certify by human observation that the square mile around the StarGate was free of major perils. A squad could do that job with less supplies while endangering far less men.

The politics had started almost at once. What about Abydan involvement? This was supposed to be their world—American marines implied an American claim. In the end Imiseba had been added to the complement as a "mission specialist." If they encountered any billboards or warning signs in ancient hieroglyphics, he'd read them.

In spite of being foisted on the team, Imiseba had

done his best to pull his weight, and for that O'Neil respected him. His was another fresh face, rising from the ranks of the warriors who'd accompanied the refugees. O'Neil didn't remember him from Skaara's initial crew of boy commandos. But then, so many of these young men had died along the way. . . .

When a knock sounded at the door, the colonel opened the door himself, and grinned when he saw Skaara. The young man wore Abydan robes, but of better quality than his mastadge-herding outfit—proper formal dress for the head of the Abydos militia.

"It's not too late, you know," O'Neil teased. "We could still fit you into our table of organization."

Skaara good-naturedly shook his head. "It's better for Imiseba to go. People have been accusing me of hogging all the fun."

Quite frankly, O'Neil would have preferred his young friend and protégé along on the expedition. But there had been considerably more political ferment about that among the refugee population than Skaara would talk about. People had been unwilling to risk one of the three established leaders in the community.

Smiling, Skaara turned to Imiseba, speaking to him in Abydan. O'Neil still had only a fragmentary grip on the language, but he did catch a traditional good-luck phrase.

"Shall we do this formally?" the colonel said with a nod to Feretti.

"Ten-HUT!" his number two brayed in his best drill-instructor voice.

Halloran and Fuentes leapt to attention. Imiseba joined them a second later. Feretti stood stiffly and saluted. "Ready for inspection, sir!"

Skaara, used to a more relaxed, personal style of leadership, rolled his eyes at O'Neil. But the Abydan leader kept a straight face as he walked down the short line. "Ready for anything, I hope?" he said in English.

Before Fuentes and Halloran could chant, "Sir, yes, sir!" O'Neil replied, "I hope so. I sincerely hope so."

He glanced at his watch. "Looks like it's time to get this show on the road."

After one last check of their weapons—safeties on for the StarGate transit—the scouts picked up their loads and headed out the door.

In the corridor outside, they found Daniel Jackson looking uncomfortable in a stylish blue suit. Privately, O'Neil knew Jackson called it his "medal suit." It had been purchased for all the formal thanksgiving celebrations since the defeat of Hathor's attack on Earth. Quite a few decorations had been pinned to the right lapel. Jackson would probably have been happier in his rumpled sports jacket and cords, but his staff had obviously insisted—after all, the President would be there.

The professor tugged at his collar. "Figured I'd

hide out from all the hoopla. It's like a madhouse out there."

"Aren't you supposed to be standing by the President?" O'Neil asked.

"Oh, please." Daniel rolled his eyes. "I sat beside the guy for supper a couple of times. Does that make him my permanent date?" He shrugged, as if trying to make his jacket sit more comfortably on his shoulders. "Besides, I don't fit in with all those movers and shakers."

"Why not?" the colonel asked. "You moved and shook things up enough so that we finally beat Hathor and her empire."

Daniel let out a quick bark of laughter. "Those were the days, huh? But I think I'm out of my league down there. I'm not ready for this brave new world we're facing. Half of the people on that dais are running for something. They just want their faces to appear in the television coverage. And the others . . ."

He shrugged again, but O'Neil didn't need words. If Daniel was up with the President, that meant he'd be hemmed in with the other dignitaries, including Kasuf . . . and Sha'uri.

They went down a flight of stairs and then faced the heavy metal blast-doors. Today the duty guards wore dress blues. O'Neil wondered what had been done to camouflage the defenses that perpetually ringed the StarGate.

A pair of Secret Service agents in dark suits intercepted the group. "Please step aside, sir, the President is arriving."

The scout team and friends were shunted off while the presidential phalanx made its entrance. O'Neil winced as music thumped and blared through the doorway. Where in heaven had they gotten a brass band? And why hadn't anybody given some consideration to the acoustics of a missile silo?

"Good God," Daniel muttered. "It's like the end of *The Wizard of Oz*, where they're supposed to go home in the balloon."

Certainly, it was a lot different from the first StarGate transit. Then the only spectators had been General West and a handful of military brass. The technicians had been working under a seal of top secrecy, imposed by Jack O'Neil himself.

Now cameramen pressed against one another, jockeying for the best shot. A packed dais backed the President.

"Sling weapons," O'Neil ordered his men. No sense coming in like a gang of terrorists. He stowed away the submachine gun he carried as a sidearm and nodded to Feretti.

"Ten-HUT!" the lieutenant said in a considerably more subdued voice.

"Break a leg," Jackson called.

O'Neil gave him a puzzled look, and the other man shrugged, responding with his usual wayward grin. "They tell me that's what theater people say before they go on stage. And, Colonel—"

25

"What?" O'Neil demanded.

"Let your people take off their packs when you get in place. You might as well be comfortable during the speechmaking."

Jackson's words were prophetic. They had to endure billows of hot air, from the President on down. O'Neil personally felt that if he heard one more cliché about opening doors and great opportunities, he'd puke on the concrete.

At last the ordeal ended, and the technicians got to work. All attention shifted to the gleaming torus of the StarGate. The alien quartz of the artifact attained an inner radiance under the heightened lighting for the TV cameras, giving the effect of a cyclopean golden brooch, or a diadem suddenly become translucent. The effect seemed somehow to diminish the ancient carvings on the concentric wheels, one set within the other.

Slowly, the inner wheel began to move. Ancient symbols, each representing a direction into space, passed under the seven gleaming shrouds that punctuated the sweep of the torus's outer circle. The first of the six symbols representing the cosmic zip code for Ballas stopped under its appropriate location. The seemingly solid scrollwork suddenly split in two, a chevron of gold clamping down to mark the sign.

The inner circle moved again, looking like some gargantuan combination lock spun by an invisible hand. As each part of the coordinate was locked in, the energy level in the room seemed to ratchet upward—a misperception, O'Neil knew.

It wasn't visceral excitement communicating among the viewers. It was a literal side effect of the energy focusing in the StarGate, first manifesting as a subsonic rumble, then finally becoming evident through the soles of the feet, increasing as each coordinate added its harmonic until any unsecured items in the silo began to vibrate. Even bedrock and concrete pre-stressed to stand the exhaust of a Titan II ICBM might be expected to quake at the gathering of energy enough to pierce the dark light-years.

But apparently, no one had briefed the President or his entourage about the physical effects of employing the StarGate technology. The chief executive's well-known features were briefly shaken out of their habitual "serious but friendly" expression into something more appealingly honest—fear.

Secret Service men clustered warily around, their hands slipping under their jackets.

The final symbol, the sun-and-pyramid sign representing the gateway's starting point—Earth—slid into place. Now the low-level rumble transformed into a glorious basso profundo note, sliding up the scale in time to the gasping breath of everyone in the room.

Strands of radiance, like slow-motion lightning bolts or questing tendrils of living light, projected from each of the locking points. They writhed across the fifteen-foot diameter of the torus, joining, expanding, until the whole circle was filled with an unearthly iridescence, a piece of jewelry on a god-like scale.

Energy suddenly spewed outward, then was just as suddenly sucked in the opposite direction in a vortex that moved to the music of the spheres. Then the gateway reached stasis, the torus holding a rippling field of energy that looked almost like the sun-dappled surface of a pond—except in this case the "pond" stood at right angles to the pull of gravity.

O'Neil had one brief glimpse of the president wiping his shaken features with a handkerchief. Then he had eyes only for his men and their objective.

Feretti went first, the other two marines about two strides behind him. Imiseba marched up to the rippling energy field, visibly braced himself, and stepped in.

Then it was O'Neil's turn. He headed up the ramp, calling a silent cadence to himself until he stood out-lined against the shimmer of the energy interface. He turned, executed a parade-ground salute, turned again, and stepped into the unknown.

Imiseba had been dazed and exhausted for his last transit through the StarGate—probably the best possible state for such a journey. He'd never distinguished himself as a rock smasher among his fellow miners—they considered him lazy. And in truth, he'd been one of the very last to pick up a stick and join Kasuf's quixotic—but ultimately effective—human-wave attack against planet-bound Horus guards.

He'd picked up a rifle from a dead U.S. infantryman during Hathor's first attack on Abydos, finding himself a member of the Abydan militia almost willynilly.

Imiseba had dabbled in factional politics after that. But he'd been lucky enough to be with Skaara the day Hathor made her second push, one of the handful armed with a blast-lance, part of the new cadre for a drastically diminished national militia struggling to keep the city of Nagada from being torn to pieces by the armed gangs in the streets.

Then the killer spaceship had appeared. After battling frenzied faction fighters and Horus guards, Imiseba had pulled every string he knew to escape the forlorn hope. Skaara had organized to cover the escape of as many noncombatant refugees as possible from the burning ruins of Nagada. A few guards accompanied the women, children, and old men.

Among them had been Imiseba.

He'd forgotten what it was like once he'd passed the energy lens at the Abydos portal. To be honest, most of that terrible night had been a blank for him.

Now he was reminded.

Traversing the wormhole between the two gateways offered the mental strain of experiencing dimensions which not only failed to adhere to standard human perceptual yardsticks, but actively threatened them with madness. But adding injury to insult, it also simulated the physical sensation of riding over Niagara Falls in a barrel.

Imiseba was twisted, pummeled, and barraged with geometry designed literally to blow his mind. No wonder the marines who'd survived the experience had christened the StarGate the "puke chute."

He landed hard on a stony floor, literally vomited forth from the Ballas StarGate—and retching up bile from his own outraged stomach. Now he knew why Colonel O'Neil had forbidden any meals before the transit.

Feretti was on his feet, his skin seemingly even more tightly stretched over his face but otherwise fully recovered. But then, Feretti was the veteran of numerous StarGate jumps.

Imiseba sucked in a lungful of cold, dusty air.

Halloran and Fuentes seemed at least as incapacitated as Imiseba—Halloran even worse so. He was spewing something—Imiseba quickly turned away. His nose got the smell of half-digested chocolate, and it was almost too much for his queasy stomach.

Apparently one of the marines had snacked on a candy bar.

O'Neil actually managed to land on his feet after he emerged, with only a brief stagger to indicate the violence of the arrival.

"As soon as you're finished," he told the miserable Halloran, "we'll establish a secure perimeter."

The young marine managed to pull himself up and appear reasonably presentable, rifle in hand.

Feretti was already shining a light into corners of the chamber where they found themselves.

He stopped at one corner. "Colonel!"

The hand lamp glowed off the whiteness of fresh bone. Some of them showed teeth marks.

"No surprise," Colonel O'Neil said. "That was suggested by the image analysts." He grinned, showing his own teeth in the lamplight. "At least dry bones means there've been no visitors in the recent past—although we do need to keep an eye out for whatever was living here."

They made their way up a series of passages which for Imiseba were familiar enough to traverse without any lights at all. Beyond the chamber of the StarGate was a wider pillared hallway, then the gently rising slope of the Grand Gallery.

Imiseba had often complained that he had been unfairly chosen for extra shifts of clean-up in the StarGate pyramid. The Abydan slave population had waged a never ending battle against wind-borne grit drifting on the passageway floors. And the gods forbid that any representative of Ra's empire should arrive and find the pavement covered in sand! Cleanup teams had been flogged and worse.

The colonel was correct that no visitors had come to Ballas in many years. If an imperial vicar had seen *these* floors, the unfortunates responsible for maintenance would have been ritually disemboweled, with their heads mounted on the nearest city walls.

Dirt had gathered inches deep on the stone pavement. Rivulets of rainwater had cut through the hard-packed, caked dust, leaving now dry cracks. Imiseba had seen the phenomenon in the streets of Nagada during the infrequent rainstorms which blew through that arid area. He never thought to see it indoors, however.

Then he noticed something else. With the side of his boot he scuffed through the dirt crust. "Colonel," he said. "The stone here—it's very different from what was used back home."

O'Neil knelt, unlimbering his own flash. The freshly unearthed stonework of the flooring showed almost like a gash through the dust. It was dark—almost black—and it gleamed as if coated with glass.

"Damned right," the colonel said. "This wasn't laid by hand. It was machine-made—cleated for traction, then vitrified."

He turned and rubbed a hand against the wall. Where the dust was brushed away, the stone gleamed as if newly hewn.

"I guess we're looking at the original design for Giza and the Abydos pyramid, without the decay," O'Neil said. "Interesting find, Imiseba."

They continued up the slope of the gallery, boots scuffing through the hard-packed earth underfoot. Apparently, there hadn't been any heavy rains in the recent past. The dirt was hard enough that it didn't show prints from whatever carnivore had been denning in the chamber of the StarGate.

And the scouts didn't spot any other traces of large animals, either.

At last they reached the tall, rectangular entrance

and stepped out onto the stone pediment. Here, weather had scarred the vitrified rock, and the pair of obelisks which had once flanked the entryway were now mere stubs.

Beyond was a very different vista from the sand dunes of Abydos—or, for that matter, of Egypt. The Ballas StarGate seemed to be located in a temperate upland. What might have been a roadway—now devolved to little more than a worn trail—wound down among a series of low hills. An orange star rode high in a nearly cloudless sky. Under its illumination the foliage seemed almost cinnamon-colored.

The air was cool, downright cold compared to the temperature at a similar time of day on Abydos. On the other hand, it wasn't as chill as the temperatures Imiseba had endured in the Colorado mountains.

The pyramid rose higher than the surrounding hills. Even the entrance provided a splendid vantage point, offering a glimpse of forest beyond the hilltops.

Imiseba smiled, drinking in the air like wine. Sharp, spicy smells wafted toward him from the trees. Ballas promised to be a pleasant world, a fertile world.

And it was his for the taking.

CHAPTER 3
DIFFERENCE OF OPINION

A week later, Imiseba's camouflage uniform had lost its crispness. There was a roughly mended line of tears along the left arm—a souvenir from his discovery that the dangling tendrils of the willow-like trees that grew on the hilltops were armed with thorns. A heavy beard had filled out his thin face. And his eyes shone with messianic fervor as he took a final moment to enjoy the now familiar landscape of hills and faraway forest.

He had a proprietary feeling for this world and wished to see it one last time without the polluting presence of the pushy Urt-men. Even when they tried to be polite, Imiseba tasted the bitter fruit of condescension.

Now he would have to turn his back on this new-found promised land and head into the darkness of the Grand Gallery. Even though they'd found no trace of the carnivores who had denned up in the pyramid—the creatures O'Neil began facetiously calling *hoodats*—the colonel had insisted that all members of the expedition remain armed.

So Imiseba would wend his way through the dimness with a rifle in his hand. His pack already awaited at the innermost hall, where the rest of the scouts had already gathered. Now he would have to trust himself to the rough, inhuman embrace of the StarGate, to return to the mechanical stinks and concrete sterility of Earth.

Even though he quailed at the thought of that bruising journey, Imiseba also felt a strange eagerness. Soon he would be with his people. And they would hear his words.

Daniel sighed as Barbara Shore strolled into his office, plumped down in the seat opposite his desk, and hooked a thumb at the portable TV on the credenza. "So, are you at least going to watch the away team's press conference?"

The return of the reconnaissance team had not been televised—a good idea, in Daniel's opinion. It was a hard enough job to get the public behind the idea of StarGate exploration without showing people being spit from the torus's maw like gobbets of tobacco juice being aimed at a spittoon.

Daniel had actually declined an invitation to attend the team's return. He had enough problems on his plate without devoting himself to more small talk with the President.

Barbara laughed when he told her as much. "I wouldn't want him in pinching distance," she said.

"I just don't want to be reminded that I'm an

American citizen for about the fifty-fifth time." Daniel shook his head. "You know that Gary Meyers and I are acting as head translators for the computer we dug out of the Rub al-Khali."

"Arabia's Empty Quarter—some of the worst desert in the world," Barbara said. "Those Setim bozos built well—the system was still working after almost ten thousand years."

"And it's giving useful answers." Daniel picked up a sheaf of papers. "Gary's out there now, getting input on designing a new generation of space shuttles using Ra's antigravity drive. They'll be sturdier and larger than the udajeets the Horus guards used to strafe us—and they may lead to an honest-to-God interplanetary spaceship."

Barbara grinned. "That's great!"

Daniel, however, was less than elated. "It would be—if it weren't for the ASAP attitude from NASA. The government is cracking the whip over everyone to get ships into space for salvage."

"I didn't think Hathor left much of our hardware up there to fix," Barbara said in bafflement.

"It's Hathor's hardware that everyone is after," Daniel replied grimly. "The *Boat of a Million Years* blew up, but something that big had to leave a few chunks floating around."

"Ah," Barbara began to understand. "And each of those chunks is solid quartzite."

Daniel nodded. "We're getting a golden quartz rush. Every developed country on Earth wants the stuff because of the virtually magical technology it unlocks."

"Tools," Barbara said. "Computer circuits . . ."

"Weapons," Daniel added flatly. "Fighter engines that make anything we've got now look like the Wright brothers. Think of a cruise missile with anti-gravity propulsion."

"Or a plain old blaster."

"People who wouldn't be bothered launching a centime's worth of payload to protect the planet are now desperate to get anything into orbit—as long as it's got a net." Daniel looked sick.

"And that's nothing compared to the crapola going on over the planetary defense system."

More than eight thousand years ago, the leaders of the alien Setim working for Ra had indentured all the survivors of their race to Ra in exchange for a virgin planet of their own to replace their ecologically ravaged home world. When it looked possible that he'd renege, the Setim wanted bargaining power. So they'd built a system of ground-based energy weapons, hidden installations literally girdling the Earth at seventy-two-degree intervals around both the Northern and Southern Hemispheres.

The aliens had hoped that their planetary defenses might be able to stand off Ra's star-traveling pyramidal palace. It might even help the downtrodden human majority.

But it was not to be. The Setim had been marched off to exile through the StarGate—exile on a planet in the midst of an ice age. The result had been outright rebellion . . . and genocide, at the hands of Hathor and the other golden-masked would-be gods promoted from Ra's human warriors.

At the time the planetary defense installations had been built, those humans who weren't Ra's direct subjects were tribes of hunter-gatherers just beginning to figure out that agriculture thing. But the nations that had come to be were now jostling one another over who had control of the remaining weapon sites.

The emplacements were generally under water— off the east coast of South America, below South Africa, in the middle of the Indian Ocean, off Australia's eastern coast, and in the South Pacific. In the Northern Hemisphere installations were located in the Western Mediterranean near Gibraltar, in the mountains of Pakistan, east of Japan, north of Hawaii, and off America's east coast. That last site was the one that had given the whole system away by blowing up an unmanned supply rocket launching from Cape Canaveral.

That incident showed that ancient technology wasn't foolproof—bugs in the installation's programming had led it to destroy numerous ships and planes over the years—creating the legend of the Bermuda Triangle. So, while erstwhile students of the occult and offbeat were reworking their theories, nations near the emplacements were trying to stretch marine boundaries to encompass these technological prizes.

"Several Japanese corporations are joining together to, ahem, 'salvage' the installations in the Pacific. South Africa is taking bids. France, Spain, and Britain are bickering over the Mediterranean site."

"Britain?" Barbara echoed in disbelief.

Daniel gave her a wry smile. "Gibraltar. And that's just the northern side. Now I hear that oil money is flowing to help Morocco and Algeria stake a claim. Pakistan is screaming in the U.N. that we somehow incited Hathor to smear the emplacement that was on their territory. At the very least, we dragged them into a war they hadn't declared."

He shook his head. "Most of the Third World is looking for a cut. They say the emplacements should be considered raw materials covered by the law of the sea they've been trying to get passed, and that the golden quartz from Abydos should be divided up according to the Outer Space treaty they've been pushing. Egypt, however, disagrees. Their ambassador wants the StarGate given back as a stolen cultural artifact. He doesn't want any Abydans, however—on the argument that the last thing the Middle East needs right now is a new faction."

Daniel looked as if his face hurt. "And we haven't even gotten to the wrangle over who owns the control station."

"Well, you found it, you imperialist, you," Barbara mocked.

"It ain't funny, Shore. Americans and Abydans deciphered the inscriptions that gave us a clue. We managed to track the defense center down in an ancient riverbed—"

"In the Arabian desert," Barbara interrupted. "And now Gary Meyers is there. So what's the story?"

"The desert there is so trackless, nobody is sure where the borders run," Daniel said in exasperation. "Besides the Saudis, Oman has put in a claim, and so has the exiled Hashemite royal house. It doesn't matter that they were thrown out of the country seventy years ago. Then there's the folks who want the U.N. to administer the master brain and use it to run the world."

"They should upgrade to Windows 95 before they start making stupid suggestions like that," Barbara said.

"It only gets better," Daniel went on. "The Setim have approached the World Court."

"Eight millennia is a long time to mislay a little item like a super-computer."

"Maybe," Daniel replied, "but it seems a couple of the ship survivors were involved in building the damned thing."

"Back after a long nap." Barbara gave Daniel an ironic look. "They may need another stint in suspended animation before the court cases get done."

"I think it's just a ploy to get some leverage in the colony stakes," Daniel said. "In the meantime—all I can say is that I don't envy Gary Meyers."

"In Saudi Arabia I wouldn't envy *anybody* named Meyers," Barbara exclaimed.

"He doesn't know who'll act as translators when the Abydans who've been helping out finally leave." Daniel settled back in his chair. "I'm hoping we can manage an orderly transition, moving in specially trained Egyptologists during the six months or so it will take to get the Abydos hegira organized."

"Speaking of which, don't you want to get the early report on the new planet?"

"We know the results already," Daniel said. "The air is breathable, and whatever was living near the StarGate didn't eat any of the team. That's really all they can report. We need cartographers, agronomists, a couple of ambitious bio-sciences types who'd like to become the first xenologists . . ."

"And publicity to get the great American people behind your effort," Barbara finished. "I really thought you'd have realized that by now."

"All right, all right," Daniel conceded. He went to the credenza—chipped plastic veneer—and turned on the television—battered plastic portable.

His timing was good. The official spokesman had just finished, and the three explorers appeared on the screen. They were physically in quarantine—something that Daniel had escaped in his time. But Jack O'Neil had given heart-chilling chapter and verse about the first away team's return to Earth. They'd been segregated to avoid the possibility of microlife contamination and forced to give a truly painful array of physical specimens. "I didn't know so much stuff could be coaxed out of one human body," was the way O'Neil had put it.

Apparently the returning heroes had been treated with more decorum than the clandestine explorers of Abydos. But from the wan expressions, they too had been wrung dry of specimens.

Questions were relayed from the briefing room to the quarantine area. The marines' responses were for the most part brief, barely going beyond the bare-bones report which had been faxed to Daniel earlier.

Then Imiseba began to speak.

"I have seen the world set aside for the people of Abydos," he said. "And it is a good world, verdant and full of growing things. It is different—both from the place of my birth and from Earth. But most important, Ballas is a planet that can become *home* for us Abydans, rather than a place where we must abide as . . . guests."

He looked into the camera with an expression of sincerity that would have made any televangelist jealous. "To my people—and to all our friends—I say, let us go *now* to Ballas. We must end the talking—and the planning. Now is the time to *do!*"

Almost immediately the phones began to ring.

Daniel had fought enough public-relations wars to identify the phenomenon. "Requests for comment," he said in disgust.

"What are you going to say?" Barbara asked as frantic staffers appeared in the doorway.

"Nothing," Daniel Jackson replied. "No comment," he amplified to the staff members who'd come for guidance. "The last thing we want is our message getting mixed up with *his*."

In his isolation quarters, Colonel Jack O'Neil debated turning in or one last shower to see if he could ease the aches and pains from his concentrated medical exam. The ringing phone decided him.

He picked up the extension, wondering who could possibly be calling. Not the press. That was one good thing about this quarantine. His wife, Sarah, could get through, of course, but she'd been visiting him in person—or rather, on the other side of a thick Plexiglas panel. The President had already made a congratulatory phone call. General West and a few military bigwigs had access, but knew better than to bother him.

"Do you know how much trouble I had getting this number?" a familiar voice demanded.

"Jackson," the colonel murmured. "Who else could it be?" Louder, he said, "Thank you for your good wishes."

"Right, yeah, I'm glad you're back," Daniel Jackson said almost in passing. "What the hell were you feeding Imiseba over there?"

"Maybe he overdosed on fresh air," O'Neil said dryly. "It's not as if we came into the press conference with scripts, you know. I had no idea what he was going to say."

"Well, I'm told that life is a continuing-education course." The Egyptologist took a deep breath over the phone. "Today I learned that in Ra's old language, 'Imiseba' apparently also means 'scumbag.' "

"Have you talked to the kid?"

"Are you joking?" Daniel demanded furiously. "He's busy on the phone, giving wall-to-wall interviews. I'm hiding out in a hotel to make this call because my office and apartment are both being swamped with calls for comment. I've spent a month trying to get this under way—and it should be months before we're ready to move. He gets on for five minutes, and everybody wants this colonization to start tomorrow, if not sooner."

"Yeah," O'Neil sympathized. "I know you've never stuck your foot in your mouth."

"Well, not in the last month or so," Daniel said defensively. "You guys had a week on Ballas. You didn't even get through the hills that surround the StarGate pyramid. We're not exactly sure what season it is there. And what about those animals that like to chew on bones? Did you see anything of them?"

"Jackson, we proved that people can breathe the air, and that there's a lot of nice real estate near the StarGate. Temperate, and a damned sight more comfortable that we found on our first expedition. I thought then that maybe Ra's people *liked* deserts, between Egypt and Abydos."

"It's easier to keep people in one place if you plop

them down in a river valley surrounded by desert," Daniel said tartly.

"I don't think you can fault Imiseba for being enthusiastic," O'Neil went on. "It's like Oklahoma when it was opened for settlement. Some people were so eager, they moved in before the official opening date—that's why it's called the Sooner state."

"If everybody jumps on Imiseba's band wagon, it will be more like Soonest," Daniel said grumpily. "I just don't want to set up a Donner party situation." He made a noise like a groan, sounding as tired as O'Neil felt. "Maybe I'm overreacting," he admitted. "Imiseba is just one voice out of several thousand. The leaders are another matter."

"Kasuf, Skaara . . . and Sha'uri," O'Neil said.

Daniel sounded briefly taken aback. "Right," he said. "Yeah. Right."

Sha'uri tried to relax in the armchair and listen to the radio. Instead, she heard the clicking of the answering machine and twitched. She had turned off the ringer on the phone, tired of its incessant bleating, and then had killed the volume on the message machine.

Since Imiseba had opened his mouth in front of the television cameras, Abydans from all over the country—and the world—had begun calling. Small groups staying in Denver to be closer to Creek Mountain, workers in Washington, groups planted in the suburbs of major cities, even the translators in

Saudi Arabia had called to hear her reaction—and to offer theirs. Overwhelmingly, their opinions sided with Imiseba.

And though few had actually said it, all of them expected her to carry the word and influence Daniel Jackson. That was one thing Sha'uri was determined not to do. She would not get close to Daniel until she was sure she would not repeat the embarrassing response she'd had at Creek Mountain. She'd reacted like the heroine of a trashy romance novel when Daniel had announced that he was going on that desperate, suicidal boarding mission.

"Not again," she promised herself, massaging her temples.

It had been a busy day, split between teaching and translating. Sha'uri was still the lead interpreter deciphering the mountains of technical hieroglyphics taken off the *Boat of a Million Years* and provided by the Setim computer in Arabia. She was also instructing a class full of eager Egyptologists in the nuances of ancient Egyptian as a living language with the addition of a large technical vocabulary.

Sha'uri was hard pressed to tell which side of the job was more exhausting. The hieroglyphics challenged her limited vocabulary and technical knowledge. She had gone from a muscle-powered technology to one of molecular circuitry.

As for the students . . . she wondered if she had ever been that young, even though some of them were physically older than she was. These scholars had grown up in such an insulated, *privileged* life. It was something she had never known, even as the daughter of an Elder of Nagada.

A slave was a slave. Even the daughter of a head slave was subject to the whims—and the lusts—of whatever emissaries Ra might send to Abydos. In fact, she had been particularly vulnerable, for she had been expected to serve the visitors.

She pushed the memories from her consciousness, her fingers trying to rub away an incipient headache.

Then the doorbell rang.

Sha'uri had relished the privacy and space when she'd moved into the small house in suburban Maryland. A short walk from the Metro station, an easy commute to her Washington office—and best of all, anonymity. With Barbara Shore to guide her, Sha'uri had been pleasant but unforthcoming with the neighbors.

She'd surprised a couple of speculative looks on people's faces after the exploration team had gone to Ballas—belatedly she'd realized that she must have been featured in the television coverage. But she had managed to avoid the welcome wagon, the civic council, and the neighborhood watch.

So who wanted to speak with her in the middle of the evening?

Sighing, she tried to push her hair into some order and headed for the door. Halfway there, she stopped, thinking of the Beretta M9 pistol in an upstairs dresser drawer—a souvenir of past wars. Sha'uri debated getting it. How ironic if she became the victim of some urban predator. Anonymity had its downside.

"Who is it?" she called toward the doorway.

"Please," the response came in Abydan.

With another sigh Sha'uri went to the door. She opened it to find herself confronting a delegation, young faces and old. Some of those kids should be in bed, or at least busy with homework. One of the women looked like her grandmother.

A face she vaguely recalled from Daniel's literacy program on Abydos leaned forward. "We tried to talk on the telephone," the young woman said, "but all we got was a machine. We decided this was too important just to leave a message. Mother knew that you lived nearby, so . . ."

The young woman took a deep breath. "We all heard the words of Imiseba. If this new world is as fair as he says, why are we not going immediately? Thus we come to ask you, and through you, to ask Kasuf, Skaara . . . and Danyer."

Danyer—the Abydan pronunciation of Daniel's name.

Yet again Sha'uri sighed.

It seemed there would be no peace since Imiseba had spoken out.

CHAPTER 4
HAT IN HAND

"I don't know whether it's a fault of my character or my upbringing," Daniel Jackson often said to anybody who would listen, "but I don't have what it takes to make an organization man. Hell for me would be unending administrative chores."

To save the Earth, he had put himself through a year of that hell, organizing the Abydos Foundation, cutting licensing deals, even working for the government in General West's Office of Bright Ideas.

True hell, however, was discovering that you couldn't stop the machinery once you'd gotten it started. Thus he found himself in the Abydos Foundation's shabby conference room, chairing an emergency policy meeting.

"We've spent a week trying to ignore Imiseba and his Soonest faction," Daniel told the assemblage. "And I appreciate your loyalty, even if all of you didn't agree with what we were doing."

The Earth-born staffers carefully didn't look at

their Abydan counterparts, who in turn uneasily refused to meet Daniel's eyes.

"Okay," Daniel said gently. "As plans go, it was a disaster. The media keeps offering more coverage on Imiseba's let's-get-going crusade, and the Abydan leadership—you know who they are—have been complaining to me that they're looking a bit foolish. More important, they've been talking to the people—and the majority of Abydans want off this planet as soon as possible. Since these are the people we're trying to help, that means an immediate shift in policy."

The off-world contingent looked at him in surprise, while the Urt-man staffers sat very still.

I can't blame them, Daniel thought. What I'm announcing here is the end of their jobs.

"I'm not the uncrowned king of Abydos, you know," he told the refugee foundation members. "If this is what the people want, we have to do our best by them." He sighed. "Which means accelerating all our colonization plans. Can we do six months' work in as many weeks?"

Daniel turned to Dave Freck, the foundation's head bean counter. "I'd hoped to use that time to accumulate funds as well . . ."

Freck shook his head. "I'm afraid the latest income projections are even worse than I'd first estimated," he said. "Licensing royalties from the toy mastadges are sufficient to keep up the stipends for the Abydans without jobs, but it's a shrinking pie. Christmas was a long time ago. The manufacturers are on to the next craze."

"So the plush mastadges are in the same limbo as Tickle Me Elmo," Daniel said heavily. "And they were our main money makers."

"Bookings for most of our speakers have been flat—we are no longer alien enough," Ankhere said with some irony. She'd been one of the refugee success stories, learning English without the help of Daniel's Abydan classes, and rising to a responsible position in the Abydos Foundation—running the speakers bureau.

She glanced at Daniel. "We had a great deal of interest in you, Daniel, after the fight on the *Boat of a Million Years.* But you declined any bookings, since you wanted time free for the colonization planning. Now—" She shrugged eloquently.

"As far as Hathor's invasion goes, it's stale news—and so am I," Daniel finished for her. "Nobody wants to hear old war stories. Now it's the colonization controversy that's hot. But the call there is for free sound bites to the news organizations."

"We are getting quite a few requests for Imiseba," Ankhere pointed out with a sidewise glance at the boss.

Daniel was silent. That name again!

He took a deep breath. "Then use him—book him for any place that will pay."

"One man isn't going to raise enough to pay for supplies and tools," Dave Freck objected. "Not even

51

if he hits every chamber of commerce in America during the next six weeks."

"And the kind of money we need can't be raised with bake sales," Daniel grimly agreed.

"We've already looked into the idea of a public appeal." Eve Patric had inherited the p.r. function after the foundation had ended its relationship with the powerful—and expensive—firm Daniel had used to whip up support for the defensive battle against Hathor. "Frankly, people are still busy celebrating. They feel they've got better things to spend their money on."

"Preparing a stock offering would take too much time," Freck said. "We might approach some people for venture capital, but I don't know that they'd go along for the long haul. And then there are banks . . . but that raises the question of collateral."

"And control," Ankhere warned. "Our people suffered a lot to get even this far, sniffing at a new world. They won't want a bunch of . . . outsiders telling them what to do."

The word "Urt-men" hung in the air, even if she hadn't said it.

Daniel stood, ending the back-and-forth. "Then I guess I'll just have to do what everyone with a bright idea and not much money does. I'll talk to my Uncle Sam."

Eve Patric shook her head. "Somehow, I don't see you getting on the phone with your congressman."

Daniel gave her a lopsided smile. "Congress would

take too long. I'll try my connections with the secret government and see what they can do."

For General West, the spoils of war had been a larger, more plush office in the E-Ring of the Pentagon. That meant he was actually in the outer wall of the structure, where sunlight might come in. He'd also gotten a new job, figuring the logistics of moving troops through the StarGate—infiltration teams, rapid deployment forces, full divisions. Some days, however, he had to admit to missing the end of his connection with the shadowy world of intelligence.

All the more when he found himself short on information he'd normally have seen as a matter of course.

Like this surprise appointment with Daniel Jackson. Their relationship was not one that lent itself to social calls. West had started out with scorn for the cocky academic with the fumbling approach. Even though Jackson had unlocked the StarGate, it had been like listening to a lecture from the Nutty Professor. When Jackson had stayed on Abydos, he'd gone from annoyance to a problem—then become an out-and-out antagonist. The man's foray into Abydan politics had been simply painful, ending with Hathor's disastrous attack.

But it had been Jackson who first identified the threat to Earth itself, and he had worked tirelessly to mobilize public opinion—coincidentally stepping in to help West against a Senate select committee out to lift the general's scalp. The Egyptologist had even worked on West's staff during the emergency, fielding suggestions from the lunatic fringe—and using them to uncover the ancient defense system left by those talking coyote aliens. . . .

West had come to a grudging respect of the nutty professor. He knew Jackson was brilliant, wayward, stubborn . . . and the quintessential loose cannon.

The question was, what did he want in this office at this time?

"Well, Dr. Jackson, this is unexpected," West said, rising from behind his desk.

"But not an unexpected *pleasure*." Jackson nodded, apparently not offended. "Good. At least we know where we stand. You want to know why I'm here. The answer is simple. Beggars can't be choosers."

"I'd have thought you'd be busy with this Ballas project—" West began, but Jackson cut him off.

"You don't have to be a master spy to know how many people are yelling for us to leave for Ballas next Tuesday, if not before. An occasional glance at a newspaper or the television would have told you that."

He scowled at the general. "If my people break their necks, we might be able to arrange it in six weeks. But we may be stuck here for six months—or we may not be able to do it at all. We're running out of money, General. When our pile came in, we used it in all the wrong ways . . . warning people about Hathor and the *Boat of a Million Years*, getting them behind the space-shield project."

"I'm sorry to hear that the Abydos Foundation is having financial problems," West replied. "But I don't see what I can do to help."

"I'm not going to circle around this with Noel Coward cocktail chatter," Daniel Jackson said. "Here it is, straight out. You can talk to your connections and shake the money tree. I supported your projects and even worked for you. This country is enjoying a quantum jump in technology thanks to all the stuff Abydan interpreters have translated for you. I'm not going to mention the thousands of Abydans who got killed fighting beside Colonel O'Neil—or the ones who died when their planet was blown up. But even in this last little skirmish, it was Abydans who dug up the planetary defense controls in Arabia—and Abydans who died defending it against the terrorist attack."

He leaned over the general's desk. "You *owe* us for what we've done for the country—and for you."

West leaned back against the headrest of his chair. "Well, it looks as if your foray into politics wasn't all wasted. At least you recognize the concept of quid pro quo—the problem is, you've pretty well blown your quid already."

"I also learned to detect when someone is trying to blow smoke up various body cavities," Jackson snarled in reply. "Maybe you wish you could slam the StarGate shut, but you don't have a choice now.

Pardon the cliché, but the whole world is watching. Everyone is gung-ho for colonization. Think of the political ramifications if the Ballas project falls on its face now—just because we're short a couple of bucks."

"Somehow, I think the shortfall may turn out to be more than pocket change," West said dryly.

Jackson produced papers from a battered satchel. "Here's our budget for a bare-bones colony. I defy you to cut the costs any better."

The general ran an eye over the spreadsheet print-outs. "I'll bring some staff in to go over these," he said grudgingly. "Then I'll have a talk with a couple of people. But I can't promise anything."

"This from a man who managed to make an entire army heavy battalion vanish off the globe," Daniel mocked.

"Those were the good old days," West came back at him. "Before we all became celebrities."

If General West's office was plush by military standards, Senator Robert E. Ashby's workplace would necessarily be rated as sumptuous. But then, Ashby didn't have to save the world. He'd merely had to convince his constituents to reelect him over the past decades, and tenure had taken care of the rest. The man had been in the Senate longer than West had been alive. Seniority had brought him power, prestige, and the plum office. Generous supporters provided the antique furnishings—though they might have been brand-new when Bob Ashby had been young.

He'd always been a loud Main Streeter, implacably opposed to Wall Street—unless there was commercial or political profit to be made. His foreign policy was downright Rooseveltian—Teddy Roosevelt, redolent of big sticks and gunboat diplomacy. On social issues Ashby consistently harked back to a more "civil" time.

Like many, West wondered if that meant the Civil War. Certainly, Ashby preferred an era when troublesome ethnic and societal groups knew their respective places.

Ashby was *not* the man West would have sought out to get help for the Abydans. He'd initially approached Senator Kerrigan, a Vietnam veteran serving on the Armed Services Committee. But Kerrigan had referred him to his subcommittee's senior member, Senator Foyle, and that old Washington warrior had in turn palmed off Ashby on him.

It wasn't the first time they'd met. Back in the Reagan days, Ashby had pushed his way onto the Intelligence Oversight Committee, loudly demanding that something be done to "straighten out those banana republics down there."

Remembering Ashby's comments about "dagos" didn't encourage the general's hopes of getting any aid. But he didn't know where else to go. His staff had crunched Daniel Jackson's numbers, and had to admit that there was no fat in his proposed budget.

There wasn't enough money to make it work, either. And with the new political winds seeming to gather around Ashby and his ilk, West wasn't sure that the government would be forthcoming.

The senator sat behind his gleaming cherrywood desk like a fat old bear in its den. The look he aimed over the half glasses perched on his bulbous nose was filled with down-home benevolence.

But Ashby's raspy voice quickly dissipated that impression.

"So what's this I hear about you transferring to Heath and Human Services, General?"

"Senator?" was all West could ask.

"You know, you bleeding-heart welfare people—I hear you want to give away a shit-pot full of money to a buncha gah-damn *aliens* who don't even belong here!"

West strove to keep his voice on an even keel. "Sir, the Abydan refugees didn't have much choice about coming here—and there's no way they can go back where they came from."

Ashby made a grumpy noise at that.

"The Ballas colony will give them somewhere to go. My staff says they've worked up a plan that's remarkable for its fiscal prudence—but they don't have the cash to make it work."

"So they come crying to Uncle Sam," Ashby snapped. "What next? Demonstrations from these gah-damned rag-heads till they get what they want?"

"A lot of their people fought and died alongside American troops," West pointed out.

"Too bad those troops were in places they never should have been," Ashby growled. Rheumy eyes fixed West with a cold look over the ridiculous half glasses. "I know you as a pretty freewheeling kind of spook meister. Sort of surprising that you get religion about Congressional approval all of a sudden." The senator displayed old dentures in a wide grin. "Or maybe you're just too outstanding a target these days."

West produced a sheaf of papers. "This is the proposed budget—"

"Bad idea giving money to people who decide they don't like it here," Ashby muttered, but he reseated his glasses and began looking through. "I don't want to hear my people screaming about wasted funds. Suppose we give 'em aid in kind?"

He ran a finger along the listed expenses. "Food. Shelter. You military boys still got lots of tents, and I bet there are still warehouses full of MREs from Desert Storm. Suppose we decommission some of them—give 'em to this Jackson feller and his towel-headed friends? You might even find some weapons for 'em. A man in strange territory can always use a gun. Be creative. Call it a pilot project. They're gonna need help knocking down trees and such-like. Get the Corps of Engineers off its fat butt and helping."

Ashby cut off with a fierce look at West. "Just get 'em out of here. We don't need any furriners sitting around sucking government tit." The senator jerked his thumb in a vague, "up thataway" gesture.

"One good thing 'bout this. Once we got 'em wherever the hell they're going, they ain't our responsibility anymore."

Daniel Jackson sat on the sprung sofa in the living room of his apartment. The place was cheap, decorated in the same secondhand style as his office. It was merely a place to eat, sleep, and hold his few belongings—just a stopover between hotel rooms. Daniel hadn't had a home since the cramped, cracked-ceilinged hole in the wall he'd shared with Sha'uri.

A tray of microwaved something or other had cooled into a gelid mass on the plastic plate. He glanced at his watch, then at the thirteen-inch TV set on top of a plyboard and cinder-block bookshelf. Another hand-me-down, the set had lost the metal strip that identified the channels on its push-button console. He had to jam a toothpick to keep in the button he pushed when he chose a channel.

It was almost time for another heaping helping of reality programming, and the newspaper television guide only said, "To be announced."

Daniel had come to dread these broadcast magazines. The syndicated ones weren't too bad, concentrating as they did on scandals and show business. But the network shows, the so-called serious ones with their fifteen-minute so-called "in-depth reports," they worried him. As if anyone could explain the eight-thousand-year history of the Abydans under Ra's empire—or even the events of the past three years—in the amount of time it took to eat a sandwich.

Several shows had attempted to present the Abydans, and their eagerness for the Ballas colony, in a handful of sound bites between commercial breaks. And as such a simplistic approach required, the newspeople had searched for a villain in the piece. Of course, they'd found one.

Daniel Jackson.

Daniel had declined several "invitations" to be dragged over the inquisitional coals by concerned anchorpeople. He'd had the Abydos Foundation announce that everything possible was being done to step up the pace of colonization preparations. His people were trying every ploy they could think of to get equipment for the expedition.

Most recently, they'd been approaching outdoorsman-type companies, touting the promotional aspects of donating tents, lamps, stoves, or clothing. They'd be able to claim credit in taming Ballas!

The response had been disappointing. Most companies would have considered helping to outfit an expedition of four, or six, or ten. But providing for several thousand was deemed an unacceptable expense.

So Daniel had been reduced to hoping for someone famous to die, or for a major political figure to be

found with his hand in the cookie jar or up somebody's skirt. But no other ten-day wonders had
arisen to distract the media and the audiences.

The pressure on him had only grown.

He wasn't the only one feeling the heat, of course.
Kasuf, Skaara, and the traditional Abydan leadership
were also being pressed to add their voices to the
debate. For the time being, Daniel had persuaded
them not to add fuel to the fire—at least until he got
a firm response from General West.

Of course, his request hadn't silenced Imiseba, or
the extremely vocal clique of supporters for the Soonest position. Nothing short of another nuclear blast
could silence them.

Daniel's stomach tightened as he recognized the
cinnamon-foliaged landscape that appeared on the
screen when he fired up the TV. It was Ballas, right
enough. The blasted piece of videotape was one of
the few views of the new planet that had been released. Then the scenery faded away, and a con-
cerned-looking newsperson popped up onscreen,
wondering out loud about the foot dragging on the
colonization effort.

The usual cast of dissidents went through their
sound-bite paces, letting the world know how disen-
franchised they were. Then came a harassed-looking
Eve Patric, giving out the Abydos Foundation line—
for as long as they allowed her. Actually, Eve wound
up sounding as if *she* supported the Soonest faction

but that Daniel didn't. Daniel couldn't blame her—much.

Shifting to various locations around the country, the show got a bunch of opinions from various Abydans on the street. What a surprise! They were for heading out to Ballas ASAP!

But then, from Washington, the producers unveiled their pièce de résistance—translator extraordinaire, war heroine, symbol, and leader of Abydan womanhood . . .

The microwaved whatever seemed to solidify in Daniel's gut as Sha'uri appeared on the screen.

A blond, sympathetic newswoman praised her for speaking out against the silence of those who should be taking the lead in this affair.

"I'm sure my father and brother want to be sure they've weighed all the options," she said carefully. "They and so many others feel a great responsibility for the fate of our people. But I don't think this go-slow policy is a good thing—for them, and for all Abydans."

"You feel that the Abydos Foundation is holding back all progress?" the blond newscaster purred.

"I think it's something that was necessary when we first came here," Sha'uri said, "but that was more than a year ago. We've learned a lot since then, and should be taking more of an active role—"

As she went on, the muscles in Daniel's neck tightened so much, it felt as if someone were sticking an ice pick between the vertebrae.

"And you hold these opinions in spite of the fact that your husband, Daniel Jackson, is in charge of the foundation?" the blonde asked.

Sha'uri's face became glacial. "Our agreement was to discuss the question of colonization, not my husband," she said.

The newswoman's facade cracked a little. "I only meant that it must be difficult for you—"

After a little more verbal fencing she retreated.

Daniel fell back on the couch, trying to get his neck to relax. "Small mercies," he muttered. "Small mercies."

CHAPTER 5
THE PASSING PARADE

The gate guard at the Creek Mountain post shook his head at the traffic jam snaking down the switch-backed road climbing the rocky slopes. "If Captain Murchison was still around to see this, he'd probably blow a valve."

Feretti nodded. He remembered Murchison, the former security chief for the base. Of course, in his day the place was supposed to be top secret, first as a missile silo, then as the home of the project to unlock the secrets of the StarGate. Murchison had been as dumbfounded as the civilian scientists to be transferred out when Colonel O'Neil took over the place.

But the old security chief would indeed have been upset, to put it mildly, by the long line of trucks and buses pointing the way to a supposedly classified location.

The secrecy had all changed, Feretti had to admit, when Daniel Jackson had told the world about the StarGate—and the dangers that lay beyond it. Creek Mountain was beginning to appear on tourist itineraries. It wasn't as big a draw as, say, Graceland, but people would drive up the winding road to the gates, hoping for a look at the magic doorway to the stars.

They didn't get inside, of course—that's why the marine guards were posted. But, Feretti speculated, if this colonization business really got off the ground, they'd eventually need to move the gateway to someplace a little more accessible.

At least someplace that didn't depend on a single road zigzagging up a mountain.

Now that road was clogged with trucks bringing supplies, the returning Abydan diaspora—and thousands of cameramen, newscasters, and freelance idiots who wanted to come and see history happen.

Another bus pulled through the gate, and a mixed team of Abydans and Earth-folks climbed aboard with clipboards. They checked the identities of the riders—Feretti couldn't believe how many people had tried to sneak in among the would-be colonists. Then came the usual protests when the busload of people were assigned lodgings. They'd all expected to go marching through the StarGate immediately. Instead, they'd have to wait until the whole group was arrayed. That meant they'd have to use the only accommodations available—the same underground barracks where the Abydan refugees had been interned when they first arrived.

Feretti thought that was a bad idea. Conditions down in the dark had resulted in a prisoners' riot the first time around. But then, he wasn't in charge of this fiasco. The military personnel at Creek Mountain were merely extending every assistance . . . as ordered.

A racket overhead brought Feretti's eyes upward while the busload of Abydans disembarked. Another helicopter with cameras sticking out. The rental places in Denver must be doing a great business today.

Then came a louder racket as an Apache helicopter gunship came down on the civilian chopper like a stooping hawk. Colonel O'Neil had made arrangements for camera crews to shoot the exodus from a nearby mountainside. He also had allowed news teams inside the base. In fact, several were going through the StarGate with the colonists. But right from the start he had wanted it understood—no cowboys need apply.

The bus was empty, and the driver attempted to jockey his vehicle into a turn on the narrow concrete porch in front of the heavy blast-doors. Instead, he managed to hang up the bus on one of the stanchions beside the base entrance.

The guard rolled his eyes at this performance "FUMTU," he muttered.

Feretti caught the joking acronym for "Fucked Up More Than Usual." He grinned and topped it. "SAPFU," he said.

The guard looked puzzled. "Don't think I've heard that one," he admitted.

"Surpasses All Previous Fuck-Ups," Feretti informed him as he walked away.

"Another news helicopter warned off," the aide reported to Jack O'Neil.

"Fourth this morning." The colonel shook his head. "Did they take it well?"

"The pilot said he just about had to pounce on them," the young lieutenant said with a grin.

O'Neil raised his shoulders in the faintest of shrugs. "As long as he didn't have to start shooting at them."

He turned to see Daniel Jackson and a couple of Abydos Foundation staffers coming down the hall. It was the first time the military man had seen Jackson this morning. To O'Neil's eyes, the Egyptologist looked like something the dog had just coughed up. His hair was mussed, his eyes glazed. Then O'Neil realized that Daniel was wearing the same shirt he'd had on the day before.

With some sympathy he asked, "How goes the gathering of the clans?"

Jackson slowly shook his head. "So far it looks like our worst-case scenario . . . cubed."

Picking up a clipboard, he began running down some of the problems noted there. "People missing planes—missing connections. Overloading the buses we've got coming from Denver." Daniel sighed. "I don't remember these sorts of problems when you were getting them out of here. How do you guys manage to get an army anyplace?"

"Well, the military does have some advantages," O'Neil deadpanned. "For instance, we're allowed to shoot stragglers."

Jackson's half-dazed eyes showed that he didn't even realize O'Neil was joking. "Unfortunately, the guys I'd like to shoot were the first ones here," he mumbled.

"It's easier to move people around when you've had the system running a few decades." O'Neil had no intention of going wherever Daniel's tired mind had headed off. "It's all the magic of FAGTRANS."

That got Jackson's attention.

"No." O'Neil waved a hand to play down the line. "It's military aconymese, on every travel order. First Available Government Transportation." Now it was his turn to sigh. "Talk to the admin officer here. Maybe we'll be able to use some empty seats to move your lost lambs here."

"Great." But Jackson didn't seem measurably happier. "It will just take a little more time—by then those bastards will have started piling the kindling around me."

O'Neil didn't have anything to say to that. Luckily, he didn't have to answer.

Complaining voices echoed down the hall. O'Neil turned to see about fifty Abydans heading along a cross-corridor. The group was about evenly divided between people wearing jeans and sweaters and more traditional types in homespun robes. All carried luggage and packages as they followed a couple of marines. Apparently, another busload of colonists was setting off for their barracks accommodations.

Equally apparent, they were not happy with what they were discovering. When they spotted the civilians with clipboards, they broke away from their guides and began gesticulating and shouting.

Then they saw Daniel, and their tone became even more venomous.

O'Neil turned to his aide. "Neither of us need to see this," he said quietly. They began to move away.

The colonel didn't have a wide command of the Abydan language—just simple constructions and the sort of swearwords and blasphemies that any soldier tends to pick up.

Words from the second vocabulary category was what he was hearing now.

Sha'uri sincerely wished that the young newswoman and her camera crew would find something—or someone—else to interest themselves. She had volunteered her services as a translator for the incoming multitudes, a little surprised at her fellow Abydans. How could they have spent a year in the United States and learned so little of the local language?

Immediately she'd felt a pang of guilt. She, like they, had grown up in a society where only one language had currency. Though they might speak a debased idiom, all in Ra's empire spoke in the god's tongue. When she and Daniel had first communicated, it had been through the ancient hieroglyphic symbols and his attempts to decode a spoken language he only knew from its writing.

Still, she couldn't still the niggling criticism at the ignorance of her fellow Abydans. She tried to bury the feeling in work, and her offer had been graciously accepted by the Abydos Foundation staffers. They were short of interpreters—the plane load of translators from Saudi Arabia had been delayed in transit.

It had been good to feel useful, to deal with her country folk, explaining the situation and allaying their fears.

Then the news team had arrived, all but elbowing away the people she was trying to help while a young, too thin woman with a microphone asked idiot questions.

"Sha'uri! Is that the way you're going to be dressed to go through the StarGate?" the girl asked, without even identifying herself.

Sha'uri looked down on what she privately considered her "work clothes"—a blazer, sweater, and jeans. Except for the hiking boots she wore—still breaking them in—most of her Ballas clothing was packed away, waiting for the transit. What she wore had been chosen for comfort on the flight from Washington, as she explained.

"It seems that your brave statements certainly led the Abydos Foundation to change its stance." The reporter—Vera-Ann Something-or-other, as she finally introduced herself—then began to rehash the questions that had been put to Sha'uri on that Ammit-bitten news show.

Having gotten some of the facts from foundation staff members, Sha'uri tried to correct this misapprehension, casting longing looks after the group she was supposed to be interpreting for.

Wait a minute—they'd diverged from their proper course!

With a quick apology Sha'uri tried to disentangle herself from the impromptu interview and pursue her charges. The persistent news crew trailed after her.

Sha'uri blushed as she heard angry voices erupt in the side passage. The people were yelling in Abydan, using the kind of swear words mastadge handlers usually reserved for recalcitrant beasts.

"Misbegotten child of diseased sand lice!" one of the men was shouting. "You torture us like one holding cool water above the workers in a pit!"

Sha'uri hurried round the corner—then skidded to a stop when she realized the target of this abuse was Daniel Jackson.

But even as she stopped, the news crew rushed past her, aiming their camera at the altercation.

Unaware he was being taped, Daniel lost his temper. "You accuse me of holding you back, oh fine and wise father of many," he retorted. "How have you spent this year on Earth? Were you learning to hunt, and build, and live in absolute wilderness? Did you study the ways of planting and nurturing plants and grains where none of their kind has ever grown before? Unless you liked the way things were in Nagada at the very end, when people were trapping vermin to eat, and even Skaara had to beg the Earthman marines for supplies."

"You weren't even there," a woman accused.

"No, I was a prisoner," Daniel said. "But I heard of these things, and I do not want them to happen again—and they will if we go off to Ballas unprepared. You have enjoyed the ease of purchasing food in markets for a year. But those markets will be far from us indeed when we arrive on Ballas. Do not expect anyone here to spend much thought on us after we pass through the gateway."

"You were no prisoner," the woman cried, as if that negated everything else Daniel said. "You were consorting with the bitch goddess, dallying with Hathor!"

Sha'uri began drifting back down the hallway, wanting to put as much distance as possible between herself and this ugly scene.

It must be hard enough for him without finding me there, she thought.

She stopped when she'd gone around the corner, a little surprised at herself to find such sneaking sympathy for her estranged husband.

Seconds later, the news crew appeared again, hard on the trail of controversy. "Could you tell us what the argument was about between Dr. Jackson and the colonists?" Vera-Ann chirpily inquired, shoving her microphone in Sha'uri's face.

For a second Sha'uri considered flat refusal, then decided on prevarication. "They expected to be leaving immediately, not realizing that all of us and our supplies must be gathered together before we go through the StarGate."

"Don't you feel this whole situation could have been dealt with more skillfully than it has?" Vera-Ann Microphone asked, her encouraging smile just begging for a crushing sound bite.

"I begin to wonder if the job might not have been done better if the workers had more time," Sha-uri said slowly.

Vera-Ann's smile dimmed. She'd expected a simple attack on the abrasive Daniel Jackson and his foot-dragging Abydos Foundation. Instead, she'd gotten a thoughtful, almost conciliatory response. This was not good television.

Another team member caught Vera-Ann's eye. "Look! There's Imiseba!"

Sha'uri was quickly abandoned in the rush to film the man of the hour. She leaned back against the wall, glad to escape the center of attention.

Then she peered around the corner, but either the wrangle was over or it had moved down the parallel corridor. Sha'uri stayed a few minutes, watching Imiseba enjoy his well-deserved moment of triumph.

He handles the interviewers well, she thought. Better than I do. And he plays to the cameras. Perhaps he smiles a little too much. But then, he should be glad that he's gotten his way—or will very soon.

Sha'uri frowned as Imiseba let loose a diatribe on wasted time. Was that exactly necessary right now? she wondered. From what she'd seen here, time had not been wasted so much as been in short supply.

Turning her back on the impromptu press conference, she headed for the colonist accommodations. Surely they'd need another interpreter there.

Imiseba waved to the news crews as they headed off to cover new aspects of the colonists' assembly. His supporters—the ones Daniel Jackson had named the Soonest party—gathered around. Mahu, a leader in the Abydan militia, clapped him on the shoulder. "That's the way to celebrate victory."

Kenna was the nephew of an Elder from one of the farming clans. He headed a faction in that small group of survivors. "You certainly showed up our would-be lords and masters."

Imiseba nodded. "A beginning, perhaps."

"Beginning?" echoed Raya, who'd headed a crew of miners.

"We've taken the first step, showing that the people can make decisions for themselves without being told what to do by that Urt-man and his friends." Imiseba's eyes glowed with a preacher's ardor. "Ballas is not Earth—or Abydos, my friends. Those who led in former days may not be able to meet new challenges." He shook his head. "Kasuf is an old man."

"But what about Skaara?" Mahu asked.

"And Sha'uri?" inquired Raya, staring down the hallway she'd just traversed.

"They are both tied to the failures of the past," Imiseba said. "The Urt-men have an interesting phrase I've heard—'the scrap heap of history.' Surely that is where Daniel Jackson finds himself now. The same may be true for Kasuf and the other leaders from Nagada."

He glanced around his circle of allies. "Ballas is not a place for Elders. A new world demands new leaders. . . ."

CHAPTER 6
ONE STEP BEYOND

It took another two days from the in-gathering of the Abydans before the colonization party was finally ready to set off. A mixed security team of both O'Neil's and Skaara's people had gone through the StarGate in advance, to prepare the way.

Politically conscious (or maybe super-sensitized, O'Neil thought), Daniel Jackson had decreed that an Abydan should be the first through. After the guards a caravan of trucks had followed, delivering the supplies the Abydos Foundation had bought or begged. Now the personnel were ready to move—or just about.

The colonists were being marshaled in a long line of march. Daniel vented a long sigh.

He'd shaved, O'Neil noticed, and at least had changed into a new shirt. "Soon it will all be off my back," he told the colonel with obvious relief.

"And some of it will fall on me," O'Neil replied with a grin.

"I keep thinking it must be a come-down for you,

commanding—what do your people call it? A heavy company?—after the expeditionary force on Abydos," Daniel said.

O'Neil only shrugged. "It's more than eight times the force I led on our first sortie through the gate," he pointed out. "That's more than enough to post guards and take care of Headache Patrol." He glanced at the media pool, journalists and newscasters chosen by lot to accompany the colonists. They would be transiting in the early waves, along with the rest of O'Neil's people.

Daniel had publicly vowed that he would be the last to go through the StarGate.

Jackson conferred briefly with a couple of clipboard-wielding assistants, then nodded. "Last chance. Is there anything we haven't thought of?"

"Barf bags," O'Neil suddenly said.

Daniel stared at him.

"Remember your first trip through the old Puke Chute?" The colonel deliberately used the Marine nickname for the StarGate. "When we evacuated Abydos, these people were half-starved, retreating from an ongoing battle after a brisk hike through the desert. They were out on their feet. Today, they're alert, excited, and probably full of breakfast."

"Damn!" Daniel muttered, beckoning his people back. "No way can we arrange for individual units—check with the supply people here. See how many trash bins we can beg, borrow, or steal. The bigger the better. And garbage bags."

He turned to O'Neil. "Can we use your name with the logistics people?"

The colonel nodded in assent. "Mops and pails might be a good idea, too," he suggested.

One of the aides—an Abydan—gave a brief, sharp laugh. "There should be lots of them left over from the Great Mastadge Crap-out last year . . . unless they were all thrown away."

The aides set out, and Daniel looked at his watch. "Another goddamned delay. You can bet I'll be hearing about it."

Hours later, the exodus was almost over. It had taken longer than the flight from Abydos, even though a good thousand people less were passing through.

More care had been taken for each individual going through as well. The blankets that would be used on Ballas had done double-duty during the transit as padding for young children and oldsters. Some had protested entering the StarGate wrapped almost like mummies, but they'd been silenced when Kasuf had borne the indignity without demur.

They were down to the tail of the line now, the really difficult cases who had to be sedated before passing through. Medical corpsmen monitored each case, and there were additional medics on the far side to receive them.

At last there were no more.

Daniel stood in the safety zone as the StarGate cycled into existence. The glowing vortex swirled out, then steadied into a rippling, evanescent lens of energy.

Taking a deep breath, he turned and directed a quick wave to the handful of Abydos Foundation staffers who remained. This skeleton crew—all Earthborn—would be the colony's lifeline, continuing to raise money and purchase supplies for the colonists.

Then Daniel stepped into the StarGate's force field and was buffeted down the long light-years to Ballas.

He arrived on Ballas with all the grace of a drunk being flung from a neighborhood tavern, sprawling on the floor of the StarGate chamber.

Maybe it's best to travel the Puke Chute when you're exhausted, Daniel ruefully thought as he pulled himself up. It doesn't hurt so much then. But your reflexes are shot when you come in for a landing.

Medical corpsmen converged on him, then stopped as Daniel rose to his feet without wavering.

"I'm the last," he announced. "You guys can start packing up now."

The Ballas StarGate pyramid had been fitted with temporary lighting and a noisy electrical generator. Daniel made his way along passageways as if he'd been there before. In a sense, he had. The Ballas pyramid had the same layout as the ones on Abydos . . . and on the plateau at Giza in Egypt. Repetition breeds familiarity.

Besides the lights, the hand of Man had evidently

been at work in other ways—primarily with a broom, Daniel thought. The inner halls were free of dirt, debris, and animal bones. And when he arrived at the tall slit of an exit, Daniel found other traces of the prep team's passage.

While attempting to widen the game trail leading down through the hills, the construction battalion had uncovered an actual road under the eons of deposited dirt. It seemed to be made of huge squares of what looked to be vitrified rock, but the stone wasn't slick. When Daniel scuffed an experimental foot across the surface, it felt more like very fine sandpaper. Yet whatever it was had stood up to the blades of the heavy earthmovers.

Ahead of him on the road Daniel could see the rearguard of the colonists' column. He caught up with them at the foot of the slope that led up to the pyramid. This was where the work of the ancients ended and the handiwork of the engineers began. Instead of vitrified stone, the pathway snaking among the hills was roughly graded and covered in gravel.

The final destination, as Daniel knew, was the evocatively named Hill 23. Based on the maps and photos the scout team had brought back, this hill had been chosen as the site of the colonists' base camp. It stood nearly at the head of a shallow, forested valley which pushed in between the hills, which meant there'd be convenient bottom land for farming, according to the experts Daniel had brought in.

There was a convenient water source—a stream winding between the hills and down into the forest. The hill was tall enough to look down on the surrounding summits—good in case of flooding, and providing a nice view. Daniel suspected, however, that the scenery had not been high on the priority list of the military engineers provided in lieu of money by General West.

Finally, Hill 23 had been the best location of its type within easy walking distance of the StarGate pyramid. Although, as he slogged along the gray gravel road undulating along the shoulders of the lower hills, Daniel began to wonder what sort of marathon walker would consider this trip easy.

The road dipped again, then climbed the side of a taller hill. Daniel spared a little breath for a brief, celebratory "Whew!"

Although, as he came closer, there seemed little enough to celebrate. The military engineers had been quick and brutal in their job of clearing and leveling the hilltop. The cinnamon-leaved trees had been bulldozed down. Most of the brush had been dumped down the hillside. A few roughly trimmed logs and branches had been left as the beginnings of a community firewood supply before the construction types cleared out.

Other than the crates and pallets of supplies and equipment, the hilltop was bare, scraped dirt, enclosed by a sloping earthen—or was that ballasten?—wall . . . a berm. Daniel recalled the term used to describe the sand walls surrounding Jack O'Neil's encampment on Abydos. It seemed that the engineers saw little difference between colonists' accommodations and an outpost firebase.

Daniel followed the rearguard up onto the hilltop, where a large crowd were milling around, regarding their new home with obvious disfavor.

"Where are the houses?" he heard one woman asking.

"Where are the stores?"

O'Neil and Skaara had their joint vanguard already at work opening the crates containing the surplus tents donated by General West. Now they manhandled one of the plywood bases from a pallet load and began to demonstrate how to assemble the construction.

The response quickly grew more negative. "You expect us to live in cloth houses? We shall freeze at night!"

"Why has there been no building? We have waited for weeks and weeks!"

"Where are the 'lectric lights?"

"Where is the TV?"

Daniel couldn't believe what he was hearing. A large number of colonists had apparently expected to move into a pleasant suburban landscape with all the modern conveniences—and free of those ubiquitous Urt-men.

O'Neil, he noticed, paid no attention to the complaints. He simply began organizing teams of volunteers to raise the tents.

A tall, deep-chested man swaggered to the fore. Daniel recognized him as Raya, a one-time ally against the greed of the United Mining Syndicate. The guy was supposed to be hot shit as a miner, but otherwise he had only distinguished himself as a pain in the ass.

"Playing with cloth is women's work," he declared flatly. "I am a miner."

O'Neil was not in the mood to play around. In his broken Abydan, he responded, "Good! You can mine holes for the latrines."

Raya seemed to swell up, his face coloring. Clenching his big, knobbed fists, he stepped forward.

Kneeling to show one of the volunteers how to secure the tent, O'Neil only looked at the miner. He had no weapon close to hand, but somehow the lack of expression on O'Neil's face made Raya falter. Perhaps the big man was suddenly remembering that this was the one who had killed dreaded Anubis in hand-to-hand fighting.

Raya stood irresolute, then took a step backward.

O'Neil kept him pinned with his eyes. "I said, you can mine holes for the latrines."

He glanced to one of the other marines. "Fuentes, give him a shovel." The colonel added in Abydan, "His friends will be glad to help."

Raya's usual boon companions had gathered around their hero to join in his expression of disdain.

Now they tried to shrink away, but were caught nonetheless as the latrine-digging party was led away.

Raya aimed a deadly look back over his shoulder as he and his friends marched off. O'Neil had made himself an enemy today.

The colonel didn't even notice, returning to his task with the volunteer tent raisers.

The rest of the process did not go smoothly, nor was it particularly easy. But by the time the shadows were growing long, there was a reasonable facsimile of a camp in existence on the top of Hill 23. Split oil cans liberated from Creek Mountain had been pressed into service as impromptu barbecue grills. Fires were lit, and a meal was being prepared. There were enough tents up to house all the colonists, O'Neil's company of marines, and even the news pool—although the media people had been somewhat put out to discover that they were expected to erect their own accommodations.

Jack O'Neil smiled over the memory of the looks on the media pukes' faces. "There isn't an International Hotel like the one in Dhahran—and there certainly isn't a swimming pool for you to film beside. This is a colony, where people will have to live rough for at least the next generation."

"If you can't accommodate us, perhaps we should go back to Earth and file our reports from there."

The aging network news anchor made it sound more like a threat than a suggestion.

O'Neil shrugged. "I guess you'll have to do what seems best. But don't expect to commute to and from this assignment. If you head back, we'll have to add someone else to the pool."

That had caused a commotion, with the media types running to complain to Jackson. Poor Daniel had looked pained over the possible public-relations disaster, but he'd backed O'Neil, who had told them bluntly, "Everyone has to pull his or her weight here. Like it or not, that means not only covering the story but living it."

He glanced at the network anchor. "You managed to live through Afghanistan some years ago. You can do it again. At least here no one's shooting at you."

In the end even the news people had gotten their tents up, with a little aid from Skaara's militia. The Abydan fighters took up positions on the dirt berm, while O'Neil dispatched a squad to act as sentries in the StarGate pyramid.

But the day's friction still wasn't over.

"Where do these Urt-men go with their guns?" a tall, skinny guy with bad teeth shouted from the chow lines. O'Neil matched the face with a photo from his intelligence dossier—Kenna, a leader of the farmers' faction. He and his followers had been pretty well marginalized during the period of exile on Earth. But he'd been regaining lost ground ever since Imiseba started beating the drums for his "Ballas or bust" campaign.

Kenna had to know what the guards were doing, but still he baited them.

"If the Urt-men are going away, we should be glad. But I do not think they are."

"They go to guard the gateway," Skaara replied, obviously disconcerted by the accusation. "We agreed—"

"*We* did not agree to give away the pyramid or the gateway," Kenna exclaimed angrily. "The Urt-men took the gate on Abydos, and we know where that ended."

He gestured angrily to the eight-man sentry crew. "If the legions of Horus guards were to come through the gateway to *this* world, that handful would not be able to stop them. Or are they to guard the way of escape in case we grow tired of their orders here on Ballas?"

O'Neil simply gestured for his troopers to continue onward, and no more was said—unless one counted the countless quiet murmurings around the campfires.

Kenna allowed himself a triumphant grin as he picked up a cup of Urt-man coffee. Imiseba had kept in the background while he challenged the Urt-men, but he knew his leader was aware. After all, Imiseba had passed along the information from his militiaman friend Mahu.

Raya had tried to confront the aliens by flexing his muscles—and he had failed.

Kenna had used his brains—and he had succeeded, not merely in facing the great O'Neil, but in making the simple folk around the fires question the intent of the Urt-man and his marines.

From across the campfire, Imiseba appeared out of the crowd. He merely nodded to Kenna and passed on.

Kenna took a sip of his drink and turned away. But the warmth he felt did not come from coffee.

A new world requires new leaders. And the more clever the leader, the higher he could rise . . .

Walking through the forest along a trail scarcely wider than his shoulders, Sheb cursed as his blast-lance was hung up once again on overhanging branches.

It had seemed like such a perfect way to avoid work when the Urt-men started conscripting people to put up their tents. Mahu had already gathered his militia unit off to one side and toward the rear of the crowd, telling his men, "This is not work for warriors. We will patrol the area around the camp. Never too soon to learn the land."

The unit had marched back onto the crushed-stone roadway and down to the base of the hill. There Mahu had broken them down into smaller groups and sent them in various directions.

Sheb's squad had been dispatched on the longest

journey, to penetrate the section of forest which lapped at the base of the hills.

"Go out with your weapons ready," Mahu told his troops. "The woods are full of animals." He smiled. "Shoot straight, and you may be able to bring back something for us to eat."

Sheb had waited until they were out of Mahu's earshot before he'd given the squad his own lecture. They were not to shoot at *anything* until they were sure it would not talk back to them. The concept of friendly fire had been one of the first things the Urt-man marines had taught the Abydan freedom fighters.

And yet, even with his precautions, the patrol had turned into a nightmare.

The men had been unhappy. They were used to the vast, open spaces of the Abydan deserts, not the dark, clammy, confined feel of the forest. Where the trees were open enough to allow a trail, underbrush choked the ways. Sheb found himself wishing he had worn his Urt-man clothes, even though Mahu had insisted that his militiamen wear traditional Abydan garb. Sweeping robes were fine for traveling the sands, but here they became smutted with ground mold and caught on every twig and branch.

Some of those branches were fanged with thorns that clung so tenaciously to the warriors' homespun that they began to look like walking bushes. And where those thorns encountered bare flesh—it was like being caught on the Urt-men's *bob-waia*.

After taking a branch square in the face, Sheb had called a halt. Most of the squad he had sent back to the camp. With the two best men he had continued the patrol, carefully marking trees so they'd be able to find their way back.

With just the three of them they made considerably less noise than the full squad. But even so, they scared off the local wildlife, finding nothing to hunt for dinner.

They completed the job that Mahu had set, scouting out the best route to the forest and exploring the largest trail through the woods. The sunlight was slanting through the trees at a long angle when they finally started back.

Sheb's feet hurt from moving over the uneven ground, and his bladder was painfully full.

"Go on," he told the others. "I have to stop for a minute." They went on, eager to return to the camp.

Sheb hoisted his robe and adjusted his loincloth. A moment later, he was directing a strong stream against the foot of a tree. Forest noises filtered in over the sluicing sound of urine against bark.

Odd how none of them had made any impression until he was here alone. There was the fading rustle of his comrades as they pushed along the trail. In the distance came a trilling noise, perhaps the call of a bird or birdlike creature. A low buzz—an insect?—sounded near his ear.

Quickly rearranging his robes, Sheb gladly took hold of his blast-lance. Perhaps what he had done was foolish, leaving himself alone in the woods. He grasped the shaft of golden quartz more tightly.

The blast-lance was a powerful weapon, but its length made it unwieldy in the underbrush. If something was to appear suddenly, would he be able to aim and fire in time?

Sheb picked up his pace, trying to catch up with the other two militia scouts.

That was a mistake. He was so busy hurrying, looking for the blaze marks that marked the path back, he never saw the root that hooked his foot. Sheb fell heavily, gracelessly, his blast-rod catching him across the belly and hip. The ankle on the foot he'd caught ached. So did his opposite knee, which had taken much of the impact.

Sheb got to his feet, trying to wipe leaf mold from his face. Instead he could feel the stuff smearing across his features.

He set off down the path more carefully, limping. He couldn't hope to catch up with the others. Sheb felt very alone now. The shade of the trees was turning to a deeper shadow, unlike the sudden night of Abydos. What happened if the light failed completely while he was still trying to pick his way?

The effort of making the best time he could on a twisted ankle and banged knee left Sheb puffing. He wished he could use the blast-lance as a true staff, but what if he had need of it as a weapon? He couldn't easily fire the lance with it pointing straight up, bearing his weight.

Even the ground was against him, sloping upward as he toiled along.

But wait! That was good news! It meant the camp had to be nearby!

Sheb peered, trying to penetrate the thickets of dense cinnamon foliage that blocked his view from the trail. Up there—ahead and above him. Was that the raw earth that marked the wall around the camp?

Then his attention was brought down to a patch of brush much closer. Branches were shaking, as if something was forcing itself through the ground cover.

"Dagi? Wah?" Sheb called the names of his fellow scouts. His voice seemed high and thin in his ears. Surely they had reached the camp by now. Why would they have left the marked trail to wrestle through the strange and hostile shrubbery?

The rustling took on a frantic note. Sheb leveled his blast-lance, certain something was charging him. A creature suddenly vaulted from the brush and onto the trail. It was covered with fur a mottled combination of cinnamon and darker browns. The body was perhaps as big as both of Sheb's fists. But there were too many legs, oddly jointed—the strange beast looked like an obscene mating of the rats that had raided Nagada's granaries and the desert spiders.

With a yell the militiaman triggered his blast-lance. A bolt of energy leapt from the stylized lotus muzzle of the weapon. It landed dead center on the disgusting hybrid's body, vaporizing it.

At the same second Sheb realized that such a small creature could not have made so much noise in its passage. He aimed his weapon at the thicket as a second form appeared, and almost triggered it again before he realized it was a small boy.

"What are you doing, wandering out here alone!" the militiaman furiously demanded.

Looking from the steaming carcass to the lance in Sheb's hands, the child began to bawl in a combination of fear and relief.

Putting up his weapon, Sheb peremptorily beckoned to the boy. He didn't trust his voice.

And his hand was shaking almost as badly as the child was.

CHAPTER 7
TEETHING PAINS

The photon had a long journey from the fusion fires in the center of Ballas's primary, through the turbulent photosphere of the star, to its face, then across millions of miles of hard vacuum, into the Ballas atmosphere, down to the surface . . . to penetrate a chink in a tent flap clumsily fastened by Daniel Jackson.

The photon continued just a little farther, an 186,000-mile-an-hour lance—which hit Daniel square in the right eye.

With a sigh he rose from his narrow, uncomfortable camp bed. No sense in trying to fool himself that he was still asleep.

Daniel collected a pair of pants and padded barefoot across the plywood floor. Even by the colonists' standards, his shelter was sparsely furnished. They had brought small pieces of furniture and personal belongings. He had brought some clothes and a lot of papers.

Even Jack O'Neil had been surprised, offering

some of the furniture from his command tent. But Daniel was content to use a converted packing case for a desk, with a couple of smaller boxes as chairs.

It didn't matter what his home away from home looked like. No one shared his tent, which was located on the edge of what the marines jocularly called "the Urt-men's ghetto."

Daniel untied the tent flap, threw it open, and sighed. Week Two of the Ballas colony, and the results were downright depressing.

He'd arrived with great hopes for this virgin world, but now Ballas was looking more like a rape victim. The base camp seemed like a scar on the hilltop. Daniel had hoped that a little time would take the rawness off. What he'd gotten was a rainstorm that turned the dusty streets into a morass.

The changing weather had also resulted in a shift in the prevailing breeze. Wafting through the tent opening came the aroma of the latrines and the crap ground for the mastadges.

Somehow, it was perfectly symbolic of the situation. Daniel remembered one marine's comment on the reversal of fortune: "Everything went from sugar to shit."

But then, he had to admit, everything hadn't been all sugar to begin with. Daniel had hoped that after arriving on their new homeworld, the Abydans would finally pull together to create a nest of safety in the wilderness. Now he had to admit that notion surpassed optimism, probably bordering on delusion.

The factions he'd hoped had been left behind were here, making all the trouble they had on Abydos. Kenna and his farmers tangled with Raya and his miners. Mahu played minor warlord among the militiamen. And Imiseba was blaming the colony's every shortcoming on Urt-man duplicity and parsimony.

There had been some bright spots. Feretti was teaching militia units the ins and outs of bush-country operations in the wake of Mahu's original and disastrous foray. Feretti was ranging farther and farther from the base camp with mixed marine/Abydan units, making topographical maps and training the Abydans to create their own topo teams, a lasting and positive contribution.

And O'Neil's tame experts, Halloran and Fuentes, were working with Abydan assistants to collect samples of the native fauna and flora for study and propagation. Long-term, another plus.

But these were easily lost in the rising tide of dissension and the specific setbacks, like the disastrous tree-felling incident. The deserts of Abydos were not likely to produce a race of lumberjacks. Such wood as did exist came from something that looked more like an urban weed tree than the heavy-trunked specimens in the forest here. What hadn't been sledged home for lumber had been turned into charcoal for use as fuel.

Unfortunately, there were no charcoal burners among the Abydan survivors. In fact, there were damned few who even knew how to wield an ax.

The first attempt at clearing some of the bottom land for farming had ended with one of the would-be woodsmen being medevaced back through the StarGate.

At least the unfortunate would keep his leg.

But the failure of the Abydans to make a dent in the forest meant another round of begging for help from General West. Military engineers would come in for a quick round of slash-and-burn, but that wouldn't improve the disposition of the colonists.

Life among the labor-saving devices of suburbia— no matter how brief—had softened them. Their spirits might be willing, but the flesh was all too weak. Not that the Abydans would admit any such thing. Their complaints focused on the disdainful Earthlings who bossed them around. It didn't matter that the marines had the knowledge and experience that the colonists lacked. They had come to Ballas to get away from the Urt-men, and Imiseba was playing that swell of feeling like Itzhak Perlman played his violin.

With another sigh Daniel turned from the tent entrance to the crate desk illuminated in the triangle of light. Complaints weren't just coming from the Abydans. Biologists on the other side of the StarGate were getting into the act as well.

Daniel had made a deal with several universities to provide samples of the local wildlife. As originally envisioned, there would have been several expeditions after Jack O'Neil's reconnaissance, gathering plants and trapping animals.

The rush to Ballas had killed that idea. Instead, Halloran, Fuentes, and their teams were grabbing whatever they could and all but shoving it through the gateway, in between their work here. The professors on the other side weren't getting the chance to conduct slow, serious examination of the alien life forms. They'd receive samples with quick-hurry-up requests to report if the meat was edible or if the plants could be used as mastadge feed, with Ballas-based research nipping at their heels.

Now, irritated at having their territory infringed by laymen, the scientists were striking back. Of course, their wrath landed on Daniel.

Just call me lightning rod, Daniel thought as he tried to draft a diplomatic reply.

The evening meal was finished, and the glow of firelight had begun to die around the camp. It had taken more than a week, Jack O'Neil thought, but the transplanted Abydans were finally returning to their traditional rhythms of life. Early to bed and early to rise might seem like charming folklore to an audience brought up on the talk meisters proliferating across the late-night scene. But it made eminent sense to any pre-technical culture where light—or rather, the fuel to make it—was an expensive investment.

Like it or not, Ballas would start off pre-technical—muscle-powered, candlelit (when they got around to making the candles), and hand-tooled. O'Neil wasn't surprised that the Abydans didn't like it, after their taste of paradise, suburban style. Well, that would be paradise lost. The colonists would just have to be led, kicking, and screaming, back to the nineteenth—or maybe the eighteenth—century.

This crass materialism had hit poor old Daniel right smack in the ideals. He'd have been just as happy to sack out in a sleeping bag on the plywood floor of his tent in the name of self-sufficiency, and couldn't understand the whiners who wanted everything, immediately, but on their own terms.

Sha'uri must also be feeling pretty disillusioned. O'Neil believed she had spoken out for the Soonest position at least as much on idealistic grounds as to embarrass Daniel. Whatever had led to the decision, he was willing to bet it now embarrassed *her*.

She had voiced the call for unrealistic deadlines. She should have realized that fast work meant a lot of rough edges. Instead, all she'd done was set things up for Imiseba—as well as giving him a perfect set of grievances now that they'd arrived here.

Imiseba . . . the young voice of revolution. He'd seen lots of similar types during his years on spook patrol in Central America. In fact, part of his job had been to silence some of those voices—permanently.

Both Daniel and Skaara had asked for a meeting this evening. O'Neil wondered if this was a case of the old, established power base turning to Uncle Sam to hear about options. He hoped not. Uncle Sammy's track record wasn't so good—just ask the powers-that-were in Iran and Nicaragua.

More to the point, General West had been pretty firm when approached for more engineering aid. The colonists were supposed to sink or swim now that they were on Ballas. Would that stance change at the threat of a hostile regime with a doorway to Colorado? The Ballas colony was supposed to be a pilot project. O'Neil wondered if West had other pilot projects going—on how to extinguish troublesome colonies.

It would be terribly easy, he knew. A bit of botulism in the rations the colonists all depended on. Or perhaps something a little more subtle—an outbreak of something nasty and viral, with Ballas being quarantined . . .

He pushed that thought away and hastily cleared his desk. Seconds later, a sentry was announcing the arrival of guests.

Daniel and Skaara entered, with Sha'uri and Kasuf. O'Neil rose from behind his desk. There weren't enough seats available in the tent, so he offered his chair to the older man.

The old guard's here, the colonel thought, settling back on the edge of his desk and considering who *wasn't* there. Imiseba. Kenna. Raya. If they were coming for help against Young Abydos, he'd have to find some way to let them down. He wasn't going to get involved.

"I got the word from General West," he said, opening on a neutral enough note. "The yellow stuff should be coming through in a day or two."

"Yellow stuff?" Kasuf echoed, in his slow English.

"The heavy earthmovers," Daniel explained to his father-in-law. "Construction equipment is usually painted yellow in America."

"Although this stuff will probably be olive drab or woodland camouflage," O'Neil agreed. Then his tone changed. "There was another part to his message. This will be the last direct aid he can offer. Powerful people are beginning to complain back home. From here on, we're only supposed to observe what happens here—and hold the hands of any visitors who might come to inspect your progress."

"Observe," Kasuf said, glancing at Skaara, who in turn looked at Daniel.

"I suppose that's what we've come to you about," Daniel finally said.

"The orders." Skaara looked embarrassed as he spoke up, which didn't make his meaning any clearer.

Sha'uri made the next attempt. "We can understand that they were necessary."

"It would have taken us forever to get the camp started up without you." Daniel's admission certainly didn't make him look any happier. "But it's led to other problems."

O'Neil sighed. "The Ugly Urt-Man Syndrome."

"The people do not like living in a military camp,

ordered about by"—Kasuf hesitated a moment—"strangers."

"Especially when there are so many Abydans around, eager to give orders of their own," O'Neil added sourly.

"You mean Imiseba and his young men," Kasuf said.

He spoke to Sha'uri in Abydan, and she translated. "They see a different world, one untouched by slavery and tradition. That is not altogether a bad thing."

"We have talked," Skaara said, indicating the whole group. "A new world does need new ways. We want the people to make more choices."

"Something along the lines of a town meeting," Daniel amplified.

O'Neil noticed that the Egyptologist and the young woman had managed to go through the entire meeting without looking at one another. How they had managed to come up with this well-meaning scheme for democracy . . .

The colonel shrugged. "If you feel we've taken up too much authority, well, you might be right. We were only trying to expedite things. I'll tell my people to soft-pedal it. What knowledge and skills we have will still be at your service, if you should request them. As to how you wish to regulate your internal affairs, we certainly have nothing to say about that. Our task is to observe."

O'Neil repressed a surge of annoyance as he looked at the relieved faces around him.

What did they think I was going to do? he wondered. Shove my dictates down their throat with a submachine gun?

His thoughts darkened. What they don't seem to realize is that observation implies reports. Reports to people who would rather we kept the upper hand here. And if their village democracy gets out of hand, who knows what West and his Washington friends might deem necessary?

The morning sunshine was growing strong by the time Feretti and his mapping team reached the hilltop overlooking the forest. Feretti was glad for the warmth—early mornings in the Ballas hills were chilly. Down in the valley below, a ground mist rose high enough to hide all but the topmost branches of the trees.

They were about halfway down the length of the valley extending its impudent way into the hills. A stream curved down among the trees, offering another entrance into the forest.

Feretti and his people were there to survey the area and trace the route, both for their own records, and the colonists.

The team consisted of both marines and Abydan militiamen. Following Colonel O'Neil's orders, Feretti and his fellow Earthmen held back as the Abydans did the work. They were to make comments or suggestions only if the militiamen started really going off the beam.

These guys were already past the final-exam stage. None of the marines had to say or do anything as the Abydans thoroughly and competently worked up a rough map of the region.

But Feretti wasn't about to let his people just sit around on their butts. As the ones ranging farthest from the base camp, they'd been requested to do a little scouting.

"Get out of the binocs and eyeball those other hills," he told his marines. "The Mighty Hunters are looking for something between a goat and a gazelle out here."

Fuentes and Halloran, the newly minted planet scouts, had quickly gotten the hunter nickname for their constant and seemingly tireless forays to collect biological samples. The big-domes on the other side of the StarGate were particularly interested in this variety of animal, reconstructed from the bones left by whatever had been denning in the StarGate chamber.

"This another variety of cootie?" one of the marines asked. The local wildlife was definitely designed on different lines from Earth animals. Everything they'd seen so far had an extra pair of legs, and seemed to have segmented bodies. They'd reminded some Earthlings of the put-together creature sets of their childhood, so the fauna was generally described as "cooties," in spite of the more scientific and officially preferred "hexapods."

The Mighty Hunters and their scientific friends

might try to label the new species they were discovering, but popular names were definitely winning the popularity contents. For instance, the fast-moving, horrifying hybrid of a spider and rat had quickly become a *sprat*—usually a *goddam sprat*, because the omnivorous, ubiquitous pests had quickly developed a taste for the contents of the colony's midden pits.

Personally, Feretti had rather liked a fellow *paisan's* name for them—*schifosa*, "garbage eater."

He dug in the chest pocket of his BDUs and pulled out a photograph of a reconstructed skeleton. "The bio boys back Earthside are wondering why we haven't seen anything like these. They figure these things would have to live at least in fairly close dragging distance from the hoodats' lair."

The marines gathered around. "Looks like something that size would be hard to miss," one man said.

The photo indicated a creature about the size of a sheep, its six legs weirdly articulated to Earthly eyes.

"You don't think they made a mistake and hooked a couple of the things together?" another marine suggested.

Ferettti gave him a look of scorn that only years as a noncommissioned officer could perfect. "Oh, excuse me, Jorgensen. I guess those professors lack the benefit of your specialized viewpoint. But now perhaps you'd better get your head out of our ass and start scouting those hills!"

"Yes, sir!" The marines scattered to various vantage points, all getting out their binoculars.

A moment later, Jorgensen burst out, "Jesus Christmas!"

Feretti appeared beside him in an instant. "What is it?"

He focused his binoculars on the area that Jorgensen indicated. There was a mound of something, mottled brown and cinnamon.

Then the mound seemed to move.

Feretti focused in harder and realized that what he'd taken for a slow undulation actually came from the movements of a group of creatures. More sprats than he'd ever seen in one place were clambering over the carcass of a larger animal.

"Hotel alpha," Feretti ordered, using alphabet code for "haul ass." He headed for the distant hillside, his rifle up and ready.

A couple of shots into the air cleared the sprats from the carcass they were feasting on.

"Hard to believe those little guys could bring down a big animal like this whatzit," Jorgensen said as the marines cautiously came closer. The still form was covered with a coarse brownish fur. To Feretti the matted stuff looked like the inner upholstery on old-fashioned chairs.

"Either that, or he suffered a damned convenient heart attack," another marine said.

"No way," Feretti replied, gently pushing the creature's head back with the muzzle of his rifle.

The throat was gone, swiped out of existence by a trio of deep-gouging claws. The marks remained in the flesh, even though they'd been nibbled around by the sprats.

"'Those little shits are carrion eaters," Feretti said coldly. "Something else killed this sucker. If they could hunt like this, why would they need our garbage?"

"'Think it was a hoodat?" Jorgensen turned from the dead animal to aim his rifle at the nearest thicket.

"Anybody's guess." Feretti looked around the dead animal. Thick ginger-colored grass left no hope of finding paw prints. "If you found a deer in the wilds with its throat torn out, would you know if it was done by a cougar, a bear, or a wolf?"

"I'd just guess it wasn't done by a rabbit and get out of there," Jorgensen said.

"But why did whatever it was leave its breakfast to the sprats?" one of the other men asked.

"I've been wondering that myself," Feretti admitted. "If it heard us coming, it must have pretty sharp ears." He made a decision. "Pack that thing up, we'll bring it back for Fuentes and Halloran. And mark this spot. I'll bet the Mighty Hunters will want to go over it with a fine-tooth comb."

CHAPTER 8
FRICTION

Sheb and his squad moved almost soundlessly through the forest, communicating by hand signals in the deep shadows. They were deep among the trees, where the shade of the russet foliage above was so intense that underbrush was starved for light. The tree trunks around them rose like vast columns, dwarfing even the pillars within the StarGate pyramid, the largest scale that Imiseba had ever seen.

He stood with a small knot of men, watching how Mahu's troops had improved. They had become woodsmen enough to attempt hunting for the animals the Urt-men called "neardeer," extremely skittish beasts whose flesh offered delicious meat.

Or perhaps, he had to consider, the constant diet of MREs had turned the fresh meat into a delicacy. After seemingly endless pouches of spaghetti and meatballs, chicken and rice, or the dreaded ham slice, even the stringy meat of mastadge haunch would seem a striking innovation.

The men closed in, completing their envelopment

of the clearing where a forest giant had toppled over years before, tearing a hole in the foliage canopy. Brush surrounded the open space, and a trio of near-deer stood grazing.

The echoing rumble of a blast reverberated through the forest, bringing the animals' heads up. They leapt with such speed that Imiseba almost thought they had teleported themselves among the trees.

Cursing broke out from the militiamen as they tried for a decent shot. Mahu's voice roared out over everything, exhorting his men not to shoot one another. A couple of rifles barked. One of the neardeer stumbled and fell. The nearest militiamen leapt on the animal, knives high, to finish it off.

"Meat tonight," Mahu said smugly as he joined Imiseba's group. "You see how well they carry themselves? They've gotten used to the Big Dark." That was what the Abydans had taken to calling the depths of the forest.

"They do not look like Abydans," complained Raya, referring to the warriors' Earth-style jeans and trousers.

"You try to untangle your robe from the thorns of a Waitaminute bush," Mahu retorted. "It would take you more than a minute, I think."

Raya only frowned deeper at Mahu's use of another terrestrial word. The Urt-men had taken the lead in exploring the forest, and their names for the plants and animals they'd found tended to stick, creating an Abydan pidgin.

Imiseba stepped in to head off the argument. "You have done well, Mahu. Now we can find food of our own—as long as the Urt-man explosives aren't going off."

"Those are my people destroying the stumps of trees the Urt-man machines have knocked down," Kenna spoke up. "You spoke of food—with some of this great grove of trees removed, we will be able to plant . . ."

He glanced at Mahu's hunters, then turned away. "A more dependable source of food, surely."

"Anything but this Ra-be-damned Urt-man food," Raya said. "It makes such stones in my belly, I feel like I'm crapping—"

"Enough!" Imiseba raised a hand. The marines made enough jokes about Meals Refusing to Exit. Yet these and some canned goods were almost the only supplies that Daniel Jackson and his friends at the Abydos Foundation had provided. Another bone of contention, and another Urt-man reliance to be outgrown.

He turned to Kenna with a smile. "I am glad your people are learning to use the clay that destroys stumps."

"*Seefaw*," Kenna said, using the unlettered Abydan's pronunciation for the marines' plastic explosive C4.

Imiseba nodded. "There may come a day when we

will be glad for this knowledge." He glanced at Mahu. "Just as we may be glad for the skills gained by your warriors." He lowered his voice. "Tell me," he asked. "With what your men know now, could they successfully fight against O'Neil and his marines?"

Mahu's eyes grew wide at the suggestion. "I could not be sure," he answered honestly. "They are the ones who taught us these ways."

If the noise of the blasting was bad among the trees, it was even worse in the clearing at the edge of the forest. Hapi was beginning to feel the stirrings of a headache.

And these idiots with him were *not* helping the situation.

Hapi was among the few farmers who had escaped the disaster which had been the final days of Abydos. Under Ra's rule, the miners and the farmers had traditionally been separate clans, with the farmers enjoying the better end of the deal. Agriculture required them to spread along the banks of the nearest river to irrigate their crops. Their life was hard, but they usually managed to hide the best fruits of their labors.

The miners, on the other hand, were concentrated close to the source of the ore which Ra demanded. They were the ones who had to deal with Ra's viceroys, the ones on whom the wrath of the god most often fell. When the people rebelled, Nagada had been blasted from the air by Ra's udajeets, his anti-gravity gliders, and the miners had no place to hide.

The farmers had barely been touched by the great rebellion until Hathor invaded Abydos with an army of Horus guards. Even then only the farmers closest to Nagada had their fields and hamlets attacked and occupied.

But when the end came, it was the far-flung farming clans who'd been doomed. Hapi had just happened to be in Nagada, hoping to sell his load of produce for an astronomical sum. Instead, he'd abandoned his load and his mastadge and run for any refuge when the legendary *Boat of a Million Years* took aim on the planet itself.

Other than the handful of fighters who'd taken arms with the Nagada miners to free their towns and a few fellow opportunists, the farm clans of Abydos were extinct. Which meant there were only a few on Ballas who knew the ways of plowing, sowing, and reaping.

And Hapi, who had spent his time of exile watching American agricultural shows on television, was the only Abydan who had any ideas about grubbing up tree stumps. After all, forests don't tend to grow in desert farmland that's been cultivated for uncounted generations.

The Urt-man engineers had done their best with chainsaws and bulldozers. But even their Rome plows, which had torn through jungle underbrush in Southeast Asia, had not been enough to clear the area completely in the amount of time they'd had. So the farmers who looked to Kenna as their leader were blowing up the more recalcitrant stumps with the magic *seefaw* paste while Hapi and his motley crew waited to use more traditional methods as a follow-up.

He had a dozen brawny miners, ropes, and chains, and the promise of a draft mastadge if he really needed one. Hapi was glad he hadn't brought the big animal directly to the field. The mastadges were doubtless unhappy enough hearing the blasts from their improvised corral. All he needed was one running amok with terror from seeing a blast firsthand.

The miners assigned to the crew were clearly chafing under his authority, testing him every inch of the way.

"Why can't we stand closer and get a good look?" demanded Djan, one of Raya's loudest supporters. "Are you more afraid than the other earth-scratchers out there?"

Hapi gave him a look. "I don't use a tool until I know what it can do—not what someone tells me it can do. Would you sit on that because they told you it was safe?"

Rough laughter from the rest of the crew left Djan's face a dull red.

A plume of dust and debris rose from the midst of the tree stump, and everything aboveground disintegrated. One of Kenna's idiots shrieked and spun as he was hit by a piece of wooden shrapnel.

Hapi turned to Djan again. "If you're so eager to join them, you might go over and volunteer. Looks like they might have an opening on their team."

The blasting team hustled off with their injured comrade, yelling for an Urt-man medic.

Then it was up to Hapi and his fellows, chopping, digging, and hauling.

The work was neither as exhilarating nor as quick as blasting. Hapi did not make it go quicker with his meticulous insistence on safety every step of the way. He didn't spare himself any of the work, either. As midday neared, he was bare-chested and sweating, perspiration creating little runnels down the nearly black loam dust coating his skin.

"Why couldn't we use the *seefaw* to get rid of these?" Djan's chest was working like a bellows after his team had pried up one of the roots of the stump they were now working to move.

"Kenna's geniuses removed three stumps—at the cost of one healthy man." Hapi was a little short of breath himself as he replied. "We've removed three—no one hurt. Which is better?"

He swung a grimy arm to take in the forest beyond the stumps they had to remove. "Sooner or later all those trees will have to go. If every three trees costs us one man, we run out of men to work and farm. This planet will win, and we'll either starve or have to go back to the Urt-men's world. Is that what you want?"

"I want it to be easier than this." Djan ran a hand

down his chest, smearing the combination of dirt and sweat. "Why couldn't Danyer bring back the men with machines to do more work? Or *we* should have had the machines! The Urt-men were teaching me to drive the big dirt pushers back home before the war started again."

"You can blame your great friend Imiseba," Hapi replied. "It would have been easier to let the machine men come here and clear away the trees before we came, while we stayed on the Urt-men's world learning the skills we'd need to make our new homes here. That was Daniel's plan, before everyone started screaming that they wanted to run here right away."

"How do you know?" one of the surly miners demanded.

"I asked," Hapi replied with a shrug. "I saw on the TV that the Urt-men farmed in very different ways than we did back on Abydos. I asked the Abydos Foundation which ways we could use here. They were going to teach all of us—but then there was no time."

"I still say we should have brought machines," Djan insisted.

"Those big things cost much money," Hapi said. "Which would you rather have? Machines or a tent over your head? Machines or food?"

"With the kind of food they've been giving us, there's no question," one of the miners said with a laugh.

Hapi ignored him. "Besides, all of those machines

drink the magic strong-water the Urt-men use. Do you see any of that sitting around here? I thought the idea of coming to Ballas was so we wouldn't have to depend on the Urt-men anymore."

Djan responded with a murderous glare. "Just like you stupid shitkickers to be so contrary. What are you doing defending Danyer? He's the one who got your precious leader Nakeer killed!"

"I think you got too much rock dust caught between your ears, *miner*." Hapi made the word sound like a new term for *halfwit*. "If you want to stand around and bellyache, I guess I can't stop you. I just hope your friends here will work. Because every day this field isn't cleared means another day's delay before we can start planting."

He gazed up into the sky. "The weather looks pretty good right now. But I certainly can't tell how much of a growing season we have left. If we slack off now, we may never get a crop in. That means empty bellies this winter. That means the planet wins again. And we go back to Urt-man's world like beggars."

"*I'll* give you a rest," Djan roared, swinging a fist.

Hapi dodged and swung back.

Shouting and cheering, the rest of the crew abandoned the stump and formed a circle around the two combatants.

"What do you do?" a heavily accented voice yelled.

Hapi, Djan, and the others whirled around to find

a mixed group of Urt-men and Abydans coming out of the forest.

All of them were armed.

"Brothers!" one of the miners called, apparently frightened that the warriors were coming to punish them for malingering. "It wasn't our fault! Djan and Hapi did it!"

Djan turned on his work mate, his fists clenched.

Hapi, however, spoke to the Urt-man warrior who had first shouted to them. "How can we help?"

"You could stop fighting one another and help us search," an Abydan militiaman called back.

Hapi now noticed that the warriors had all halted at the new treeline.

"What are we supposed to look for?" Hapi asked.

"We found another kill in the forest—a neardeer— and traces suggest that it's the work of a hoodat," the militiaman shouted.

The work team suddenly cast nervous glances at any surviving underbrush.

"It's not here now—but it had been heading this way," the militiaman went on.

The Urt-man leader spoke up, pointing at the churned-up earth. "In dirt . . . its foot . . ."

"What Lieutenant Halloran is trying to say," the militiaman explained, "is that the hoodat may have left footprints. We've seen blurred traces in the forest, but with all this soft dirt . . ."

Hapi shook his head. "Many people have been through here. Another crew was blowing up stumps." He glanced at the others. "We'll help them look."

As he slowly looked over the naked earth, Hapi cursed himself, the Urt-men, and Hoodats in general. He'd insulted that oversized idiot Djan for wasting time. But that was what they were all doing now. It was foolish.

Just as Hapi was straightening to call off the search, Djan suddenly called out. "Hapi! Everyone! There's something here!"

The Urt-man, Lieutenant Halloran, began shouting in pidgin Abydan, assisted by the Abydan warrior who'd translated before.

"Don't move! You may step on other tracks!"

Hapi felt even more foolish for not having thought of that. He looked around himself, but the only footprints he saw were from the blasting crew.

The searching warriors made their way carefully to Djan and cordoned off the trace he'd found. After some more grubbing about, they decided that Djan's find was the best print they'd find.

Lieutenant Halloran produced an Urt-man picture box, a camera, and began recording the impression in the ground.

Hapi leaned into the protective ring of warriors, craning his neck to get a look at this all-important footprint.

Something had sunk deep into the rich black earth—a large, padded paw of some kind.

Hapi gasped. From the looks of it, his head could fit into that print!

Lieutenant Halloran kept clicking away. "Did your people have cats on Abydos?" he asked his translator.

The Abydan warrior frowned. "Hathor was known as the Cat. That was the form of her god mask."

"Well, this is the paw of a cat. And a damned *big* cat at that."

CHAPTER 9
DISAPPOINTMENTS

The StarGate cycled, thrusting its vortex of energy from the golden quartz torus, settling into a glowing soap-bubble lens, and then suddenly ejecting a human form.

Daniel Jackson skidded on the floor of the Ballas StarGate terminus, then caught himself. When he turned to the guards he expected to find, his expression became one of surprise. "Since when have you taken over as gate guard, Colonel?"

Jack O'Neil felt a bit surprised, too. The professor had only been gone for a couple of days, but seeing him again, the reality didn't match the colonel's mental image.

Maybe that's because you still see him as the overgrown kid who bulled his way onto the first StarGate expedition, good-looking but sort of—unformed. He'd had the face of someone who did most of his living in books.

Now more bone showed in Daniel Jackson's face, and it wasn't just from an MRE diet. Fine lines showed on the Egyptologist's features, the sort carved by harsh experience of life's little surprises.

O'Neil wondered how many of them had been carved on his recent visit to Washington, D.C.

"I thought you might appreciate seeing a friendly face to welcome you back," the colonel said. "Besides, I wanted to find out how successfully your mission went."

The fine lines on Daniel's face suddenly deepened, making him look years older. "I can give you the news in three letters . . . B-A-D."

He shifted his satchel to his other hand and strode over to O'Neil. "You were right about West, Jack. He's exceeding his orders in giving us the help he has. All he could do was refer me to some power monger in the Senate, a jovial racist named Robert E. Ashby."

O'Neil nodded. He'd heard the name.

"The guy is good—a real politician. Sat me in his office, talked with me, pleasant as could be. Didn't quite go so far as to call me a squaw man, though that's what he was probably thinking. Didn't quite call the Abydans a bunch of welfare-grubbing raghead furriners. But he left no doubt that there would be no more government assistance for the Ballas colony. 'We got our own fish to fry,' he explained in his most elegant down-home manner."

Daniel's shoulders slumped. "Then I went to talk to my people at the Abydos Foundation . . . and wished I hadn't. According to Dave Freck, our income couldn't get much worse. Fund-raising got a brief shot in the arm from the excitement when the colonists left, but afterward—" He shook his head. "All people seem to remember is the negative coverage Imiseba and his people stirred up."

He glanced at O'Neil, his face twisted in a wry grimace. "For the Congress and the great American people, it's all the same — 'out of sight, out of mind.'"

"Can't the foundation do anything?" O'Neil asked.

Daniel sighed. "Dave's had to let people go as it is. When I asked him about getting a little variety into our food, he told me that the reason we're getting so many MREs is because they're coming free from the government. We're one of their biggest recipients—us and Ethiopia."

In spite of his sharp laugh, it was obvious that Daniel didn't find the situation funny. "You know what really burns my ass? After giving those news crews the best of what we have, we're getting virtually zero coverage on the national media." He seemed to shrink in on himself. "I didn't expect that things would be like they were during our first week, when we actually had news anchors on-site, doing their broadcasts from beautiful downtown Ballas. But for the last week it's been zilch, zip, nada."

O'Neil cleared his throat. "Which may explain the piece of bad news I've got waiting for you."

Daniel gave him a guarded look. "What now?"

"The press pool—or most of it—wants to go

home. The broadcast media people say their management has pulled the plug, but I think part of it is that they find their accommodations pretty damned uncomfortable."

"It's the best we can do!" Daniel protested.

O'Neil shrugged. They'd had this argument several times over the past month. "Then, too, there's not much in the way of pretty pictures for them to film. The day-to-day work of building a colony is pretty grim, rough, and untelegenic."

Daniel nodded, resigned. "Not exactly the stuff of sound bites."

"Anyway, except for a couple of technical writers, most of the press want to go home."

"Maybe that's just as well," Daniel said. "It means we won't have to put up new accommodations for the visitors who've asked to come over."

"Visitors?" O'Neil echoed.

"Observers," Daniel amplified. "People who want to set up their own colony, who'd like to see how well we're doing on the budget we've got." He paused for a second. "Setim."

"Ah," O'Neil said. "Then I guess we can't charge them rent."

Daniel laughed. "No," he agreed. "But I'll bear that in mind for anybody else who asks to come and look at us."

His mood quickly soured, however. "Those damned news people. All they did was show the worst side of everything."

"They look for excitement, not solid achievement. And the last exciting thing around here was that footprint Halloran found."

Daniel gave an inelegant snort. "Damned idiots made it sound like the Werewolf of Ballas was on the loose, coming to eat us in our beds. That didn't get people to open their wallets. Although quite a few gun nuts called the foundation to see if we were declaring open season on the hoodats."

"Maybe a package hunting tour . . ." O'Neil suggested with a straight face.

After darting a sharp look at him, Daniel reluctantly smiled. "Before we invite the hunters in, we'll need some actual targets to offer them."

"Quite right," O'Neil agreed. "What we need is something spectacular to bring the TV cameras back—something the network audience can understand. Something they've seen on old science-fiction shows. What do you think? Should we discover a hidden treasure, or find a secretive alien race living underground?"

Against his will, Daniel began to laugh again. "That's just what we need," he said. "That's *just* what we need."

On the way back to the base camp, however, Daniel's grim mood reasserted itself. "I really did it this time," he said sourly. "Even better than I did on Abydos. There I just shot off my mouth and nearly set up a civil war. This time I talked several thousand people into posing on top of the World Trade Center with one foot on a banana peel."

He looked back over his shoulder at the StarGate pyramid. "I tell you, Jack, I almost didn't want to come back here."

"I can understand that you've had it rough—" O'Neil began, but Jackson cut him off.

"What the hell do you understand?" the typically mild-mannered academic snarled. "You've got a wife and a home back there, and a straightforward job to do here on Ballas. All I have on either side of the StarGate is screw-ups and failures." He put out a hand. "Damn! No! I hardly know what I'm saying anymore. You haven't had it easy in your life, and I haven't been very helpful most of the time. I wonder how you put up with me. Remember how you used the alphabet code to tell me off once? Delta Foxtrot Bravo. DFB. Dumb Fucking Bastard. You were a hundred percent right."

"Come on," O'Neil said, appalled by the other man's sudden collapse of morale. "You saved the Earth. And you might have pulled things together on Abydos if Hathor's assassins hadn't upset the applecart."

He looked at Daniel's tired face, remembering the frantic last-minute work that had gone into preparing the summit meeting between Kasuf and Nakeer, the farming clans' head Elder.

"Whatever happened to that constitution you were trying to get the Elders to approve? People are saying they need something new for a new planet. Maybe that's a point you can bring up at this town meeting you've got planned."

Daniel glanced at him, a flicker of hope in his eyes. "God, I don't even know where I've got the files on that. Or if they even got saved from Abydos when everything went down the toilet."

"I'll send a request to General West," O'Neil promised. "He was getting intelligence reports on every step your constitutional convention took." The colonel gave Daniel a smile. "It will be nice to see them put to constructive use for once."

A large bonfire rose in the central square of the camp—what would probably be the parade ground if this were a military installation, Daniel thought. Sparks and embers flew upward from the log fire, short-lived stars against the overcast night sky.

At least their first experiment in participatory democracy hadn't been rained out.

He looked at the people gathering in the large circle of firelight, most of them still work-stained from the day's labors. Hot water was still in short supply, and not everyone was ready for what the marines called "Johnny Weismuller showers," downpours of cold water that forced anguished Tarzan-like yells from even the most prepared bathers.

It's supposed to be a town meeting, but it looks like everyone gathering to see the medicine man perform big ju-ju, Daniel thought, with a sudden glance at the Setim observers' team. These people came from a technical society that had surpassed Earth. What must they think of the crudeness of life on Ballas?

He shuffled the papers in his hands, notes on the proposed constitution. As soon as the reports exhumed from General West's files had arrived, Daniel had discussed the constitution with Kasuf and Skaara. They in turn had spoken with Sha'uri and other Abydan leaders. All agreed that this was a good subject for the town meeting.

Daniel just wished that *he* didn't have to be the one leading the discussion. Kasuf had participated in creating the draft constitution, trying to adapt the ideals of the founding fathers to the realities of Abydan life. But as the only surviving Elder, he was going to chair the town meeting. Skaara and the others pleaded ignorance of the details, while Sha'uri, who had helped translate Earth texts on constitutional law, just wasn't willing to work with him.

Like it or not, Daniel again found himself in the spotlight.

The mass of people settled down—almost all the adults on Ballas—and Kasuf raised his voice.

"Let all who have entered the circle of light be welcome," he intoned, using a traditional Abydan greeting. Elders often chaired open meetings of townsfolk, especially among the farming clans. But they were more like editions of the people's court than deliberations on policy.

"Let those with concerns for our commonality

stand forward, not with the aim of contention, but with earnest cause—"

Kasuf didn't even get a chance to finish his invocation. People were rising all around the ring of spectators, calling, "Elder! Elder!"

The older man glanced around, nonplused. He had agreed with Daniel that the notion of a constitution should not be the first thing to be discussed. But he hadn't expected such a wild rush of causes being brought forth. Stretching forth a hand at random, he pointed at a guy who looked as if he'd spent the day grubbing in the dirt.

"I am Thouty of the miners, and I have a question to present. We have moved to Ballas to be free of the would-be rulership of the Urt-men. Why is it, then, that an Urt-man still controls our money? Should it not be given over to our Elders, or those whose lineage can claim the most Elders, for an accounting?"

"He probably spent it on himself!" a voice cried from the rear of the ring.

Daniel flushed, looking down at the seedy corduroy jacket and khakis he had worn to the meeting. Yeah. Didn't he look as though he were rolling in dough?

An angry Kasuf ignored the comment from the peanut gallery, again warning all who heard him to speak justly, and not simply fling accusations without merit.

Another colonist stood forward, calling, "I should like to speak forth, Elder."

Kasuf gave his assent.

"I am Merab of the farmers," the newcomer introduced himself. "I do not think that Danyer has stolen money. But did he use it wisely? Vast amounts were raised and placed in his stewardship. Some of it went to support us in our exile in the Urt-men's world."

"And what of the rest?" a voice cried.

"What of the rest? What of the rest?" The words grew into a resounding chant.

Merab stood until things calmed down enough to let him continue. "Danyer also gave away much money to warn the Urt-men of the danger from Hathor, for they did not know or believe that such as she even existed."

"That is money we could use right now!" someone else in the crowd interjected. "We could have real houses instead of tents or those wooden abominations."

The last few weeks had seen an attempt to use some of the chopped-down trees as the basis for log cabins. But there a sizable reality gap had opened between the neat diagrams in the survivalist manuals and the leaky, smoky, shelters that had been constructed.

True, the cabins weren't as comfortable as the adobe-style desert dwellings the citizens of Nagada had known. But that wasn't the yardstick that was being used. The cabins were being contrasted with the twentieth-century tract houses occupied by the Abydan exiles.

Kasuf glanced at Daniel to see if he wished to respond.

Daniel was angry enough to do exactly that, and damn the consequences. "Yes, great sums had been amassed—given by Earth merchants in the way of business. And yes, much money had been spent to awaken the people of Earth to the danger that Hathor represented. Was it wise to spend this money? Better to ask what would happen if it had been *not* spent. We would not be here on Ballas. Some of us, perhaps, would be toiling for the Empire, and for Hathor. Most of us—any who had raised a hand against Ra or his Horus guards—would be dead."

That left the crowd murmuring.

"Yet we spent our treasure for the good of Urt-men's world. Might not the Urt-man Elders return some portion to make our lot easier?" Merab asked.

Daniel sighed. "I have spoken to some of these Elders, and they are as generous as most men. There is a saying among my people— 'Out of sight, out of mind.' After we departed for Ballas, they and most of their people would be just as glad to forget us."

"But they send their warriors to mount guard over us!" an angry miner interrupted, thrusting a hand toward Jack O'Neil.

"And they send the beast-men to spy on us!" a less brave soul shouted.

Daniel glanced to where the Setim delegation sat, a wide, empty space around them as if they were ringed by an invisible cordon.

"There are a few scouts, for some of Earth's Elders would learn of different worlds," Daniel admitted. "The Setim came of their own will, wishing to find a world of their own, and eager to learn of the problems in setting up a colony."

Another miner stepped forward. "I and Djan of the miners will tell them of a problem. They should bring many machines to do the work that we break our backs doing!"

Lots of voices joined in with agreement on this point.

"Danyer gave our money away, so we could work harder than we did when we were slaves!"

"Is there something wrong about working hard?" Daniel shouted back. "When you were slaves, everything you had and were belonged to Ra. Ballas is something for *yourselves*. Isn't that worth working hard for?"

"*We* work, while the Urt-men tell us what to do!" somebody yelled.

"He keeps us weak, with that lousy Urt-man food!" another call came from the lunatic fringe.

"We want to be free, but you tie us to Earth!" a more educated voice shouted.

Daniel looked numbly at Kasuf. The town meeting had turned into a referendum on how well Daniel had done for the Abydans lately. All hope of discussing a constitution was being swept away on a flood of passion and discontent.

Too late Daniel realized it was hopeless even to

argue. The malcontents were attacking from too many divergent viewpoints. He was being vilified for not buying enough goodies from Earth, and for making the colonists *too* dependent on Earth products.

A classic no-win situation, Daniel now saw. He gave up arguing, electing to endure the storm of abuse until Kasuf could decently call the public pillory to an end.

Soon enough, the Ballas colonists ran out of constructive things to say. They hooted down Skaara when he tried to speak, calling him "the Urt-men's puppet."

Finally, the meeting degenerated into plain name calling. The crowd tried out "Away with the Urt-men!"

But that didn't make a good chant.

They settled on a battle cry that had a remarkably modern ring to it.

"Urt-men go home!"

"Urt-men go home!"

"That went remarkably well," Imiseba told his lieutenants later that evening.

"I thought there would be fighting when Kasuf declared the conclave at an end." Mahu sounded a little disappointed that his expectations hadn't been fulfilled.

"There would have been if O'Neil had sent his warriors in to enforce Kasuf's bidding," Kenna said. He showed his stained teeth in wide grin, just as he'd done throughout the meeting, sitting behind Kasuf in the Elders' conclave.

He had enjoyed the show, and was only disappointed that a shower of rocks hadn't landed on Daniel Jackson.

Merab was one of his followers, and he had played his part perfectly, sounding so reasonable while inciting the crowd against Daniel and the Urt-men.

When they had met after the crowd dispersed, Imiseba had patted Kenna's shoulder in silent approbation.

"It turned out better than we could have hoped," Imiseba praised his followers. "Daniel became the worst sort of Urt-man—angry and arrogant. Kasuf looked like his protector, and Skaara appeared to be a puppet."

"Yet still, it was Skaara's men who enforced Kasuf's edict to end the conclave," Raya pointed out. "He still has loyal followers—followers with weapons."

Imiseba nodded. "Then we must make that clear to the people—and make those followers of Skaara as uncomfortable as Daniel felt tonight."

"The people," Kenna sneered. "They are mere mastadges, to be led by the wise. At least we stopped Daniel and his friends from offering up that ridiculous ruling code. Can you imagine any of those yammering fools there tonight choosing who should be Elders?"

"We will need those people you deride before we

become the leaders here, Kenna," Imiseba reproved. "Tonight, we got them used to the idea of crying out against the rotten leadership of the past and the Urt-men they bow to."

He cast his eyes around the coterie of ambitious young men around him. "Now we must bring them to a willingness to fight for our cause. We even have a rallying cry." Imiseba smiled and raised his fist. "Urt-men go home!"

CHAPTER 10
OVER THE RIVER AND
THROUGH THE WOODS . . .

Daniel was frankly nervous when he'd gone to greet Seventh Officer Ankhere and the four members of the observation team that she had led to Ballas. From what he knew of Setim military hierarchy, "Seventh Officer" would put her somewhere around the level of a lieutenant. Better than high brass dropping in, but still worrisome.

Since the battle on board the *Boat of a Million Years*, Daniel had had little contact with the Setim. The members of the alien race who had manned the craft dealt mostly through Gary Meyers and the translation team at the ancient computer in Arabia.

When the red-furred visitors arrived through the StarGate, he had been struck again with wonder to see ancient temple art seemingly come to life. Set had been the most alien of the Egyptian gods—understandable now that Daniel knew the models for the deity came from another star system. With his furred form and muzzled countenance somewhere between a Russian wolfhound and Wiley E. Coyote, Set always seemed the most enigmatic of the ancient gods.

Ankhere, on the other hand, had been quite practical—and downright forthcoming.

"Perhaps you think it odd that an officer of my low rank heads this embassage," the young female officer had said as Daniel and Colonel O'Neil had played official greeters. "There were several reasons why I was selected for the position. Third Officer Sened wanted a younger officer—fit for extended field reconnaissance. We hope to get a look at all of this world, as well as your colony. I will be submitting my report directly to the Third Officer."

Sened was the highest-ranking officer among the surviving Setim. If Ankhere was here as his deputy, that gave her more than enough status, as far as Daniel was concerned.

Ankhere went on, a subtle change in her tone, although Daniel couldn't recognize the alien expression on her face. "Besides, my training and service was as an interstellar astrogation officer. As such, I would be of little use on Earth at this time."

There was another shift when Daniel didn't respond. "I served under Second Officer Nekhti in Astrogation. And perhaps you recognize Tenth Officer Bak."

Nekhti, son of Ushabti, had been the Setim officer who'd captured Daniel during the boarding action on the *Boat of a Million Years*. He'd been the first to hear the true history of what had passed since Ra had put the Setim crew into stasis eight thousand yeas ago. Nekhti had launched the mutiny that had climaxed in Hathor's death and the destruction of the gigantic starship, had led the group who'd sabotaged the engines. But he hadn't escaped when the *Boat of a Million Years* went up.

"Without Nekhti's bravery none of us would be here." Daniel glanced at the Setim petty officer with the gray flash on his muzzle. "And I do remember Bak. He fought most bravely."

Ankhere raised a furred hand. "Without your warning, Dr. Jackson, my people might have ceased altogether. We all owe you a debt."

Halting outside one of the former media tents, now occupied by the Setim, Daniel took a moment to prepare himself. He was going to call in that debt if he could.

Even on a canine face, Daniel could see the look of inquiry. "How may we help you, Dr. Jackson?"

"I understand you'll be undertaking some field reconnaissance today, Seventh Officer."

"Anything to escape these abominable stinks," one of the ratings in the background muttered, a little too loud.

Ankhere bristled.

"I know that certain of your senses are sharp," Daniel plowed on. "Nekhti had been able to detect my scent aboard the *Boat of a Million Years* some time after I escaped. We—the colonists and I—request a favor. In the reports on Ballas, you've probably come across references to a predator creature—"

"Commonly called a hoodat." Ankhere gave an almost human nod.

"Perhaps you also know that we haven't been able get a sighting of one of these beasts, much less a sample. But we were thinking . . . with your acute senses . . ."

Daniel floundered to a halt, unable to find a polite way to ask the Setim if they'd mind taking the role of talking bloodhounds.

Ankhere took him off the hook. "Bak, Niay, and Teye have all been trained in the arts of ground tracking. If our pack finds a scent, we will be happy to follow it."

Bak stood in the Setim form of attention and salute, head up, his throat exposed in the ritual form of submission.

Even in this position he couldn't help the occasional twitch that wrinkled his muzzle. In the millennia since the grizzled petty officer had gone to rest in the arms of Ra, the human pack had found all sorts of new stinks to surround its members. The sharp, unwashed body odors of the *fellahin* in Ra's empire had been distinctive enough. Earth-humans now wore strange scents and potions to hide their natural aromas. But they bathed themselves in the sweet, choking effluvia of their internal-combustion engines, their clothing exuded chemical reeks from its own making or from cleaning, and some of them even added odd-smelling gunk to their fur topknots.

For a trained nose like Bak's, it was enough to cause physical illness.

But the worst of Bak's ire was reserved for those fools who collected tubes of dried leaves, set them afire, and inhaled the resulting fumes. The stench clung to their skin, their clothes . . . and, as Bak had discovered to his great vexation, even to their surroundings.

His predecessor in this tent had been a smoker. The fresh smell of burnt tobacco overrode even the mustiness of long storage. When they removed the human sleeping racks from the shelter—Setim had other accommodations—Bak had discovered a metal container heaped halfway full with dead cigarettes. He'd almost retched before hastily removing the receptacle.

Nor were the Earth-humans the only offenders to his nose. The interaction of the Abydan colonists, with their standards of odor, and sweat, the stinks of the chemically neutralized wastes in the latrines, the spoor and droppings from the mastadges, presented a gallimaufry of smells to lighten the head and assail the stomach.

Bak looked forward to the trek through the untouched wilderness. It would clear his head—and his nose.

"Come out of there," Ankhere ordered him, her

own muzzle wrinkling at the smoke residue. "What did you make of Dr. Jackson?"

"He was different from the time I saw him on the ship," Bak replied, joining his superior. "I could smell tension on him then. Now there is a feeling of frustration."

"A fear of failure. I am not surprised after what we saw and heard last night." Ankhere looked around at the crude camp. "We will have to make sure we have considerably larger financial backing for our venture."

The humans insisted on joining the pack on its foray. Their leader was an Earth-human called Halloran. Bak detected the oily aroma of whatever he used to lubricate his projectile weapon . . . and the sour aroma of stale cigarette smoke.

He did his best to stay upwind.

The forest trails were a liberating experience. They reminded Bak of his long-past youth, of outings by his school pack, before the disasters which befell their planet.

As the Setim pressed deeper into the russet-shaded darkness under the trees, Bak caught other nuances on the air—blood, and a trace of something that raised the hackles on his neck.

He began quartering back and forth along their path, trying to determine where the scent came from. Niay and Teye joined him, their muzzles rippling to reveal fangs as they too detected the alien spoor.

"That way!" Teye nodded off beyond a deep thicket. "The blood is fresh!"

The Setim set off at a ground-eating lope with the humans rushing after.

Blood and a rank, unpleasant odor filled Bak's consciousness. It was the smell of a predator; more, the scent of a killer.

Bak ran along, testing the air and ground. The quarry's trail twisted back and forth. The wind shifted, and blood cried out through his honed senses.

"Here is a kill," one of the Abydans in the group called out. "A neardeer, clawed and slashed."

Bak blocked out the blood, concentrating on that other, elusive scent. There—that way!

He called to his fellows, raising the blast-lance he had brought along. Best to be ready for battle with whatever cast off a scent like that.

Patches of sky appeared between the branches ahead of them. The path became choked with brush. Now he had both visual as well as olfactory evidence that the quarry had passed this way—recently and quickly.

Branches were broken, as though a large body had forced its way through the underbrush.

Bak gave cry again, waiting for backup from his packfellows. The others joined him, leveling their blast-lances. They moved forward into orange sunlight.

The scent of the quarry was thick in the air.

Then they found themselves at the edge of a small river. The trail vanished.

Bak gave a yelp of frustration.

Ammit eat the beast! It had escaped!

*   *   *

"That damned hoodat seems like a canny beast," Jack O'Neil told Daniel as they headed up the ancient road to the StarGate pyramid. "I mean, that swimming trick—knowing the river would break its spoor—clever, huh?"

"More like annoying," Daniel growled. "All we have to show for the exercise is another dead neardeer." He thought for a moment. "Do you think this means we've got even bigger predators to worry about? Ones the hoodat has to run away from?"

The colonel just looked at him and shook his head.

"Maybe we'll get an answer today," Daniel went on. "Professor Leighton is supposed to give his verdict on the hoodat, based on his examination of the two kills and the casting of the paw print that Halloran found."

"That doesn't sound like enough to base *anything* on," O'Neil objected.

"After we saw that print, we figured we needed an expert on cats," Daniel responded. "And Leighton is it. If he thinks he knows enough, I'd be inclined to believe him."

They arrived at the tall slit cut into the side of the pyramid, then down the ramp and passageways. Messages and supplies were still coming through on a regular basis, and the guards had made a constant joke about "the old 12:45."

The StarGate was already going through its light show when they arrived, and a moment later a deuce-and-a-half truck came bouncing through. This driver was evidently familiar with gateway phenomena. He'd gunned the gas enough to get up the ramp to the StarGate, then cut the ignition and coasted through. Even so, the medium truck landed on only two wheels, bounced, and then finally righted itself.

"Take your time unloading, guys," the driver said in a hoarse voice. "I think I'll just sit here quietly for a while."

Daniel went up to the pale-faced man, torn between a wish to let him recover and his eagerness to see what Dr. Leighton had deduced. Reports and mail always rode in the front cab.

At his request, the driver fumbled through the mail pouch and came up with a large envelope, which he passed through the window with still trembling hands.

Daniel pounced on the report as if he were a big cat jumping an antelope for lunch. His brows knit as he read through the typewritten pages.

"So, did this Leighton guy draw a picture of the hoodat for you?" O'Neil asked with a flippant grin.

"A word picture, maybe. It's definitely a cat, or nearcat, you might say—like the neardoor. Leighton gave an estimate of the size—"

"Bigger than a bread box?"

Daniel gave the colonel a look. "Bigger than a leopard. Heavier, too. He explains that the biggest leopards weigh in at 190 pounds with a four-and-a-half-foot frame, excluding the tail. From the kind of kill and the paw size, Leighton believes our cat comes in at 325 pounds with a frame almost six feet."

"On a human, that height and weight would equal a big, fat slob," O'Neil said.

"On a cat, apparently, it's all muscle. The stats Leighton mentioned would equal an immature lion or tiger, or a full-grown saber-tooth, if they were still around."

"Anything else?" O'Neil asked.

Daniel correctly interpreted that to mean, "Anything useful?"

So he decided to start with the trivia. "Did you know that in the genetic scheme of things cats are the most closely related mammals to humans, except for the apes and monkeys?"

"If I ever meet a hoodat, I'll mention that to him. Does your doctor friend give an estimate of how likely we are to bump into one?"

"He gives sample home ranges for terrestrial big cats," Daniel replied, reading on. "A leopard generally hunts in a range between four and twenty square miles. Tigers use between four and fifteen hundred square miles. He suggests the hoodat falls between the two—unless the specimen we're talking about is immature."

"Then he may grow to a larger range," O'Neil said, frowning. "Four square miles—that's a problem. Puts this bad boy very inconveniently underfoot. If we're lucky, maybe he uses the larger range—he could be just passing through."

"Leighton lists another consideration." Daniel looked up from the report. "That he may be a she. Tigresses with young adopt a very limited hunting ground, to stay near the little ones."

"Which only adds to our problems," O'Neil said seriously. "Assume that when the Maple came through the gate, it scared Mama and the kids out of a nice, secure den. If she keeps the smallest range you mentioned, that probably puts our camp right in the middle of her hunting ground."

Daniel glanced back along the passage toward the outside world, even though it wasn't visible. "And somewhere nearby is the replacement den with the kitties, just waiting for someone to trip over it."

O'Neil nodded grimly. "If Mama is around, God help whoever does that."

A sardonic smile appeared on Daniel's face as he finished the report. "At least Dr. Leighton takes an optimistic view. He says this looks like a very interesting species, and he looks forward to the day when we can send him a sample."

"I just hope this doesn't end with a hoodat hanging a bunch of trophy human heads on his wall." O'Neil flicked the edge of the report with his finger. "Does your expert have anything else to say in there?"

Daniel shrugged. "Just that he got in touch with the guys chopping up the neardeer and goaty things we've found, and they were surprised to hear about something eating their species. It doesn't seem to fit in with the picture they've been drawing of the Ballas ecology. Apparently, they feel that his picture of the hoodat is a bit like . . . overkill. He responds that in a world of plant eaters, there's always room for a carnivore."

O'Neil nodded, his eyes going to the mixed team of marines and Abydan militiamen unloading the truck.

"You didn't mention why you were coming up for the 12:45," Daniel said.

"Gardening equipment," the colonel replied. "Specifically, more stump remover. Hey," he called to an Abydan tossing a crate to the floor. "I'd treat that C-4 a little more gently if I were you. Plastic explosive is supposed to be inert until it's primed, but a wise man treats *any* weapon with respect."

"P-p-plastic explosive?" yelped the truck driver, having apparently picked up only those words from O'Neil's ten-second lecture on C-4. "I took this damned truck bouncing through hell with a load of *plastic explosive*?"

The transport section man settled back in his seat, his face even whiter than when he'd arrived.

O'Neil turned to the unloaders standing at the back of the truck. At least they were taking things a bit slower and easier now. He glanced at the metal ice chests that were going back to Earth—more of Halloran's and Fuentes's biological samples.

"Good. There's no need to make a rush job out of it," the colonel told the men, jerking his head in the direction of the truck's cab. "*He's* not going to be in any shape to drive for a little while yet."

In these contentious days Qa'a stood out among his friends and neighbors because he held to no political opinion. He refused to be drawn into discussions on what must be done. When people inveighed against Daniel, or farm-clan rivals, or others began grousing about the overambitious faction leaders or complaining about conditions in the colony, Qa'a listened, shrugged, and went on with whatever work was at hand.

He was a militiaman in a company which had always remained loyal to Skaara, but he didn't go in for faction fighting. He stood guard on the earthen walls of the base camp, patrolled the forests and hills, and often was sent to unload the trucks that came through the StarGate.

Qa'a had a sort of dour outlook on life. When people began wrangling instead of working, his response was usually impatient.

Imiseba considered Qa'a the best undercover agent he could hope for.

So, that night when the lights began dying around the camp, the young firebrand was especially interested when Qa'a strolled by, signaling that a meeting was necessary—right away.

Imiseba excused himself from his comrades and set down one of the dark, dusty side alleys among the sea of tents. When he returned a short while later, his eyes were gleaming.

"I have information," he told his inner circle. "Today, the Urt-men brought many crates of the blasting clay—the stuff they call *plasteek*,"

"*Seefaw*," Kenna said. "The stocks have grown very low, since they have been felling more trees. Hapi's way of grubbing up the stumps is very slow, and my people have been finding large rocks and boulders as they begin to plow."

"Well, now the Urt-men and their friends have *seefaw* in plenty. They unloaded most of a truckload today. And what do you think? They stored it in chambers within the pyramid of the StarGate." Imiseba's eyes were dancing with laughter as he looked around among the triumvirate of his lieutenants. "Why, you'd think they didn't trust us poor colonists."

"They don't," Kenna said venomously. "And when we spread the word among those *shikken*-brains around the campfires . . ."

"They'll do nothing," Imiseba cut him off. "All of us have seen that already. Anyone will murmur. Sometimes they'll speak out. We've even gotten the mob to shout against Daniel, O'Neil, Skaara, even Kasuf. But unless we come up with some overwhelming reason, they will not fight against them. Why is that, Mahu?" he asked, turning suddenly to his would-be military commander. "Would your people fight?"

"Against the Urt-man warriors—the marines?" Though the night was cool, sweat stood out on Mahu's features. He wanted to look confident, to say

"Yes!" But if he did, and Imiseba demanded an attack, he would not be able to deliver. Among these conspirators, that would not merely mean losing face.

It might mean losing his life.

Imiseba took Mahu's hesitation as an answer. "Why do people fear to fight the marines?" he now asked Raya.

"I do not fear," Raya said, louder than he needed to. "I would happily break that Ra-be-damned O'Neil over my knee. But"—here his face lost its fierceness—"we do not fight just O'Neil and the handful here. Urt-man's world, and many, many warriors, lie just beyond the StarGate."

Imiseba gave a brief, fierce nod. "But if there was no StarGate, we could be free of the Urt-men, free of the ones they have placed over us, free even of worry about the Empire and its vengeance. Think of it, my friends. Just this world, with our people, and us to rule."

His lieutenants leaned closer, as if they were warming themselves at his fire.

"We have the strength—" Imiseba looked at Raya and Mahu.

"We have the knowledge of the Urt-man explosives—" He looked at Kenna.

"All we need to do is shut the StarGate and lock out the worlds beyond."

Imiseba smiled in hard triumph. "And the *seefaw* will be our key."

CHAPTER 11
HARD WORDS—AND DEEDS

The oil lamp flickered as Daniel Jackson sat at his improvised desk, going over reports. It seemed as if that was the last of his improvisations that had worked. The Ballas colony was not sustaining itself, falling further and further behind every day.

To take a simple example, there was the oil that Daniel was burning in this late-night session. It came from Earth. Daniel had carefully specified that oil lamps rather than kerosene jobs be brought, because he didn't want to be dependent on terrestrial petroleum products.

But so far they had found nothing to replace the earth-supplied lighting oil. They might end up with tallow dips, or smoky torches—a waste of firewood. Nothing effective, nothing efficient. It was like that with a long list of substitutes he'd hoped to find locally.

If they used animal fat for soap, that meant even less candles. And when one considered the successful hunting rate, not enough of both. Clothing—so far they'd found neither a plant fiber nor an animal coat that could be spun into anything useful. If they had to depend on animal hides, most of the colonists would be naked.

That meant importing sheep or something, which in turn meant shepherding—another new skill for the Abydans to learn. Could he divert mastadge handlers to that job? What would the sheep eat?

More important, what would the shepherds eat?

He read a report on the progress of the colony's agriculture, which could be summed up in three words. There wasn't any.

Reading between the lines, he could see the problem. The stump story told it all. Trial and error had finally taught the woodchoppers how to fell trees with a minimum of damage to themselves. But wrangling between the farmers and the former miners held down land clearance to a snail's pace.

Maybe O'Neil was right to bring on the C-4. Blow up a couple of the worst idiots. No, that wasn't the way to think. The colony needed the biggest gene pool possible for long-term survival. Even idiots.

Besides, it wasn't the long term Daniel was worried about right now. If they didn't get a crop into the ground soon . . .

Unbidden, pictures of Nagada toward the end rose in his mind's eye. The Nagadans were a desert people—as such they tended to leanness. When conditions were bad and food was scarce, those on the short end of the stick became stick figures.

Daniel had heard stories of people trapping and eating life forms that shortly before they'd considered vermin. Could that happen here? Perhaps, if Congress pulled the plug on the lifeline of boring but supposedly nutritious MREs. What then? He tried to remember if anyone had declared the sprats edible.

A recurring nightmare replayed before his eyes, even though he was still awake. The failure of self-sufficiency. A cutoff of supplies for Earth, for either political or financial reasons. Slow starvation, until a pitiful handful of emaciated Abydans came stumbling back through the StarGate, slamming the door on the brightest prospect humanity had ever faced.

That's if the Abydans were even allowed back, given the attitude of Senator Ashby and his friends. Maybe they'd find the way to Earth barred, which meant extinction, not starvation.

Not everybody on earth had lost interest in the Ballas colony, however. Daniel turned to the stack of correspondence requesting information on everything from budgeting for supplies to the effects of StarGate translation on pregnant women.

It seemed as though everybody who had reason to feel unhappy on Earth wanted a planet of their own. And, given the plethora of StarGate coordinates he'd found, perhaps they'd find one.

Daniel riffled through the letters. Every -ism and ethnic group. Black nationalists who want to separate themselves from racist America. Boers in search of the ultimate *apartheid*. In Asia alone, every marginalized group from Tamils to Tibetans were apparently searching for their own promised lands.

Speaking of promised lands, there were the proposals to create all-Protestant, all-Catholic, and all-Islamic worlds, not to mention the Wiccans, who wanted a world with permanent Celtic twilight.

Every European country which once had an empire leapt at the idea of new worlds to conquer. Then there were the unrepentant communists, the folks who felt fascism never got a fair shake, or feudalism, anarchism, paganism, libertarianism . . . probably nudism too, Daniel thought sourly.

There were even large companies who wanted to know about the bottom lines on colonial ventures. Maybe it was an interest in a new field of investment. Or maybe some CEOs were dreaming of their very own corporate states . . .

Whatever the reasons, Daniel found himself drowning in correspondence. Dave Freck seemed to forward him more every day.

Daniel suspected his bean counter was indirectly suggesting a fresh influx of cash and colonists. But bringing additional colonists, especially Urt-men, into the present troubled situation seemed to Daniel like pouring oil upon the fires.

Squaring the thick pile of paper, Daniel put it aside again. Somehow, such an eager market should be able to yield the foundation some sort of financial return. Maybe a journal on the problems of colonization. Get the staff of experts they'd been using to write learned articles. He made a note to talk to Dave about it—

If they could divert precious resources from the endless day-to-day struggle for survival.

Daniel remembered the glib way he'd invoked the Donner party during the arguments over planning the colony. Now he faced the grim reality of becoming an unrecognized prophet. He'd been there before, attempting to lecture the establishment of Egyptology. But back then, if nobody had believed his words, nobody had starved—except for Daniel Jackson, unemployable Ph.D. Now, however . . .

Rubbing his eyes, Daniel wondered for the thousandth time whether he'd have been wiser simply to have hired an administrator for the colony and stayed home.

No lamplight flickered in the tent which Skaara and Kasuf shared. The older man had already gone to sleep, exhausted by his day's work. Sha'uri and Skaara stood outside the tent, illuminated by the dying flames of a campfire. They barely noticed, embroiled in a flaring argument.

"Daniel, Daniel, Daniel," Skaara snapped. "To listen to you, everything is his fault."

"Not all," Sha'uri had to admit. "It could be that we picked a bad world. Ra never chose to bring humans here. Maybe it was all right for his race, but not for us."

"I don't think that Ra chose worlds that were easy

for humans to live on," Skaara argued. "That would make it too easy for us to get out from under his thumb. On Earth he terrorized a good-sized region, but he only ruled in the Nile valley—which was surrounded by deserts and cut off by a sea to the north."

"We don't know much about the other worlds in the Empire," Sha'uri said, "but we know nothing of Ballas. I don't blame Daniel for that—although he was the one who picked the name out of the list."

"If Daniel didn't find problems with this world, you can blame your friend Imiseba," Skaara retorted. "*He* stampeded everyone into rushing here, after seeing only what could be seen from the StarGate's Entrance Hall. And ever since he's arrived, all he has done is complain."

"You call Imiseba *my* friend, but wasn't he one of your followers?" Sha'uri shot back. "Wasn't he one of your militiamen?"

Skaara's lips thinned. "I've been asking around about Imiseba, especially since the town meeting. The stories are . . . interesting. When Father rose, staff in hand, to lead the people against Ra and the Horus guards, it seems that Imiseba was one of the last to go. He couldn't even find a stick as a weapon. Some people mock him still, calling him 'Twig' because that was all he brought."

Sha'uri had noticed Imiseba's odd reaction whenever the word came up.

"When Hathor landed her ship, Imiseba wasn't a member of the militia. But he went out to loot among the dead, and found several rifles. We took him in then, but even so, he flirted with other factions. For a while he was very friendly with Gerekh."

That was a name Sha'uri knew. Gerekh had been a profiteer and warlord, becoming more and more powerful as things had grown worse in Nagada. By the time the end came, he had controlled a sizable part of the city, with a number of armed followers.

"If he was so friendly with Gerekh, how—" Sha'uri began.

"Dumb luck. Imiscba was with me, dickering about something or other, when the city went mad. He joined the riot squad I led, probably because he didn't think he could survive in the city alone. When I went to rescue our supply of blast-lances, he was there, so he got one."

"And somehow he survived all the fighting and the retreat," Sha'uri said sarcastically. "Why do I suspect he wasn't in the front lines?"

"He managed to avoid our final attack. Somehow"—he looked as if he'd tasted a rotten fruit as he repeated the word Sha'uri had just used—"he ended in the guard detail with you and the noncombatants you led to Colonel O'Neil."

"Clever," Sha'uri grudgingly admitted.

"And dangerous," Skaara added in a low voice. "Don't underestimate him, or you could wind up as Mrs. Imiseba."

Sha'uri stared at him.

"He's ambitious—he wants power," her brother

warned. "If Daniel, Father, and I were to . . . suffer accidents, Imiseba could end up leading the colony." Skaara's face took on a brooding look. "And the easiest way to cement his control would be to marry someone connected with the former legitimate leaders."

"You go too far, brother," Sha-uri said.

"I merely speak of things that happened in Earth history," Skaara replied. "And back home on Abydos. Do not let your emotions blind you, Sha'uri. If Imiseba or his friends make overtures, see them for what they are."

"And what should I do instead?" Sha'uri inquired in a cutting voice. "Stand by Daniel as a good, dutiful wife?"

"Daniel has done some foolish, even hurtful things," Skaara admitted. "But even when he spoke against Father, he stood up and did that *himself*. He didn't rely on faceless voices from the crowd."

"You take his side against me—?"

Skaara shook his head. "I take no sides. All I ask is that you look to your feelings. Do not let others use them to manipulate you."

Sha'uri opened her mouth for a hot reply. She *had* watched her feelings, she thought. How often had she squashed back a sneaking sympathy for Daniel when others abused him?

She realized that was a rather one-sided watchfulness, and was silent for a moment. Finally she asked, "What do you think of Daniel?"

"I think he is a man, with the shortcomings of any man. I know he has done his best for the people of Abydos." Skaara glanced at her. "All of them."

He sighed, looking away from her and into the fire. "Given all that has happened, could anyone have done better?"

The illumination in Jack O'Neil's tent was bright and unwavering—electric, powered by batteries. The discussion going on, however, went wildly back and forth—producing more heat than light at the moment.

Seated behind his desk, O'Neil faced Mahu and a delegation of his militiamen. The Abydan captain was indulging his penchant for oratory. "You say this is to be our world, yet you still exclude us from the gateway. When will we be good enough, honored colonel?"

O'Neil stifled a sigh. The complaint was valid enough, if anyone but Mahu had made it. One of his tasks on Ballas was to leave a strong, trained militia force to act as gendarmerie and guards. The problem was, such a force did not exist. And Mahu was one of the major reasons why.

He regarded his group of warriors as a personal fief, resisting anything like a unified chain of command while aiding and abetting any other would-be warlords with groups under arms.

On the other hand, Kasuf and Skaara had made it clear that it just wasn't politic to point this out. Mahu and his coalition of independent companies would somehow have to be assimilated. Somehow.

Personally, O'Neil saw Mahu as a loudmouth who liked to talk while leaving the dangerous job of fighting to the other guys. Astonishingly, neither the leader nor his company had suffered serious damage in the final, forlorn hope of an attack against the Horus Guards in the mines of Nagada. The colonel would be just as happy to squash him as an annoyance and get on with the work of reorganizing the militia along workable lines.

Unfortunately, O'Neil couldn't follow his instincts. And he couldn't let Mahu go away mad, or his complaint about the Abydans "not being good enough" would be all around the campfires by breakfast.

O'Neil glanced at Feretti, Halloran, and Fuentes, who stood beside his desk. Halloran coughed, his face almost as red as his close-cropped hair. "Gate guard has always been the major draw on our manpower," he said. Fuentes nodded.

O'Neil knew that Halloran meant "drain" rather than "draw." A heavy company did not leave a whole lot of warm bodies to take care of all the jobs, official and otherwise, the marines had found themselves doing. Between Feretti's topographic training team, the other lieutenants' sample grabbers, and the men giving those Abydans who would listen a basis in handicrafts and survival, he was hard pressed to maintain any kind of security at all.

For instance, the damned hoodat was still on the

loose. It would be nice to detail a couple of people to finding the animal's new lair, preferably without becoming brunch, instead of depending on Halloran and Fuentes to fit the search in around their other missions.

But the StarGate was still the prime point to be secured, even more than the camp itself. If disaster befell the colonists, they'd all have to retreat through the gateway. If the StarGate was closed, they'd have neither escape nor support.

O'Neil moved his eyes to Feretti. The sharp-featured lieutenant kept dourly silent, but he raised his shoulders in an almost invisible shrug.

Looks like I'm elected to be the diplomat, O'Neil thought.

He said, "Perhaps the time has come let the militia take a more active part in guarding the gate. I will present your idea to Skaara in the morning, suggesting that one shift become the responsibility of the Abydan people. He can ask for volunteers from among all the warriors, then organize them appropriately."

Mahu's deeply tanned face changed color—an angry flush, though he said nothing. O'Neil's proposal would be a victory for centralization, with Abydans of all political stripes mounting guard, instead of the power grab Mahu had intended. "It is a start," he choked out at last.

"An excellent start," O'Neil said blandly, enjoying

his small triumph over this small adversary. "Let us make it so."

Daniel had a variety of reactions as he heard someone working on the tapes that held his tent flaps closed.

Where the hell did I leave that pistol? he wondered, fumbling along his crate desk. Surely things hadn't gone so sour that he had to worry about assassination, but . . .

Admixed with that was worry that some new disaster was about to be dropped on his desk, preferably without awakening the whole camp.

Finally, there was plain old annoyance at being interrupted while trying to catch up with his paperwork. Didn't he do enough all day without having to hold people's hands in the middle of the night?

All those responses vanished when the flaps opened, and he saw his uninvited guest.

Sha'uri.

She was wearing jeans and a sweater, but had wrapped an Abydan homespun shawl around herself against the chill of the night air.

Daniel remembered a time, not all that long ago, when the girl he'd barely met had let her mantle slide from her shoulders, revealing a sweet, delicate body to the stranger from the StarGate.

"I don't want to bother you," Sha'uri said almost brusquely.

Too late, Daniel thought.

Sha'uri wrapped herself more closely in the brown robe, as if the air inside the tent were colder than that outside. "I was walking . . . and thinking. And then I saw your light was on."

As if on cue, the flame in the oil lamp began to gutter. Daniel quickly began adjusting the wick. Almost out of oil. He'd have to get some more tomorrow.

"I just wanted to say—perhaps I made a mistake." Sha'uri's apology sounded almost surly. "My feelings—I've been unfair to you. I overreacted during the final fight against Hathor, when you volunteered to go aboard the *Boat of a Million Years.*"

Can't say that I minded that, Daniel said to himself, but he only nodded silently.

"And then, during the arguments on how and when to set up the colony, I went too far the other way, to show my independence. I should never have gone on that stupid TV show and complained about the job you and the Abydos Foundation were doing. You're trying your best at a very difficult job—and it's not as though we're making it any easier," she said with a wan smile.

As an attempt to cheer someone up, it was a signal failure.

Well, Daniel thought, if she's trying to be honest with me, the least I can do is offer honesty in return.

"When you were undoing the flaps, for one second I wondered if it was someone coming in to kill me," he admitted. "Because, let's face it, I haven't been making a lot of friends around here. The town meeting showed that clearly enough."

Daniel shook his head. "Oddly enough, I realize I don't mind being yelled at so much. I just hate the fact that everyone seems so *divided* on what we've got to do. It reminds me of how things went to hell on Abydos, all the factions arguing all the time instead of doing something—anything—to solve our problems."

"So you thought of assassination," Sha'uri said quietly, her expression one of pain.

"I'm a damned idiot!" Daniel swore at himself. "I didn't mean to bring up bad memories—"

"You didn't try to kill Father," Sha'uri pointed out, surprisingly reasonable. "That was Hathor's people. As for the factions, they seem to exist after every revolution."

"Well, they're certainly back with a vengeance now," Daniel said gloomily. "The last time they were screwing around, it was just about power. Now, unless we all pull together, we could end up starving."

"They say hunger concentrates the mind powerfully," Sha'uri offered.

Daniel glanced up in surprise. Sha'uri had stopped joking with him long before she'd left the hearth and home. Since then her humor, such as it was, had always been of the slashing variety.

More than anything she'd said, this was the fragile offer of some kind of truce.

"I'd rather not find that out," he replied. "My

clothes have gotten baggy enough as it is, and re-placements are light-years away."

They shared a quiet smile, and at least for the moment that was enough.

CHAPTER 12
UNANTICIPATED
CIRCUMSTANCES

The wind was up with an intensity that usually
threatened thunderstorms or tornadoes back on
Earth. The tall, stilty trees down in the valley rocked
back and forth, branches shaking, the entire huge
canopy of foliage undulating like a stormy russet sea.

For Feretti the effect was intensified because the
rocky crag on which he stood jutted into the forested
valley like a headland into deep water. He had to
brace himself as he peered through his binoculars to
check the sky. But there were no anvil black thunder-
heads scudding into view, no deadly funnels stretching down from the heaven. Apparently, it was just a
windy day in the neighborhood.

"Different planet, different weather," he called to
the rest of the topo team, who were sheltering in the
lee of the hill. "Let's just hope there's not a whole
season of this."

From his vantage point he ran his binoculars along
the length of the western side of the valley. Those

hills were no longer terra incognita. He and his team had surveyed them all, learned their secrets, and codified them.

Then he turned toward the new territory they had to conquer, the eastern hills. The land displayed the same gently rolling characteristics, though there were a couple of taller, squarer ridges shouldering up among the hills. The face of the nearest ridge had weathered, creating a gentler scree slope running down to a rounded hilltop below.

Feretti plotted a course up the fan-shaped earth spill, where the eroded debris was covered in grass and dotted with trees. And at the very top . . .

The lieutenant blinked, refocusing his lenses. For just a second he'd seen a patch of black against the cinnamon foliage.

One of his marine assistants came up into the wind, each step a deliberate movement against its force. "See something, Loot?" he asked.

"Not sure." Feretti knelt, opening out a copy of the rough chart the initial survey team had made. The marine dropped beside him, helping to hold the sketch map while Feretti made a notation.

"I only got the barest glimpse, but I think there's an opening in the face of that ridge."

"A cave, you mean?" The marine squinted, trying to make out what Feretti had described.

"There's bushes or something in the way. This wind just moved them in the right direction." Feretti folded up the map and stowed it away. "It's worth checking when we get up there," he said. "Maybe it will turn out to be the hoodat's second home."

Mahu blinked as he stepped into the Entrance Hall of the StarGate pyramid, which made him frown. In the last couple of months he'd become unused to powerful artificial light at nighttime. That would change when he became one of the people running things. They would move the electricity machine to the camp, to light the tents of the rulers by night.

No, not tents. The houses of the rulers, the palaces. Some of the miners must know the secrets of shaping rock instead of just hacking it out of the way. They would build fine stone walls, and large windows gleaming with light. At night lesser folk would walk by in awe at the beauty of Commander Mahu's home.

An interrogative cough behind him recalled Mahu to the present. This was no time to dream of glories to come. Tonight he would earn his place. Tonight they would destroy the StarGate.

It had taken awhile to assemble the right roster of guards for the night shift. Inflexible sorts had to be . . . diverted. Sometimes it required only a quiet word in the right ear, a suggestion, a promise, a threat. Not necessarily to the inconvenient militiaman—there were families, friends, loved ones.

Only a couple had required accidents.

In the end, Mahu was surprised at the number of supporters Imiseba boasted, people he'd never have suspected. But then, neither would Skaara nor the Urt-men.

Now they were gathered, a corporal's guard, to take over responsibility of the StarGate as usual—nothing to arouse suspicion.

They marched into the lights in a ragged line, a crowd of individuals seemingly flung together by fate. The marine noncom in charge shook his head at such slovenly performance.

Ah, Mahu thought, at least our guns are clean.

The marine noncom produced a clipboard and pen, giving Mahu a dubious glance. Ankha, one of the bright young men who'd learned his English from Sha'uri, stepped forward to take care of the necessary paperwork.

Shouldering their arms, the marine guards left.

Mahu deployed his sentries as he had done on other nights, just in case the Urt-men should come back for some reason. But he stayed in the Entrance Hall, trying to pierce the almost complete darkness outside. Ballas had no moon, and the sky was overcast.

Truly, it was a night for conspirators.

Long minutes passed. Though he tried to adopt an appearance of quiet confidence, like the great captain he fancied himself to be, Mahu found himself fidgeting. There were times when he wished he'd bought and learned to read an Urt-man timepiece.

At last the call of a *hoopeh*, an Abydan bird, sounded in the distance. That meant the Urt-men had passed on to the graveled road. The call was answered from nearer in the darkness.

Mahu dashed into the passageway that led deeper into the stone and called down to Ankha. "Gather our men. The others come."

He arrived back in the Entrance Hall in time to greet the new arrivals. Three were Kenna's farm clansmen, skilled in the use of *seefaw*. The fourth was Qa'a.

"My people await you in the downward passage," Mahu greeted them abruptly. "Where is the *seefaw*?"

The Urt-men had maintained their stockpile of the explosive in the pyramid, doling out only small amounts of the putty-like stuff for the job of clearing the land. Qa'a strode ahead to where the militia guardsmen stood.

"Down here," he said, "and off to the right."

The packs of explosive were stacked in a shadowy corner of the Grand Gallery, behind one of the monumental pillars.

"Not too close to the gate between worlds," Qa'a explained. "But not too close to thieving hands outside."

He opened the pack, and the men began carrying foot-long blocks of the stuff back to the StarGate chamber, aided by the floor's slight but definite slant down into the bowels of the pyramid.

"How much do you need?" a puffing militiaman asked as he returned for a second load.

"All of it!" Mahu commanded. "We must be sure the gateway is destroyed—or at least sealed forever."

Kenna's expert with the explosives, a tall, lean farmer, gave him a skeptical look, then nodded.

Soon enough all the cases were emptied. Mahu went down the Grand Gallery, through the antechamber, and into the stone room where the Star-Gate stood.

The golden quartz of the three-man-tall torus seemed to have developed some cancerous growth. The gleaming circle was blotched in several locations with large globs of odd-smelling, putty gray goo. Blocks of *seefaw* were also piled at each corner of the room that housed the gateway.

Kenna's technicians were at work stringing fuses and crimping on blasting caps for each block. Apparently the detonating devices had been kept in a different location. Qa'a and the knowledgeable ones had collected these materials themselves.

Mahu leaned over the one who seemed to be the leader. "Soon?" he inquired impatiently.

That earned him the sort of look all experts bestow on those who joggle their elbows during ticklish jobs. "Soon enough," the rangy farmer replied. "With stuff of such power, it is best to be slow and cautious. Haste has cost one of our comrades an arm."

"And probably his head, when he recovers enough so the one the Urt-men call 'Gunny' can get at him," another of the bomb makers said.

Then the younger man looked a little surprised

and laughed. "I suppose Gunny won't, at that. When this goes off, our people will get *him*."

The sound of the blast was supposed to be the signal for several groups of chosen men to deal with the Urt-men and take into custody doubtful elements among the colonists—like Kasuf, Skaara, and Sha'uri.

"Relax, Mahu," Qa'a advised. "Let the Urt-men get their sleep—while they can."

As soon as the demolition preparations were finished, Mahu demanded that he be the one to light the fuse. He was determined that *he* should be acclaimed for closing the StarGate and beginning the new reign on Ballas.

The rangy farmer in charge of the sappers gave him a cigarette lighter with ill-concealed relief. He knew the power of the packages he'd prepared and wanted to be far away when they went off.

Impatiently, Mahu counted off the militia guards and their auxiliaries as they passed through the Entrance Hall, out onto the stone pier beyond, and then disappeared into the darkness beyond.

The farmer who'd set up the charges had warned Mahu of two things. He had to delay the detonation until the team had gotten well away—at least halfway down the great hill—and he could not stand in the entrance when he triggered the blast. The open passages leading from the StarGate chamber might act as a gigantic rifle barrel, channeling some of the explosive gases and flame.

The fuse had been set so that it ended in the shelter of one of the massive stone pylons flanking the entrance. Mahu nodded. The point of doing something that goes down in history is to survive and exploit it, not to be remembered posthumously.

He went down to one knee, clutching the lighter, crouched against the coming fury he expected to unleash. But as he dropped, he caught movement in the corner of his eye. Something had broken the tall, narrow shaft of electric light streaming through the entrance.

Mahu dropped the lighter, his right hand freeing the pistol he'd tucked into the sash around his waist. Was it one of the Ra-be-damned Urt-men turning up for some unknown reason? Perhaps it was one of Raya's or Kenna's followers, come to make sure he suffered a fatal accident in his moment of triumph.

Snarling, Mahu sprang to his feet, his pistol raised.

And faced the stuff of nightmares.

The creature before him stood tall as a man, but it would never be mistaken for human, not standing naked and furred. But it was not one of the dog men, the russet-furred Setim who had come through the StarGate after the last battle with Hathor.

This thing had fur that shaded from brown to gray in a subtle striped pattern. Its face was built along the lines of the Lady Hathor's cat mask, but the head seemed misshapen—strangely deeper. Its upper canine teeth were a pair of jutting fangs at least four inches long.

Here was the hoodat. *And it walked like a man!*

Mahu broke the grip of the bone-chilling fear which had kept him frozen. With a high-pitched, woman's scream he fired his pistol.

But his bullets passed through empty air where the target had been. The creature leapt at him with unimaginable speed and fury, one huge paw sweeping upward, claws extended. They ripped out his throat, but the claws were unnecessary. The force of the blow was sufficient to break his neck.

Mahu slammed against the stone pylon, already dead as the creature slashed again, eviscerating him.

Then it turned at the sound of human voices returning.

"Mahu! Why did you fire?"

"What's the problem?"

A tall, sturdy figure—Qa'a—stepped into the square-cut pool of light. He held a rifle across his body as he peered into the shadow of the pylon. "Mahu, why do you delay? If they heard your shooting in the camp—"

Wild yells erupted behind Qa'a as the nightmare form launched itself from the darkness, both paws upraised. Claws tore through Qa'a's flesh and stove in his ribs before he could even bring his rifle to bear. He was down, a bloody ruin, as the creature bounded out of the light and vanished off the stone pier.

Its flight was followed by a hail of bullets. The adrenaline-pumped militiamen charged into the darkness after the beast, shouting and shooting wildly.

The tall farmer who had led the demolition team pulled out his pistol, but he did not join the pursuit— nor did he allow his team members to do so.

"The blast!" he called after the out-of-control militiamen. "No one has triggered the blast! All we've done is warn the Urt-men!"

Scattered shots were his only answer.

He stepped toward the primed detonator, then glanced down the road. The lights of approaching Humvees were already illuminating the ancient roadway up the pyramid entrance.

"The Urt-men are already here," he said in disgust. Muttering low curses, he herded his men off into the darkness. There were other ways down beside the road. With luck they could be back in the camp with no one the wiser.

Feretti stopped the Humvees before they entered the shaft of light from the pyramid entrance and brought his men forward on foot. In the distance he heard an M16 on full auto running through its clip.

He shook his head. What the hell was going on up here? A colonist argument gone out of control? A StarGate invasion? An unannounced inspection?

If it was the last, he felt a twinge of sympathy for the inspecting officers. They were dodging a lot of lead out there.

No one seemed to be guarding the ingress to the

pyramid—at least no one alive. Feretti sent a couple of men to secure the entrance, then knelt beside the nearer figure sprawled on the stone pier. He recognized Qa'a—and he also realized the Abydan was not one of those designated for guard duty.

There wasn't much hope in asking him what had happened, however. He was still breathing, but blood was bubbling on his lips. If they could evacuate him to an Earth-side hospital, he might survive this night's work. But at the level of medicine available on Ballas, he was a goner.

"Die, beast!" A yell from the darkness brought Feretti's head up as a wild-eyed militiaman came charging into the light, rifle leveled. Apparently, he'd seen only a silhouette crouched over Qa'a's body and leapt to the conclusion that the night hunter was back for a meal.

A shot from Feretti's M16 caught him in the chest and sent him tumbling back into the dark.

"Sir!" The marine who'd gone to the other crumpled body had just found the fuse he'd failed to light.

Feretti's usually tight face seemed to compress another inch. He quickly redeployed his men, leaving most to guard the entrance while he took a couple of volunteers down to the chamber of the StarGate, reeling fuse all the way.

An indrawn breath hissed through his teeth when he saw what the Abydans had done. Well, they'd sealed Qa'a's death warrant. No way would they be using the gate before he passed on.

The lieutenant whipped around, heading back to the outer world. "Got to get word to the colonel right away," he said. "We need everybody we can trust up here ASAP to scrape that damned glop off the gate before dawn."

"Sir?" The marine knew that the Loot had a mania for keeping things clean and in their place. But this seemed excessive.

Feretti rounded on the man with a glare. "At 12:45 p.m., that thing is going to light up like a Christmas tree. There's gonna be all sorts of energy running through it. Maybe you'd like to see how that energy reacts with a coating of C-4. *I* don't."

Somehow, Jack O'Neil wasn't surprised to find both Kenna and Raya in Imiseba's tent. The place had been set up as a command post—except now the guards outside had been disarmed and sent on their way.

O'Neil figured that the blast from the StarGate pyramid was supposed to have been the starting bell for Imiseba's putsch. But when the sounds of shooting had erupted around the pyramid, those plans had gone down the toilet. Many of his followers had taken the rifle fire as a sign of failure and quietly gone to bed. Others had gone to their gathering points only to find alerted guards—or to be coopted by Skaara's militia officers and ordered to guard the walls.

O'Neil had decided it was time for a chat with

the would-be leader. Knowing the energies that the golden quartz could contain, O'Neil didn't believe that any amount of C-4 could have damaged the Star-Gate. He wasn't so sure about the stonework of the pyramid, however. No one would have been going through the glowing torus if the plotters had managed to bring down the roof of the chamber.

He strolled through the tent flap with his submachine gun dangling negligently from his hand. "Lot of excitement tonight, huh, gentlemen?"

Imiseba stood behind a large improvised table, his eyes darting from O'Neil to the M9 Beretta pistol acting as a paperweight.

"I just got the radio report from the pyramid. They had a visit from a hoodat. Poor old Mahu was mauled—"

O'Neil abruptly switched from the easy drawl he'd affected to a colder tone. "If you're going to go for the pistol, just do it and get it over with. If not, why don't you just move away? You're beginning to get annoying, and that's not smart to do to someone with one of these." He hefted his weapon.

Imiseba scuttled back from the gun.

"Now, where was I?" O'Neil asked, resuming his lighter tone again. "Oh, yes. Mahu. Clawed to death. Qa'a, too. Funny about him. He wasn't supposed to be there. But then, a lot of odd things were going on up there tonight, it seems."

A strangled sound came from Raya, but he subsided when O'Neil glanced inquisitively in his direction.

"We're cleaning it up now. Mahu's company will be disbanded, the men moved into other units." Skaara's units, with reliable men to keep an eye on the newbies. At least, O'Neil hoped they were reliable men. The discovery of Qa'a at the pyramid had come as an unpleasant surprise.

"Skaara is talking to Daniel about calling another town meeting to discuss how to defend ourselves against dangerous animals." His gaze took in the three chagrined conspirators. "I'm sure you'll be glad to cooperate."

O'Neil backed out of the tent—no sense turning his back on any of *those* characters—and nearly crashed into Skaara, who was rushing up with a squad of his militiamen.

The Abydan leader looked askance at O'Neil's submachine gun. "You didn't . . . *do* anything to them, did you?"

Shaking his head, the colonel grinned. "I saw no reason to create any martyrs," he said. "Mahu died by his own stupidity, and won't be regretted." He looked at the gunmen backing Skaara. "And you?"

"A small precaution to keep those three from talking to their followers before tomorrow evening's town meeting." Skaara also smiled without mirth. "A reception team, you might say."

"Tent arrest," O'Neil said.

"Do you blame us?" Skaara asked. "As you say, we cannot kill them. There are so few of us as there are."

"And we'll need every able-bodied man we can get," the colonel said in agreement. "Because now we have to hunt that sonofabitch animal down."

CHAPTER 13
THE GREAT CAT HUNT

Daniel had to admit that this town meeting was a great improvement over its predecessor. But it wasn't a case of practice making perfect—rather, the attitude of the participants had undergone a sea change. The former combative mood was gone. The colonists huddled around the bonfires, eager for the light, afraid of what the outer shadows might hide. These people were quiet, edgy, eager to hear what was being done.

So Skaara told them. "Perhaps we took too much for granted after the Maple machine scared off the hoodats in the StarGate pyramid," he said. "We thought the creatures would avoid us and our activities. But the events of last night have shown this is not the case. Thus, we have doubled the perimeter guards on the earthen wall, and will begin logging operations to create a palisade. The marines will also increase their sentry force at the pyramid, where the attacks occurred."

No more talk of militiamen guarding the StarGate, Daniel thought. At least for the time being.

The announcements of increased security were greeted with a favorable murmur.

Daniel glanced over at Imiseba, Kenna, and Raya, who sat at Kasuf's feet. They had nothing to say about the marines reasserting control. Indeed, at the mention of the pyramid all three of them had looked at the ground.

The conspirators had come frighteningly close to cutting Ballas off from the universe and precipitating a deadly breakdown of the colony. Even if the safety net offered by Earth was on the threadbare side, it beat nothing at all. Daniel shuddered at the vision of the colonists trying to get through an early winter with no supplies whatsoever.

It was ironic, he thought, that the Earth-side connection—and their lives—had been saved by a wild animal they'd now have to hunt down.

That was the second item on the town meeting's agenda. The colonists began to discuss how many people could be freed from work tomorrow to act as beaters and hunters in what was already coming to be called the Great Cat Hunt.

Everyone with energy weapons would be left to guard the camp or the StarGate. Those with rifles would be distributed among hunting parties and protectors for the unarmed noisemakers.

Hunters would take positions in the western hills. Beaters would begin at the edge of the cleared fields and march into the forest, make a racket. They would make an enveloping motion, curling around to drive whatever might be in the forest toward the hunting parties waiting in the hills.

Sheb, formerly of Mahu's militia company, asked to be recognized. "It seems that much work has gone into this plan. But there are a few things that might bear more thought. One, not many of our people have gone into the woods. It is hard to proceed through the thickets, but very easy to get lost. All should wear Urt-man's clothing—jeans, heavy trousers, sturdy shoes.

"My other point is more of a question. You think that people shouting and banging on pans will drive this hoodat creature away. But this did not work last night, did it?"

One of the marines gave a rehash of the suggestions that had come late that afternoon from Dr. Leighton, who based his suggestions mainly on tiger hunting in India, and why they thought this was the best approach. Daniel had read the report and noticed that the spokesman did not mention that Leighton had wished for heavier-gauge rifles in the hands of the hunters.

But even Daniel hadn't been able to tell if that was because the doctor was advocating greater stopping power, or whether Leighton was afraid that automatic fire would ruin his potential specimen. . . .

Sha'uri yawned, inhaling the delicious smell of freshly baked bread. She had arisen with the bakers today, setting off early for the communal kitchens.

They would have to put out a special effort this morning to feed all the hunters.

As she and several others started lighting the cook fires, marines came in, jackassing several heavily loaded freezer cases. One of the men saluted. "Colonel O'Neil's compliments, ma'am."

Sha'uri opened one of the cases and discovered a treasure trove. Fresh eggs, somehow transported unharmed through the StarGate, and butter. The others held whole hams and slabs of bacon.

The whole room was silent as the cooks considered this addition to their larder. Then they leapt to work, chattering excitedly about the generosity of the Urtmen and the day's outing, when they would act as beaters.

Sha'uri did not join in. She would not be going out of the camp that day. Colonel O'Neil had decreed it. Her only consolation was that Skaara, Kasuf, and Daniel would also be prisoners within the earthen walls. O'Neil wanted no chance of "accidents," as he delicately phrased it.

She sighed and began stirring a pot full of oatmeal. If this was all she was allowed to contribute, she would at least make sure the hunters set off with a hearty meal.

Considering what the hoodat had done to Mahu and Qa'a, some of the hunters might not be coming back.

"NABU," sighed Corporal Fred Ames as he glanced from the sea of humanity threatening to tread down the colony's planted fields to the teams of armed men still picking up supplies down in the camp.

"Who's that, sir?" asked young Castellano, assuming his superior was talking about an Abydan he'd seen in the crowd. The marine's short stature, wide-eyed interest, and apparent boundless store of innocence made him seem even more youthful than he actually was.

"Not who, what," Hank Young, one of the older marines, corrected him. "NABU—non-adjusting balls-up." He shook his head as he took in the chaos. "God! This is taking them about as long as it did to get everybody through the Puke Chute."

The hunt had been scheduled to set off at dawn, and the sun had already been up for an hour.

"Lieutenant Feretti has set off already," Ames said. "We're not getting any younger." He went to Lieutenant Fuentes, who was acting as traffic manager, and returned with a smile. "We're now an official advanced unit," he reported. "Hotel Alpha."

At least they had a map. Feretti's top team had been very, very busy getting most of the western hills surveyed.

"You think we're gonna bag ourselves a hoodat?" Castellano asked as they passed through the camp entrance.

Ames shook his head at the kid's eagerness. "It'll make a nice change," he said, "to be able to shoot at something that won't shoot back."

* * *

The beaters were still being organized as the last of the hunter units marched off. Hemaka's eyes widened as a rifle-carrying figure darted from between the tents to join his group. "Sheb! What are you doing here?"

Sheb gave a shame-faced grin, hefting his M16. "I traded my blast-lance with Pairi for the day. He's got the footrot and didn't want to go marching all over the hills."

"And what do you get out of the deal?" Hemaka asked suspiciously.

"I get to go where I can do some good," Sheb replied. "I've been outside the camp more than a lot of people. You know how they feel."

Hemaka nodded. Nagada had been a town of strong, thick walls. They had been necessary, with the killer sandstorms that blew over the desert. The walls had also crept into the culture and the blood of the inhabitants. Many of the colonists preferred to keep within the camp and its shallow earthen berm, feeling more at home there than in the unfamiliar forest.

"Besides, this will be my first chance to get deep into the hills," Sheb went on. "You know how Mahu always kept us on a tight rein, wanting us close to the camp." His gaze took in the entire bustle of the camp. "It's good to see everyone working *together* for once."

Again, Hemaka nodded, smiling at his friend. "I suppose we can always use another man. Come on."

With a grin like a kid playing hooky, Sheb shoul-dered his weapon and marched off.

Imiseba's feet hurt. Since his return from the first Ballas expedition, he'd made a point of wearing Aby-dan homespun and sandals. He hadn't even brought any Earthman's clothes when he had gone through the StarGate. Now his borrowed marine boots, the LPCs—leather personnel carriers, as the servicemen joked—were raising a painful crop of new blisters after the first mile of hiking. And the trousers of the woodland BDUs he wore were binding in the crotch.

He wondered if O'Neil somehow had planned this.

His discomfort was bad enough, but he had to share it with Kenna and Raya, who had punctuated every step with bitter complaints.

"I'm a planner, not a fighter," Kenna protested as he stumped along, holding his rifle as if it were some foreign thing that might pollute him. The skinny farmer was also dressed in borrowed finery—a pair of woodland camouflage pants with a red-checked shirt that clashed horribly.

Raya at least had clothes that fit—he'd taken along some of his Earth wardrobe. Over a pair of heavy-duty work pants he wore a knit sweater that looked remarkably like Abydan homespun.

But even the big miner didn't look comfortable, though he was probably in the best shape for this little exercise. His face was sullen, examining every bullet in his magazine, sure there was an underhanded motive for their inclusion in the cat hunt.

"I saw where we are to go in the hills. They put us between two groups of Urt-men," he complained for the fiftieth time. "Why would they do that?"

"To keep an eye on us, perhaps," Imiseba replied in a toneless voice.

"Maybe." Raya gave his companions a dark look. "Or, perhaps they will not shoot straight when this damnable creature appears. Perhaps some round will go astray," he said with a significant look.

If such should happen, I hope it hits you, Imiseba thought venomously.

"The Urt-men warriors have a term for that," Kenna agreed. "They call it 'blue on blue' when they accidentally fire on their own."

"If O'Neil did not kill us two nights ago, he won't bother now, accidentally or otherwise," Imiseba finally snapped, sick to death of their babbling. "He prefers to fight an enemy he knows."

Come to think of it, so do I, Imiseba realized in the sudden silence around him.

He gripped the stock of his rifle, trying to will himself back to familiarity with the weapon. He'd carried a blast-lance when he'd marched with Skaara, and usually armed himself with an easily concealed pistol nowadays.

But he'd gone through rifle training when he prepared for his sojourn as a scout, and he hadn't been a bad shot.

His finger slid over the outside of the trigger guard. It would be nice to extract a little vengeance from the Ra-be-damned beast which had so catastrophically altered his plans. . . .

Feretti surveyed the face of the ridge through habitually squinted eyes. There was the scree slope, pointing like an upward arrow toward the clump of foliage that might or might not hide a cave.

When the plans for the cat hunt were being laid, Feretti had remembered the notation he'd made on his chart and laid it before the colonel. Here was the result—an advance scouting party to check out the ridge, which had yet to be visited by the topo team.

"Okay. That's it." Feretti's voice was clipped, even harsher than usual. Perhaps it was the extra weight he was carrying—the AN/PRC-77 field radio, or the "prick-77," as it was known. Or maybe the tension came from the reason why he was humping along with one of the few radios available on Ballas.

Feretti and the three men with him were the farthest-flung unit of the hunting operation. If they found a cave, they were to investigate. If it was inhabited, they were to deal with any occupants and then seal it off, depriving the hoodat of a potential hidey-hole.

There were twice as many of them as the men the hoodat had killed, and the scout team was on its guard. But if that cave was more than just a pocket in the hill, and if it had tenants, Feretti and his people would be playing tunnel rats in the dark with a big, nasty cat. Just them. No backup.

The team reached the top of the nearest hill, and Feretti unlimbered his binoculars, straining for a glimpse of the blackness he'd spotted once before.

Nothing.

They started up the scree slope. Feretti felt oddly naked climbing the grassy incline, dotted with an occasional tree. It was his military instincts cutting in. Anybody hidden in the brush at the apex of the slope would have an open field of fire.

Right, Feretti chided himself. And if the cat had his own prick-77, he could call in an artillery strike and cover the slope in pureed marines.

He stopped the group about thirty feet below the suspected cave mouth and counted off two men as a covering force. "Anything comes out of those bushes, you waste it," he commanded.

Then Feretti and the remaining man carefully made their way into the brush.

"You were right, Loot," his companion, Lambertson, said. "There's the hole."

Feretti left Lambertson guarding the entrance while he made sure the rest of the thicket was empty. Then he called up the covering group.

The black mouth of the cave was taller than Feretti, and wide enough to accommodate someone with much bigger shoulders than he had.

Like a tiger, maybe, he thought.

"Lights on," he ordered.

Each man on the team had a rifle equipped with a flash under the barrel. Four beams illuminated a sort of rampway of grit leading down into deeper darkness.

"Cover me," Feretti ordered.

The interior of the cave was much larger than the small aperture had suggested. Feretti got a feeling of space around himself as he quickly ran his light in a semicircle along the floor. The drift under his feet gave way to a gritty, level footing.

Too level, a little voice in his brain warned.

Then he encountered the wall.

It wasn't rock, or anything natural he'd ever encountered. It was like a neutral plastic, translucent in the beam of Feretti's flashlight. There was a milkiness farther within the wall that blocked the light—and his view. The thing rose straight up and curved slightly as it merged with an equally planed ceiling.

"What the *hell*?" Feretti muttered.

It wasn't a cave, it was a room!

He called his people in, even as he ran a light over the other walls. What the hell could it be? A bunker? Underground storage? A cesspool for a long-vanished house on top of the hill?

Even smeared with dirt, the walls were still recognizably made of that translucent plastic. Except, on the wall where he'd come in, there were several panels of a different material. They couldn't be doors. . . .

Feretti felt a chill. *But they could be windows.*

In the course of his career he'd visited countries

where jungles had overgrown the ruins of lost civilizations. He'd seen ancient cities of mud brick which had over time collapsed to form hills rising above river valleys.

But how long would you have to wait for enough airborne soil to settle until it buried a six-story structure?

He waved the men forward. The entering team members were just as astonished as he was.

"Artificial," Lambertson said.

"I don't think this is a hill at all," Feretti agreed. "I think we've got a buried building." He shook his head. "I always wondered what would happen if you didn't dust for ten, twenty thousand years. Now we know."

They found the door on the far side of the room, offset from the broken window. It was one of those sci-fi things that slid into the wall, but in this case the panel only slid halfway.

A sill of dust had blown into the track that the door ran along. Feretti noticed that it was scuffed.

"Heads up, people." Aiming his rifle and light, Feretti stepped through the narrow doorway.

A faint echo of his order came back from a distant wall. This was a much bigger room, maybe some sort of public space.

What the hell had they gotten themselves into? Could this be a base of the mysterious forerunner race that had spawned Ra? A town? A city?

The guy they really needed in here was Daniel

Jackson. But what they had was a fire team of marines tasked with a ticklish mission. And that mission had just grown a hell of a lot more difficult if the beast had a whole building to hide out in.

I hope we don't shoot up some archeological treasure if we do find the hoodat, he thought.

The beam from his flash petered out into the darkness as he waved it before himself.

Follow the floor, he decided.

But the floor, too, ended, maybe fifteen feet from the door, at a shin-high parapet. Waving his men forward again, Feretti advanced to the retaining wall and shone his light down.

Whatever Ra's people—or whoever had lived here—had been like, they apparently didn't have a problem with heights. The center of the buliding was a vast well, going down several stories.

Not much of a safety rail, Feretti thought, kicking the low parapet. Set in the top was a thin strip of familiar material—golden quartz.

Maybe it generated a force field to keep the unwary from a long tumble.

"Loot!" The cry brought him back from the edge.

Lambertson stood at the wall they'd just passed through. The plastic on this side wasn't milky, however. It was clear as glass. And Lambertson's beam, passing through a film of dust on the surface, spotlighted an alien face. It was wholly alien, but similar enough to humanity to give Feretti the creeps.

The basic design suggested a lizard—ash gray, scaly skin, eyes like pools of black oil, with dissipated-looking pouches below. There was no nose, but a sort of pressed-in snout, with what looked like gill slits below. Then a too wide, lipless mouth, running down to a receding chin.

"What the hell is it, sir?"

"I'd guess it's the people who built this place."

They added their lights to Lambertson's, illuminating a tableau of gray-skinned forerunner people—a 3-D image of some kind, not, as Feretti had first thought, actual people embedded in the material. He knew how thick that wall was—it wouldn't accommodate a grouping of aliens. Not even skinny ones.

They moved along the wall, spotlighting new tableaus. Here one of the aliens had its mouth open, revealing far too many ridge-like teeth.

Feretti was more interested in the background—hills, some with fanciful little buildings on them, leading down to what looked like an ornamental lake. Looming behind were a couple of larger buildings, like accretions of living crystal. Is that what this place looked like under its coating of dirt?

Squinting his eyes harder, Feretti frowned. Could one of those images *be* this building? Over time, lakes turn into swamps, swamps into forests. He tried to overlay the image with what he knew of the topography of the forest valley.

"Sir!" That call was even louder, more excited.

Feretti turned to discover that his men had moved even farther along the wall. There were more gray aliens strolling along. But bringing up the rear was a new figure in brown- and gray-striped fur and carrying something after the aliens. It was like watching a saber-toothed tiger attempting to do an impression of Jeeves the butler.

"Oh, man, look at this!" Lambertson was even farther in the lead. The imagery changed to show a group of grayskins seated with all the dignity of operagoers, their black holes of eyes avidly taking in the spectacle of a couple of big cats—hoodats?—tearing at one another with fang and claw.

"Sick bastards," one of the marines muttered.

"Well, it looks like they left their pets behind when they pulled out of here," Lambertson said.

"Enough of this," Feretti said sharply, tearing himself away from the almost clinical violence of the image. "I want to see what's at the bottom of this central well."

Pooling their lights together, they succeeded in illuminating the floor several levels below. It was a vast open space, dotted at irregular intervals with intricate, enigmatic contrivances made of golden quartz.

"Looks like they left a *lot* when they blew town." Feretti stared down in wonder that the—what? Operations center? Power station? Art Gallery? Home-appliance superstore?

Then he realized there was something wrong.

There were empty spaces among the golden relics, odd patches free of dust. . . .

"Pull back," he ordered.

But even as he spoke, his words were drowned out by the crash of blast-bolts.

CHAPTER 14
HUNTERS AND HUNTED

Castellano gave an involuntary groan as he shifted stance in his position. Corporal Ames, lying prone on the top of the hill, turned his eyes from his binoculars to glare at the younger man.

"Too bad you don't have a mini-megaphone, Castellano. You could yell through that and wave a red flag to let the hoodat know we're here."

"Come on, Corp," Young protested. "It's not like we're running an ambush. It's an animal, for chrissake."

"Yeah. And animals have good ears." Ames looked balefully at Castellano again. "I should have sent you back after you took that skid down the hillside."

"It's just a sprain, Corp." Castellano shifted again and gritted his teeth. "It's not like we're off on a fifty-mile hike. All we have to do is keep position."

"Yeah," Ames grunted, "and the longer you're down there on your ass, the stiffer that ankle is gonna get." He grimaced. "Don't think *I'm* carrying you back."

"Aye, sir," a chastened Castellano said. "I'll find a stick or something—"

He broke off, staring away to their right. "I thought we were supposed to be anchoring the flank."

Ames turned from the stretch of forest he'd been observing and saw what had caught Castellano's attention. There was a brief flash, a glint of metal on the next hillside—a hill that was supposed to be empty.

He trained his binoculars on the spot, and was rewarded with the blurred image of something moving very quickly through his field of vision.

Whoever it is, he's certainly hauling ass. Maybe it's one of Feretti's people. But he was carrying a radio. Why send a runner?

Ames shrugged. Whatever the reason, it was a lot of effort for nothing. That hillside was cut by a gorge a good twenty feet wide. The runner would have to double back and find a way around, wasting time.

At least he'd be able to get a good look at the guy when he had to stop.

The corporal refocused the lenses where he figured the runner would have to halt.

But the guy didn't stop. He seemed to expect the gorge, taking it right in stride.

He sailed out of the view again, leaving Ames with only a confused impression of brown and gold. What the hell—had one of the Abydans wandered out of position and decided to commit hara-kiri?

He refocused again to catch a clearer view of the stranger coming in for a landing after a jump that would have taxed an Olympic athlete. He also saw that the brown was fur. The gold was some kind of armor. The face seemed to be a distorted version of the gold quartz mask the would-be goddess Hathor had presented to the world. And the long, gleaming length in the creature's left hand could only be a blast-lance.

"Heads up!" he yelled. "We got unwanted company on our right flank!"

Still worse, the unwanted company was coming straight at them.

Ames dropped the binocs and grabbed his rifle as Young changed position, crawling on elbows and knees.

Castellano was already firing. "Damn!" he swore almost in admiration. "That guy is fast!"

He was that.

The intruder was by no means dressed in camouflage, but he was hard to see as he used every rock, tree, and fold of the land to cover his advance. When he moved, Ames might have believed the guy had teleported, except every once in a while he'd let loose a blast-bolt on the fly.

The corporal was getting angry. These were three *marines* here. They should have hit this furry Rambo at least once.

Then a blast-bolt tore in and incinerated the turf beside Ames's right elbow.

He rolled out of position, to see another bolt land to the left of Castellano's station.

No way the two could have been shot at the same time. While they'd been concentrating on the frontal assault, more of these characters must have been infiltrating along the hilltops to the right.

"Pull back!" he said in a hoarse voice. "There's more than one of 'em! We've got to get the word out!"

More blast-bolts created little burning divots as Ames tried to find a position that offered cover from both prongs of the attack. They'd have to cut and run—

He suddenly felt sick. There was one of them who *couldn't* cut and run—not with a sprained ankle.

"Castellano!" he said.

"Get out of here, Corp!" the kid said, taking three quick shots. "Warn the others. You said you weren't gonna carry me—we'd make too big a target for these bastards."

Ames and Young scrambled until the brow of the hill blocked them from direct fire. Then they began to run.

Behind them, they heard Castellano's rifle suddenly switch to automatic fire.

The beaters had started the day boisterous and cheerful, whooping and hollering as they banged their noisemakers.

But after a couple of hours the novelty had worn off. They were rationing their energy now, finding a rhythm for their *clangs*, *thwocks*, and *clunks*, until the forest seemed to resound with an offbeat symphony for pots and pans.

Or perhaps cacophony would be a better word.

Kynebu had learned the English term from one of those word-a-day calendars he'd used as a translator, working with Sha'uri and Barbara Shore. In his own language he called it "that Ammit-bitten Ra-be-damned racket!"

At least his partner in protecting the noisemakers, Nebitka, had finally stopped chipping in the occasional rifle shot to punctuate the din.

Kynebu disapproved of wasting ammunition in principle. He had also been one of the few trusted men who had prepared Mahu and Qa'a for burial. He'd seen the damage the hoodat's claws could deal out.

Anyone who wanted to go strolling through hoodat territory should do so with a full magazine and rifle ready.

Conversation had flagged among the beaters, except for quick warnings and assorted curse words as people encountered thorns, branches in the face, or animal droppings.

"I'll feel better when we get this damned thing," Nebitka admitted. "And even better when we have a real wall around the camp. This place is not the same as back home. If you ask me, Imiseba made a mistake pushing us to come here. Too cold, too damp, and all these trees! On Abydos you had open space and could see what was coming—"

A blast-bolt shattered the trunk of the tree that stood between them. Flying splinters tore like shrapnel through Kynebu's face, but even as blood began to flow over one eye, he tried to aim his rifle toward the point from which the bolt had flown.

Kynebu caught the glint of a gold helmet-mask. Had the Horus guards somehow come to Ballas?

Then he saw the full inhumanity of the figure rushing him with such unbelievable speed. A hoodat. An armed and armored hoodat!

He fired at the same time a second bolt caught him in the side of the chest. Kynebu spun, falling.

The last thing he saw was the beaters, women and oldsters, fleeing in terror.

From the hilltop where he and his friends lounged, Imiseba peered curiously to the south, his attention drawn by a fusillade that reminded him of last year's Fourth of July.

"Won't be much of that animal left by the time they're finished," Kenna announced.

But instead of dying away, the sound of firing grew more intense—coming closer.

"What deviltry is this?" Raya asked uneasily, picking up the rifle that had rested across his knees. "I told you that Ra-be-damned O'Neil was planning something."

Imiseba gazed intently at the figures now appearing over the crest of the tallest hill to the south, whose ridgeline hid the rises beyond it. A stream of men came into view, running as if Ammit itself were on their tails.

Others burst into view on the flanks of the hill, running wildly for the cover of the forest.

"Whatever is happening," Imiseba said, "I do not think it was Colonel O'Neil who planned it."

The quartet of marines stationed on the southern shoulder of what Imiseba considered "his" hill had seen the movement, too. The warrior in charge sent one of his men to see what the commotion was about. By the time he returned, fugitives were swirling past on the lower slopes.

Whatever the marine reported, it moved his superior to immediate action. He pulled up the whip antenna of the radio he carried and began passing on the news.

Imiseba discerned that not all the running men were Abydans. Figures in woodland camouflage were also passing by. He recognized one face in the crowd, a man who had fought to the end at Nagada, then gone unflinchingly to battle the Horus guards.

But here this man ran with his mouth open, as if he wished to scream but couldn't draw the breath. As he passed Imiseba's position, he threw away his rifle to run faster.

Imiseba turned to his friends. "This is nowhere to be," he said, moving to join the line of flight to the north, to the base camp—and perhaps to the Star-Gate beyond.

Feretti opened his eyes to almost impenetrable darkness, the stink of burning cloth—and the reek of charred meat.

He tried to move and instantly regretted it. Part of those burning smells came from *him.*

He'd been incredibly lucky, taking two hits and only being grazed. One had passed between his right arm and his chest, leaving burns on both.

The other had flash-fried the outside of his left thigh. "Lambertson, Unger—Wysovsky!" He whispered the names of the rest of his team.

No answer. And the thickness of the scorched stench in the air suggested why.

He was the only survivor.

How long had he been out? The base—the colonel—*everybody* had to know what he had seen in the brief illumination from the tip of the blast-lance.

Apparently, the hoodats hadn't just carried the ancient aliens' packages and staged the occasional ultimate fighting exhibition for them. They'd also fought battles for the old ones; what he'd seen was one of the cats in full combat array.

Trying to move only his good arm, he picked up the handset from the field radio. "Eagle, Eagle, this is Chesty Actual." He gave his call sign. "Over."

No response. Had they heard him? His voice had

sounded like something more appropriate for giving last words than for a battle report.

He cleared his throat, wishing for a glass of water, and tried again.

"Eagle, Eagle, this is Chesty Actual. Over."

Still no answer.

Horrible possibilities began running through his mind. Had the camp been overrun by armed hoodats? Had his radio been another casualty?

As best he could, he ran a hand over the case in the darkness. No holes. No scorch marks.

Then there was the third possibility. He was underground, or at least under dirt, in the middle of an alien building of unknown construction. Could that perhaps have an effect on getting his call out?

There was only one way to get an answer.

Slowly, painfully, he began pushing himself in the direction where he fervently hoped the door was.

Jack O'Neil stood in his command tent with his hands behind his back, one clenched painfully tightly to the other. He'd been out on the berm when the sound of the rifles began echoing down the valley.

It had started out slow and deliberate, the kind of fire you'd expect when a target—say, a big cat—moved into a rifleman's sights. Then the tempo had accelerated and gotten louder. More people shooting, and not picking their targets. To an educated ear, that was a sign of trouble.

Even in a retreat, a withdrawal, an advance to the

rear, fire has a cadence—units lay covering fire to keep the enemy's head down while other units pull back. It's an attempt to control the attacking force, and more important, it lets the retreating soldiers feel they're in control of something.

When weapons go full automatic and reach a crescendo, that's a sign of desperation. Either the defenders have been overrun, or they've been routed.

O'Neil stepped away from his vantage on the berm, muttering, "Looks like Private Murphy has put in his appearance."

Clausewitz called it "friction." Von Moltke said, "No plan survives contact with the enemy." It was the nightmare of any military man. Whatever could go wrong, would.

O'Neil had hoped, however, that he wouldn't have to worry about military disasters on a big-cat hunt.

Daniel Jackson and Sha'uri had been on the berm as well, and after one look at the colonel's face, they followed him to the command tent.

"What's going on?" Daniel asked when they caught up with O'Neil. "All that gunfire—rifle fire," he amended when the marine winced, "should have been enough to kill a big cat—or a dozen of them."

O'Neil nodded. "Which means we've got some kind of situation out there." He looked at the improvised desk where the base's radio operator was carrying on a set of staccato responses to various reports. "I figured I'd come here and find out what the hell is going on."

The radio man shook his head. "The hunting parties are under attack, but I'm getting weird stories as to who's doing the attacking. Guys in armor—animals—Horus guards."

"It would be nice to think that someone is playing a little joke on the net," O'Neil said grimly. "But it's not April Fool's."

Feretti felt as if he'd been propelling himself across the floor for hours. Sweat poured from his face, and his tongue felt as if somebody had wrapped a sock around it.

A dirty sock.

His progress had not been easy. Several times his chosen route had been blocked by still figures on the floor—the remains of his team. He ransacked his memory, trying to place where each of them had been at the moment the ambush had been sprung.

At one point his questing hand had come upon the lens of one of the flashlights they'd used to illuminate their way in here. He'd fumbled around, trying to find the switch, or the rifle the light had been attached to.

Instead, he'd found fused metal where a bolt had torn the rifle barrel and fore part of the lamp away from the rest.

Where was Moses when the lights went out?

In the fucking dark.

Feretti forced himself along, one good arm, one good leg, while the damaged parts all screamed with pain, and each movement was punctuated with a little gasp.

Got to find the door. Get outside. Use the radio.

Where's the radio? Right here. On the strap. Pulling it along. Prick-77. Right name for it. Feels like a seventy-seven-pound prick, and just about as useful.

Was he even going in the right direction?

Then came the first explosions of rifle fire, single discharges at first, then speeding up and swelling in volume.

Feretti corrected his course, instinctively following the old Napoleonic dictum—"March to the sound of the guns."

Of course, Napoleon and company had meant field guns, artillery. Damn, this radio was heavy. Like trying to pull a tandem tractor trailer single-handed.

He remembered reading somewhere that a bee could haul three hundred times its body weight. Surely he should be able—

His hand landed in a dusty groove.

He'd reached the door!

Maneuvering around the half-closed panel was almost beyond Feretti's endurance. But he made it, then the endless journey across the empty floor, up the ramp of spilled earth . . .

Sunlight peeked down at him between the fronds of the bushes guarding the cave mouth.

Feretti got on the hook. "Eagle, Eagle," he repeated the call sign for the base. "This is Chesty Actual. Over!"

But not yet out.

CHAPTER 15
NO JOKE

"Chesty Actual, this is Eagle."

A raspy voice came through the staticky connection. "Let me speak to the Six."

The radio operator turned to Colonel O'Neil. "Sir, it's Feretti. Do you want it on the hook or over the speaker?"

O'Neil stabbed a finger at the speaker on the improvised desk.

"Chesty Actual, this is Eagle. Go."

Feretti's voice crackled from the speaker unit, curiously breathy. "Sir, if people have told you we're being jumped by cats with blasters, believe 'em."

O'Neil leaned forward. "Feretti, what's the situation up there? Over."

"Team's wiped out. Cave wasn't a cave. It's a building, buried. But there were pictures. Aliens, maybe the ones who built the StarGates. Ugly bastards."

The radio man's eyebrows rose. Swearing on the communications net was a major no-no.

O'Neil waved it away. "He's wounded. Listen."

"Maybe they're dead. But they had servants. Big cats—saber-tooths. They've got body armor, blast-lances . . ."

Daniel was amazed that they got such a detailed report on what Feretti had seen and experienced. Especially when just getting the words out was such an obvious effort.

As the recon man described the underground complex and its machinery, Daniel was struck by a joke O'Neil had made when the news crews pulled out. That they'd stay if we'd found a lost treasure or an underground civilization.

They'd probably wet their pants if they knew about this, he thought. We may have found both.

The muscles were bunched all along O'Neil's jaw as Feretti finished. He held the mike in his hand as if he wanted to strangle it.

"Job well done, Chesty Actual. Now, you hang in there. We've got a cat infestation to clear up, but we will be there to get you. Repeat, we will be there. Over."

A ghost of a laugh came through the speaker. "Not a problem, Colonel. I ain't going nowhere. Chesty Actual, Out."

O'Neil's face was a mask of concern for the isolated marine. Daniel understood. There were few enough alumni of the first Abydos mission.

He tried to change the subject. "Too bad we didn't

find the secret city when the cameras were here. Or even better, when just the recon team was here."

The colonel shook his head. "There is no secret city," he said. "Those cats don't belong here any more than we do."

Sha'uri stepped forward, staring. "What do you mean?"

"Let's take it right from the beginning. What did the Maple probe find when it arrived on the other side?" O'Neil answered his own question. "There was something denning in the chamber of the Star-Gate. Those were our friends the cats."

He looked at the two civilians. "That leads to question number two. Why hang out in a drafty pyramid when you have an underground installation? For the same reason we did—Halloran, Fuentes, Feretti, and Imiseba—when we came through. Those cats are a reconnaissance mission—and not a friendly one. They cleared out pretty fast when the StarGate began cycling for the Maple to come through. They didn't make contact, which argues both bad intent and small numbers."

"I don't see that," Daniel said.

"If they had bad intent and large numbers, they'd have attacked us much earlier—say, when we were first coming through the StarGate. If they had good intentions, they'd have greeted us. Look at our own experiences. When we went to scout Abydos, we tried to communicate with Sha'uri's people."

"After you were spotted," Sha'uri pointed out.

O'Neil nodded, conceding the point. "On the other hand, we didn't kill the first two people who saw us."

He went on, pressing his point. "And both on Abydos and Earth, which have large populations—when a hostile force appeared, where did we fight them? Near the StarGate. We tried to keep them from coming through, and when they did, we tried to drive them back."

"Maybe these people have forgotten the StarGate," Daniel suggested. "The population could have shifted away. New York—or even Cairo—didn't exist when the pyramids were built."

"They've had more than enough time to organize a response before now," O'Neil said. "A force attacking with blast-lances argues a technological base. Why didn't they fly in a division? Or even a regiment?"

"Maybe they got their weapons from this ruin Feretti found."

"Forgive me, Daniel, but these characters don't seem to be acting like archeologists, more like military scouts checking a location for salvage. Feretti said that there were empty spaces in that hall of machines. That sounds like equipment they'd already set aside."

He frowned. "Their problem is that ever since we arrived, we've been sitting on their ride home—the StarGate. I don't know what triggered them now, whether it was the general hunt or Feretti finding that buried building. But the cats have stopped observing us and started attacking."

"Then why are they pushing our people back toward the camp—toward the StarGate?"

"Numbers!" O'Neil rapped. "They don't have enough people to sucker us away and *keep* us away. So they're using infiltration tactics—attacks on our flanks and rear to roll up our scattered hunting parties and get through our superior numbers."

His face changed. "Damn it! They've left whatever they were going to salvage because they have something more important. Information that another race is using the forerunners' StarGate network."

Sha'uri spoke up. "There's only one thing I don't understand. Ra was supposed to be the last of these forerunners. Why didn't he have any of these cat servants, or at least mention them?"

"He did have a facility for using other races—the Setim and humans—as cat's paws." Daniel winced. "Excuse the expression."

"Maybe he set off in the *Boat of a Million Years* before the others of his race started using servants." O'Neil shrugged. "Or maybe he just didn't like cats."

He grabbed up one of Feretti's maps. "Now that we know what the cats are up to, we've got to stop them—preferably well short of the StarGate. We still have a reserve force—the men with energy weapons here in the camp." The colonel turned to his radio operator. "Tell our people to disengage. Form a new main line of resistance between Hills 53 and 69. Get the word out—use runners, if you need them."

O'Neil tapped his finger on the map symbol for the pyramid. "We also have to send reinforcements for our people at the StarGate." He looked grim. "That's our last-ditch position."

Sha'uri turned from O'Neil's battle planning to see Daniel pushing his way through the flaps of the command tent. When she caught up with him outside, he was muttering, "Damn, damn, damn, damn," like a litany.

"Daniel," she began, but he cut her off.

"I knew there would be problems trying to settle here, but this is even worse than I expected."

He turned to face her, his eyes full of pain. "You and your people have suffered enough from my meddling. I thought I could somehow make it up if I could find you a safe haven—a nice galactic backwater. Instead, it looks as if I've dropped you right in it again."

Sha'uri regarded him gravely for a moment. "Daniel, it's true you've done enough to . . . piss people off." She spoke quite deliberately, choosing the vulgar idiom. "But you don't need to take the blame for things you couldn't have known about or hoped to avoid."

She shook her head. "Keep going that way, and you'll end up like that guy in the movie who wished he'd never been born. If you had not used your brains and knowledge to unlock the StarGate and come to Abydos, Ra would still be ruling his empire." She paused for a second, raising a hand to her throat. "And all my people would still be slaves."

Unwilling to meet his eyes, she looked down. "Certainly, our freedom had come at a fantastically high cost, and we may not always use it well. But I've never doubted that you've always tried your level best for us."

"Yeah, and look what a great job I did," he said bitterly. "You were living on a planet that people wanted—because of the golden quartz. After helping to get Abydos blown up, I pick another world for you—stocked with incredible technological relics and a bunch of aliens who are willing to fight to get them."

"You'd have done a better job of looking out for us if we'd allowed you to follow your original plan," Sha'uri admitted. "Maybe that would have given us some warning before we all came trooping over here. But we made a lot of trouble for you and screwed up your plans." She nodded off toward the distant sounds of combat. "Just like we seem to be making trouble for the cats. Who knows? Maybe we'll screw up their plans, too."

She looked at him levelly. "After all, we have the incentive. We are fighting for our home."

Private Voorhees had yet to tangle with the cats in combat, and his attitude proved it. "Lieutenant Fuentes has been on the horn to Base. They say there's only a few of the Pussies out there," he declared as the squad settled into their ambush sites.

Corporal Ames's lips quirked in a mirthless grin at Voorhees's words. He never got over how quickly the marine grapevine created rude, lewd sobriquets for their enemies, almost as soon as those enemies hove into view.

He was also somewhere between amused and annoyed at Voorhees's baseless (and in his opinion, brainless) confidence. There might not be a lot of the enemy, but to quote an old movie line, every bit was "cherce."

Ames hadn't enjoyed his enforced walking tour of half the hills in this western range, courtesy of an enemy that had rolled up the hunters' skirmish line like an old-fashioned window shade.

Of course, the hunters had been facing the wrong way, and a lot of their strength—the Abydan citizen-soldiers—had taken to their heels in the terror of the first reverses.

Now Colonel O'Neil and Skaara were getting them in hand and bringing some reinforcements. But they needed time. That's what Lieutenant Fuentes's squad was supposed to do—earn them a much needed breathing space, while at the same time giving notice that the Pussies weren't the only ones who could pull surprises.

Ames wished they had a little more punch—grenade launchers, a heavy machine gun, maybe a mortar. But he might as well wish for air cover and a naval bombardment. The heavy company that had come through the StarGate had been envisioned as a teaching, mapping, and guard unit. Prolonged combat against a professional enemy had not been in the crystal ball.

He lay crouched in the shade of a russet-colored bush, scanning the terrain ahead for signs of movement.

The squad had been positioned to spot and block any attempt at an end run around the defensive position now beginning to gel to the north and east of them. This time, if the Pussies decided to try to fall on O'Neil's rear, they'd be knocked on their own—and given a lead enema into the bargain.

Ames let out his breath in a soft hiss when he caught a glint of gold in one of the hollows between the hills.

"Company," he announced in a hoarse whisper. "Check the base of Hill 87."

Those who had binoculars swung them to survey the hill in question. The rest of the men devoted themselves to their rifles. The plan was to catch the enemy out in the open and hose him down with firepower.

Ames thought of Castellano and silently slid his weapon off "safe."

The golden glint was stronger now. Ames focused his binoculars and saw that they'd hit the jackpot.

Two of the armored forms were heading their way.

But these Pussies weren't moving with the blinding speed that had characterized the initial attacks. They were husbanding their energy, moving along at a curiously boneless, ground-eating lope.

Sure, Ames thought, no need to strain yourselves now. You're just moving on to your next attack. Take it slow and easy, you bastards. Right until you amble right into my sights . . .

The lithe forms traversed the hollow, then dropped from view behind an intervening hill. Then they came into observation leaving a stand of brush, only to disappear again.

Each time they were a little closer. Each time Ames's binoculars showed him more—gave him additional inhuman details. The Pussies' legs were jointed differently—that would explain their odd gait. Their hands seemed misshapen. The bone structure there must be different even from the Setim.

Odd, Ames thought. You couldn't watch television or go to the movies without seeing aliens, big sluglike things sitting on thrones, worms with teeth bursting out of people, or cheaper humanoid varieties with squint lines around their eyes or rhinoceros skin on their foreheads.

We ought to be immune by now, he thought, staring through the lenses. But there's nothing like seeing the real thing. When I first caught sight of those dog-faces, the Setim, I could feel the little hairs rising at the back of my neck. And they were friendly!

These guys, though . . . Maybe it was the heads.

The sleek lines he associated with cats were bulged and reshaped in these aliens, as if they were carvings in the hands of an inexperienced sculptor who had never seen cats before. Whatever was hidden behind those shining gold masks, it seemed to whisper on an almost subconscious level, "monstrosity . . . abomination."

Ames put the binoculars down. He was running away with himself there. That wasn't the way to launch a successful ambush. Keep it cool. Don't care much about which part you get under your sights. Just waste the whole.

He didn't need the binoculars to spot the Pussies now. They were visible to the naked eye, loping along, not a care in the world. Again, they disappeared behind the adjacent hillside.

The waiting riflemen tensed as the aliens entered the clearing below. It was perfect for the marines' purposes, bare of cover. The pair of armored aliens moved deeper into the killing zone, nearing the spot Lieutenant Fuentes had designated to trigger the ambush. They might as well be standing naked on an open stage.

Ames set his rifle sights right on the chest of the lead figure.

Come on, you cat-faced monsters, he thought, almost crooning the words.

They were almost there . . . Just a little closer . . . Now!

He squeezed the trigger, putting his shot dead center in that golden breastplate. Around him he heard the snarl of other rifles hurling lead at about two thousand miles per hour in the direction of the unsuspecting aliens.

Yes! His target was flung back as if it had been struck by an invisible sledgehammer.

Scratch one alien!

He looked up over his sights to see if the other target needed acquiring. But no, it too was flying back to thud into the hillside.

The hard, mirthless grin again twisted Ames's lips. One for the kid.

Then the grin faded as his lips went slack, dropping open in disbelief. "Son of a bitch."

The first Pussie, the one he had personally dropped with a chest shot, was pushing itself up.

Ames fired again. His second shot caught the armored figure in the shoulder. He could see the big cat slew round from the impact—and the bullet skip off that damned armor.

Other shots were rattling as well.

The damned things should be wounded.

The damned things should be dead.

Instead, they were moving, like men caught in a heavy hailstorm, to regain their blast-lances—the same sort of original-design energy weapons that had been captured aboard the *Boat of a Million Years*, Ames realized.

There couldn't be flesh and blood under that armor, even if bits of fur stuck out here and there.

No, this response was a thing of gears and cog wheels, of machinery that couldn't be killed.

The Pussies were up and moving now, using that unnatural speed to rush their attackers in stop-motion instants.

Ames thumbed his fire selector to full auto.

Behind him, he could hear Lieutenant Fuentes on the field radio. The Loot's tone was somewhere between fury at the latest screwball Fate had pitched at them, and superstitious awe at what he was seeing.

As Ames slapped another magazine into his rifle, he thought of one of the thousand and one versions of Murphy's law adapted for the military.

Suppressive fire—doesn't.

CHAPTER 16
"RETREAT, HELL!"

"Bulletproof," Jack O'Neil fumed as he stood in his command center listening to the radio reports filtering in. Off in the distance a new hail of rifle fire began to patter. "The goddamn things don't need nine lives, they're bulletproof!"

Those enemy warriors were also incredibly mobile for leg infantry. Though their attempted Hail Mary play had been delayed by the ambush squad, the enemy's assault was playing merry hell with the colonel's attempt to create a solid defense.

O'Neil knew there weren't that many of the cats. But they seemed to be in a lot of places, almost at the same time. Unfortunately for the marines and their Abydan allies, most of those places were weak points in the defensive line.

Distant rifle fire told the story better than the radio. Aimed shots had predominated when the Main Line of Resistance had reformed. Now came a cacophony of full-auto fire as confusion set in again. The men were trying to hold on, but they couldn't maintain their positions against an enemy that kept threatening their flanks and rear.

O'Neil stepped out of the tent and up to the berm surrounding the base camp, listening to the sounds of battle in the distance and taking a long, hard look at the .50-caliber machine guns he'd dug in up there. These monsters fired a projectile that was bigger, heavier, and more heavily charged than the marines' rifles, or even their light machine guns. How would the cats' breastplates hold up against armor-piercing ammunition striking at a rate of 550 rounds per minute?

It was tempting to consider ordering a few of the .50-cals up to the battle line, but that would leave the camp almost undefended except for the handful of energy-weapons specialists he'd held behind. Better to see what blast-lances and rifles could do against the enemy first.

O'Neil looked out across the fields of fire for the heavy machine guns. The cleared fields and newly planted crops would provide little cover. . . .

As he looked, the first group of beaters, running and screaming, came fleeing out of the woods.

Lance Corporal Mitch Rodakis shrugged his shoulders against the weight of the blast-rifle power pack, trying to move the straps to a more comfortable position. There didn't seem to be any.

Trudging up the hillside, he cursed all clever engineers. Yes, he could see it was important to develop a facsimile of Ra's blast-lances that could be built by Earth technology. But there was a big difference between toting something on the order of a spear and humping around the equivalent of an oversized flame-thrower.

Rodakis had earned his stripe just as world television was full of the image of energy-weapons types swooping down on the space shuttle to rescue Daniel Jackson's team in the Arabian desert. His mind filled with those images; when he was offered a chance to qualify on the blast-rifle, he'd leapt on it.

As the old military adage has it, never volunteer. Mitch Rodakis never got any closer to a space shuttle than the pictures he saw on TV. But he'd grown intimately familiar with the new, improved, and heavier battery backpack.

He hitched the straps again. It never felt worse than when he had to hump it up hill and down dale. Which, of course, was all he'd been doing. From the hills ahead, Rodakis could hear the rattle of rifle fire. It seemed to be coming closer. Well, at least that meant less of a trip with this dead weight on his back.

Rodakis had just reached the summit of yet another hilltop when he saw fugitives appearing over the top of the next rise. First they came in ones and twos. Then a whole compact group came into view, moving at a fast jog-trot. They were Abydan militiamen, many of them looking over their shoulders as they ran.

As they approached Rodakis, one of the Abydans—an under officer, perhaps—addressed the marine in English.

"It is no use, Urt-man. These cat-things strike like
the demons of the night. We fought them until they
killed our captain."

The Abydan gave a low moan. "Weneg led us
from the day we rose against Ra. Without him . . .
we go to the camp, where there are families and children to protect."

And a wall to fight behind, Rodakis thought. Even
as the Abydan spoke, his companions continued to
bug out. The English speaker gave a worried glance
to his surroundings when he realized he was the last
one left.

"Come with us," he said. "There is nothing you
can do here."

Rodakis considered the prospect of humping his
weapon back over the hills he'd just traversed. Then
he shook his head, taking refuge in a traditional marine response. "Retreat, hell! I just got here!"

"Then good luck, warrior." The Abydan sounded
as if he thought Rodakis needed a lot more than that.
"We shall tell your fellows where you fell," he called
back, quickly advancing to the rear.

"Great guy—a real morale builder," the marine
muttered, ranging across the hilltop in search of any
decent cover. The big winds of a couple of weeks
ago had blown over a tree, revealing a large snag of
roots. The dirt and wood offered decent protection,

not to mention a decent blend with the woodland camouflage Rodakis was wearing.

No sooner had he positioned himself than he heard the sounds of thrashing foliage and snapping branches. The Abydans' retreat across the hilltop ahead had been channeled by a big patch of wait-a-minute bushes. Troops with an enemy on their tail aren't eager to waste precious minutes disentangling themselves from thorns.

Apparently, the enemy had no such problems. The cat in his golden armor just crushed his way through the wicked thorn patch, making his own path.

Rodakis rested one arm on an exposed root, his hands tightening convulsively on the grips of his blast-rifle. Maybe those Abydans had a point. There was a sort of supreme, unconscious arrogance in the way the Pussie bulled its way forward, the sort of mindless, unstoppable purpose of Godzilla creating his own personal route through downtown Tokyo.

Hell with it, Rodakis thought, triggering his weapon. I'm a marine. The crash of his energy discharge was like a literal bolt from the blue, spilling and discoloring a fist-sized patch on the cat's breast-plate. He lowered and let fly with his blast-lance even as Rodakis triggered again. The Pussie's shot vaporized a thigh-thick root above and behind Rodakis's shoulder. But the marine had been tracking his target. His second blast struck the section he'd damaged with his first discharge almost spot-on. This time the armor didn't hold. Neither did the fur, flesh, or bone beyond. And the soft tissues within, they simply exploded as their liquid components flashed to the boiling point in a split second.

Rodakis had never heard of the dance macabre, and certainly didn't know what to make of the wild contortions his target went through. It was as though the creature's muscles were trying to break every bone in its body—or maybe it was the armor, trying to operate without conscious control?

Even as that thought occurred to him, Rodakis triggered two more blasts to the creature's head.

"Scratch one cat," the marine muttered, glancing around. "Now, who the hell do I report it to?"

In his command post, Jack O'Neil visualized his still eroding defense from the radio reports coming in. It was mainly a battle of morale—units exploding rather than men. Half the Abydan militia was either running, lost, or left behind. But they were still alive, available to fight another day.

If there was another day.

The good news was that fighting men with energy weapons could put down even an armored cat. The bad news was that the armor didn't just protect the feline aliens. The golden quartz wasn't just solid plates. It made up receptors and servomotors that boosted the cats' already impressive physical abilities.

Augment the speed of a charging tiger, and you've got an enemy that's fast indeed.

Dangerous too.

In this hilly, rough country the advantage should have gone to the leg infantry. But those gilt longjohns the cats were wearing, while not quite offering the powers of a Superman suit, went a long way toward making up for their meager numbers.

The armor gave the cats the capabilities of—well, armor. They could fight like tanks in terrain reachable only on two legs. Standard firepower did about as much damage as a water pistol—hell, the damned stuff even strengthened their legs, giving them the mechanical advantage in mobility. Worst of all, they understood their technical edge and used it mercilessly. The cats were outnumbered, but when they chose to fight, they just overwhelmed the troops then engaged—and forced other troops to abandon positions by threatening their flanks or rear.

They could take the best his riflemen could dish out, and still make them retreat.

The only thing that seemed to work against them was energy weapons—in those situations where a gunner and a cat could be brought together.

Since the enhanced cats could run rings around a human, those conjunctions took place only from very bad luck or very good ambushes.

The cats simply avoided strong positions and routed weaker ones in a sort of otherworldly blitzkrieg, with armored panthers acting the part of the German panzers. Bottom line, they were doing to the human troops what Hitler had done to Poland.

Meanwhile, O'Neil had no idea of what was going on in the forest. Sha'uri had managed to rally some of the militia guards who'd come running with the first wave of panicked beaters. They were now searching for the other noncombatants still in the woods. Even a cursory tally showed there were lots of women and old folk yet to be accounted for.

And there had to be at least one cat among the trees too. Probably more.

Another of Murphy's rules of fucked-up warfare came to the colonel's mind: The enemy diversion you are ignoring will always be the main attack. By this point it seemed clearer and clearer that the aliens were merely playing with the bulk of the human troops, much as an earthly cat played with its mouse prey. Then what was the real target?

It came down to two choices: the camp or the Star-Gate. He turned to his radio operator. "Get a message to Halloran and the guards at the pyramid—beware of infiltrators at any time. I'll also be sending him reinforcements."

The tech glanced at him. "From where, sir?"

O'Neil drew in a long breath through clenched teeth. "We're calling back the energy weapons from the front lines."

His radio operator blinked. Removing the only weapons that worked against the Pussies would deal a fatal blow to the rifle companies' morale. They'd feel they'd been left to die in place.

The muscles on the colonel's face were held so tight, they began to ache.

"As for the riflemen, they're to withdraw toward the camp, delaying the enemy as much as possible while sending detachments into the forest."

It was about time we found out what was going on in there, he thought.

I just hope it's nothing too ugly that we learn too late.

Everything seemed wrong to Pairi, from the course of the battle in the distance to the unfamiliar length of the blast-lance he carried.

It had all seemed so simple when he'd traded places with Sheb to escape the Great Cat Hunt. Sheb had wanted to tramp through the hills. Pairi wanted to be close to his pregnant wife, Ahouri. Their child might be the first born on Ballas.

But then things had begun spinning out of control. The cats had declined to be hunted, and apparently began pursuing the hunters. Warriors with energy weapons had been sent out, but luckily, Pairi had not been chosen. Thonufer, the petty captain in charge of Pairi's squad, had made his reasons clear. Pairi didn't know how to use his weapon, and would be more hindrance than help. Pairi hadn't been offended—it was only the truth.

Now new orders had come down. The handful of remaining Abydan blast-lancers were to take defense positions around the great pyramid. Any Urt-man marines with their bulkier weapons had already been dispatched.

"O'Neil is leaving the camp almost undefended." Pairi spoke with all the worry of an expectant father, but the complaint came out as a whine.

Thonufer glared back at him. "Listen, father of fools. The colonel and Skaara are not so foolish as you may think. I heard the orders go out. The ones with weapons like ours are being recalled from the hills."

"Then we shall lose the hills and the men there," Pairi declared, thinking about his friends and comrades in the new militia company he had joined. Poor old Sheb!

"They have their orders, too," Thonufer said. "Right now there are only three important places on this world. There are the fields, for we must eat. Then there is the camp, where we must live. But most important of all is the place we are going to guard."

"Why do you say that?" another blast-lancer asked.

Thonufer let go a long-suffering breath. "Even if the planted fields are destroyed, we could still get food, so long as the StarGate is open."

"You call it food," a voice from the rear of the group muttered.

" 'An empty belly brings savor even to a moldy crust.' " Thonufer quoted an old Abydan proverb. "Even more would it do to hot, filling food."

The noncom returned to the thread of his argument. "Even if we lost the camp—"

Pairi broke step as if an arrow had pierced his heart. "Do not even suggest such a thing!"

Thonufer went on. "We could always fall back on the pyramid. If need be, we could retreat to Urt-man's world." He raised a finger. "But if we lose the StarGate, we lose food and escape. And in return we'll probably receive a plague of cats, as soon as these ones get back to wherever they came from and report finding us on this planet."

Unconsciously, the group picked up its pace on the gravel road winding through the hills. Even so, they could never have outrun the golden figure suddenly streaking after them from the summit they'd just passed.

The joker in the rear who'd made the remark about the Urt-men's food need never worry about it again. The back of his head was vaporized at the first bolt.

More blasts landed among them. Pairi realized they were being attacked on three fronts.

He fumbled around with his weapon, groping for the trigger stud.

Thonufer loosed a bolt that knocked the rear attacker right on his golden arse. Then discharges from the other two cats nearly tore the petty captain in half.

That was too much for Pairi. With a yell of sheer terror he threw his blast-lance from him and ran, right past the downed ambusher, thinking only about the camp and its earthen wall.

He didn't even hear the others running after him.

The figure that had been downed in the brief firefight rose effortlessly to his feet. His commander examined the damage—some melt in the shoulder pauldron, and a few minor mechanisms deranged. She pronounced him fit to go on. The warrior turned to the escaping aliens, ready for more battle, for the only real injury had been his pride.

The leader dismissed the fleeing aliens with a curt gesture. They had struck only to prevent reinforcements from reaching their objective. In doing so, however, they had given warning of their existence.

The leader wished that the other units had finished their tasks and joined for the attempt on the main objective. But these aliens had offered greater resistance than expected.

In spite of the time needed to take the long flanking movement through the rougher hills, her team had arrived first. The hill attackers she placed no reliance on, other than as a diversion. But her fellows in the forest . . .

The third warrior had gathered up the weapons abandoned by the aliens. With a quick, augmented movement he snapped the lances over his armored knee.

The leader cast one last glance along the road to the aliens' place of dwellings. Then she turned toward the road to the pyramid. Though she and her fellows would not be following it, that was one way to the prime objective.

And no matter how few resources might be available, the prime objective must be taken.

From the berm of the base camp, Jack O'Neil stared out across the drab vista of recent seedlings and the muddy expanse of yet-to-be-tilled raw soil. Every remaining able-bodied male was on the line up here. Daniel Jackson was manning one of the big .50-cals, with O'Neil's backup pistol tucked in his waistband.

If the enemy stopped dicking around up in the hills and made a determined thrust, they'd be here in no time.

O'Neil rose a little straighter. Maybe that would be a good thing. The moment of decision. If the machine guns held them up at the treeline and energy-weapons people caught them from behind . . .

The colonel rejected that tempting thought. Those cats might be thin on the ground, but they'd shown themselves capable of making more than enough trouble. Suppose the machine guns didn't stop them . . .

He vented a long sigh of relief as figures appeared in the clearing. The first recalled troops. They were all Abydans, all armed with blast-lances.

O'Neil didn't care whether they'd arrived quicker because they'd been holding back from the battle or because they had less to carry than the marines with their bulky blast-rifle backpacks. They had weapons that could blow holes through the cats' armor. And with their arrival the base camp now had the advantage of those weapons.

As the men moved around the berm to the camp entrance, O'Neil moved to spell Skaara on the machine gun he was manning long enough to let the Abydan meet the newcomers. They'd already discussed where the reinforcements should be positioned, and the arriving men would respond better to orders from someone who spoke their language. Looking out across his planned No-Cat's-Land over the sights of the big fifty, the colonel debated other plans. Was it worth broadcasting over the radio net that the camp was now better defended?

He didn't think the aliens would intercept the message—or understand it even if they did. But it might make a difference to the Abydan riflemen out on the firing line to know that their loved ones were safer.

Maybe that was one to discuss with Skaara when he returned.

Here he was, with a couple of blast-lancers at his heels. O'Neil noticed that the Abydans looked happier to be inside the walls. Good. He'd need every steady man he could assemble on the ramparts. Although it was pushing it a bit too far to call these glorified mud piles ramparts.

Skaara located his men on either side of the heavy weapon, and O'Neil got up and let the younger man take his place. For the start, at least, the men with energy armament would position themselves to protect the machine guns and gunners. As to how it would end up, well, that was in the lap of the gods. . . .

Another quartet of Abydans and a couple of marines with blast rifles came into the clearing. They seemed in a bigger hurry, heedlessly trampling the newly planted crops in their rush to get closer.

Hope there are no farmers on the wall, O'Neil thought, or we may see some fratricide in progress.

One of the marines, a tall, balding man, spotted O'Neil by the machine gun. "Colonel! Sir!" he called, waving frantically.

"What is it?" O'Neil called back.

This would be a bad moment for a sniper to put in an appearance, he suddenly found himself thinking.

But the man below was already shouting up his report. "Movement in the forest, sir! Lot of bodies by the sound of it. Figured we'd better tell you right away."

Better figuring might have led to a quick reconnaissance to deliver more solid information, O'Neil thought. But after the way the cats had been tying his fighters up in knots, he could understand the other man's reluctance to push his luck.

"Get around and hole up at the entrance," O'Neil ordered. "You and your pals are our official reserve."

The colonel turned to the defenders along the berm—a pat of butter spread along a loaf of bread.

"You heard the good news," he said. "We can expect company—maybe lots of it. Don't fire until you hear the command."

Behind the confident front he was projecting, O'Neil sent up a heartfelt silent prayer. Oh, God, don't let me be wrong. A company of cats with blast-lances—even less—could overrun us with ease.

There was movement at the treeline. O'Neil snapped the binoculars hanging from his neck up to his eyes.

"Hold your fire!" he roared. "I repeat, hold your fire!"

The enlarged image through the lenses showed the tired, haggard faces of the missing beaters.

Well, they couldn't come home at a better time. But they didn't seem very happy to be home. And they were really too far away to see what was being aimed at them, so it wasn't what they were facing that worried them.

More and more of the missing noncombatants stumbled out into the open, forming two big, ragged blobs.

Something was wrong here. Very, very wrong.

The voice came from behind him, startling O'Neil out of his surveillance.

"Sir!" It was the other marine who'd run through the plantings, one of the six men supposed to be guarding the door. "Bunch of Abydans just came running up. Said you sent 'em as reinforcements for the pyramid, but they got jumped before they got there."

The colonel raised the glasses to his eyes again, running them over one of the little islands of humanity advancing across the clearing.

Right in the middle O'Neil detected a glint of gold. He began to mutter every curse word he'd ever learned. The lost people weren't just arriving, they were being herded into position—for use as a giant pair of human shields!

CHAPTER 17
CLOSE QUARTERS

Daniel Jackson swallowed once, then finally found his voice. "Jack," he called from his end of the firing line, "what are we going to do?"

"We're going to radio the pyramid and tell Halloran that trouble's on the way." O'Neil turned to the runner who'd delivered the word from the gate. "Pass it to the radio operator. Now!"

The Marine ran off.

"That's not the question I was asking," Daniel said.

"I know." The edge in O'Neil's voice could have been used to saw down a couple more trees at the edge of the clearing.

Daniel clutched the handles of the big, brutal weapon, as if he were afraid the damned thing would somehow get loose and start shooting people on its own.

"If they attack the camp . . ." O'Neil's voice trailed off, but Daniel could fill in the gap. If the cats struck against the camp, the colonel would have to fire on them—and the civilians—to protect the colonists inside. Whether or not the .50-caliber armor-piercing rounds could penetrate golden quartz armor, they'd be more than effective on the human shields.

"Suppose they don't?" Daniel desperately asked. The two blobs of terrified people were not directly approaching the walls, but splitting, as if they intended to go around the camp.

Of course, a cynical voice pointed out from the back of his mind, splitting up also doubles their axes of attack—and forces us to divide our defense.

But if the cats simply used the noncombatants for cover . . .

"Hypothetical question," Daniel said. "Suppose the cats came without the shields, not attacking the camp. What would you do then?"

O'Neil's face was tight. "I'd still have to fire on them."

"And if you couldn't stop them and they still passed without attacking?"

"I'd get down on my knees and thank God for letting me survive in an undefensible position—after warning the guards at the StarGate," the ever practical colonel replied.

"So what's the difference here?" Daniel wanted to know. "They're passing and you can't stop them. If they attack, yes, we'll have to fight. But if they don't . . ."

"I've got a hypothetical for *you*," O'Neil said. His face seemed to have aged in the last few minutes. "What if they marched up with those hostages and demanded that we surrender? Or another—they pass with those hostages and demand that our people surrender the StarGate."

Daniel frowned. "That's pretty far-fetched—"

"Then here's a situation that's not." O'Neil's voice was rough. "If I let them pass with their human shield, they'll be able to walk right up to the pyramid. So all I'm doing here is shucking the responsibility onto Lieutenant Halloran's shoulders."

"Those are human beings out there!" Daniel shouted.

"So is Halloran," O'Neil responded. "I have no intention of turning him into the next William Calley—famed for the worst civilian massacre since My Lai." The colonel seemed to be steeling himself. "If blame has to be assigned, it should go to the commanding officer."

"You can't—" Daniel protested, looking around. "Where's Sha'uri?" he suddenly asked.

Lieutenant Phil Halloran got off the horn and turned to the men in the Entrance Hall of the Star-Gate pyramid. "We can expect callers," he announced. "Pretty soon, I'd imagine. They managed to surprise the militiamen who were coming to reinforce us—sent 'em running back to base."

"And how many Pussies accomplished that, sir?" Lance Corporal Tamayo asked.

Halloran hated the crudity, and he didn't bother

to hide it in his voice. "Three of the cat aliens hit them from as many directions."

"If that's all we've got to worry about, why don't we go out looking for 'em?" Private Erhardt wanted to know. "We've got at least a three-to-one superiority over them."

"Those poor bastards up in the hills had lots better odds than that," Halloran warned. "But the cats obviously have gotten past them. And at least a couple more are trying to get by Base."

"Colonel won't allow *that*," Erhardt said.

"Colonel O'Neil says we can only depend on ourselves," the lieutenant went on. "So we button up."

That meant moving the radio in from the Entrance Hall, which was the only part of the pyramid where it worked. It meant leaving three men in the hall, covering the entrance and the gas-powered generator. When it had been installed, the idea had been to keep it near the doorway to vent the exhaust. Now the machine was just one more thing for his men to guard.

The rest of the squad would be spread along the Grand Gallery and in the StarGate chamber itself.

Halloran himself took the last-ditch position by the StarGate. Besides himself and Weber, there were three technicians in the room, standing in readiness in case they had to crank up the gateway to send a message or, in case of absolute disaster, evacuate personnel.

The lieutenant had offered these men what he had

available in terms of weapons for close-quarter battle. Two men carried shotguns, and the third had a Heckler & Koch submachine gun. Nobody knew if these weapons would be effective against the cats' armor, but it made the men feel less naked.

All of the security detail carried blast-rifles. Halloran had qualified on the weapon during his stint for planetary recon, but hoped it would never be more than a weight to be lugged around. Now, deep within the stony bowels of the pyramid, he shrugged into the heavy backpack.

If the weight of the world hadn't been on his shoulders before . . .

"Why the hell should *we* be the welcoming committee?" Erhardt complained as soon as the others had taken their stations.

"I thought you were all gung-ho to go out there, kicking ass and taking names," Tamayo mocked. "Well, you get your wish—first to fight."

"First to get wasted, you mean." Erhardt scowled, running a hand through his blond brush cut. "Outside, we'd have a chance to move around, see what we're shootin' at."

Tamayo laughed. "You *want* to go hauling one of these leaf blowers around these hills?" He hefted the weapon as emphasis.

The third man on the team swatted the power pack on his back, shaking his head. "Never volunteer."

"You think it's better, just sitting around—"

"Passive defense," said the third man with a grin.

"Without half the defenses we'd usually have," Erhardt finished plaintively. "I figured after the old man sent the news back about cats who shoot, the brass would get the tanks and artillery rolling." He shrugged. "At least some sensors and claymores."

"This was supposed to be a nice, quiet planet," Tamayo pointed out. "You don't set up claymores to get animals—even tigers. Besides, there's too many civilians around. Do you think kids—"

A loud scraping sound came from outside.

The men flattened behind the barricade that barred entrance to the inner passages.

"Told you we should have built a door for that thing," Erhardt whispered. "Now when the flash-bangs come bouncing in—"

"Pussies haven't used any grenades so far," Tamayo said impatiently.

"Where we gonna find a thirty-foot-tall door?" the third man asked, glancing up to the stone lintel high above them.

That's how he saw the golden cat face peering in at them from up there.

"Holy—" he began, trying to tilt his weapon upward so it would bear on the intruder.

A blast-bolt penetrated his Kevlar helmet and exploded his brains.

Erhardt and Tamayo both fired almost reflexively, laying down a pattern to cover the open entranceway. They did a good job—for ground level.

But the sniper wasn't where their fire was focused, and he had them targeted, perfectly.

A bolt blasted open Erhardt's power pack and fried him under it. The explosion jolted Tamayo out of position for the bolt that was supposed to do for him. It ripped into a sandbag in their barricade, leaving a tiny fulgurite—a fused-glass impression of the beam—behind.

Tamayo now realized that the fire was coming from above. He half scrambled, half rolled into the passageway beyond, triggering off a trio of blasts as he moved.

That kept the sniper upstairs busy. But two more cats seemed to appear as if by magic inside the doorway, blast-lances leveled.

Tamayo flopped down the inclined ramp of the Grand Gallery, trying to keep the entrance covered. "They're in!" he screamed to the men farther down.

In the Entrance Hall, a bolt hissed into the generator, just above the fuel tank. The whole pyramid seemed to jump for a moment, and a hollow explosion echoed down the passages.

The temporary lighting strung down the central rampway went dark.

Tamayo found himself kissing stone pavement. He forced himself up, shaking his head. Where the hell had his helmet gone?

He had no idea. All he could hope was that the explosion had messed up the cats more than it had messed up him.

* * *

The leader berated her teammate in the doorway as she turned back to help the sniper, who'd been hurled from the lintel by the force of the blast.

He rose, but slowly. It was obvious he'd been injured.

Barely within the mouth of the objective, and their strength was already being worn away!

Brusquely, she gestured for the bungler to advance. The flames of the primitive contrivance he'd destroyed no longer blocked the entrance to the lower crypts.

With an arm thrown out to steady her third, staggering companion, she advanced, blast-lance at the ready.

When the blast and the darkness came, Halloran gave a fatalistic sigh.

"We knew we'd lose the generator if those cats got in," he said.

"Won't be easy, running this sucker by flashlight," one of the techs warned.

"Hopefully, we won't need it," Halloran said.

He was interrupted as a runner brought the news. "Three hostiles—and they've gotten two of our men."

Silence greeted his announcement. They'd lost twenty percent of their force as well as the lights.

"Cheap charlies," Baird complained in an undertone from his position behind one of the pillars flanking the Grand Gallery. "That damned Jackson should have sprung for a better lighting system. And we all should have had our own set of goofy goggles!"

He referred to night-vision goggles, which made the wearer look like a cyborg from a low-budget science-fiction show. To Baird they always looked like a cross between strap-on binoculars and sniper scopes. What really burned him was the fact that Morrisey had them . . . and he didn't.

"It was supposed to be a peaceable world," Morrisey muttered. "Who the hell expected to be running around, playing grab-ass in the dark?"

Up at the head of the inclined passageway, blast-bolts began flying. All Baird could see were the discharges and a set of dazzling afterimages. He threw a couple of shots toward the entrance, hoping no humans got an attack of Rambo fever and charge through his line of fire.

Somebody lit a flare, throwing a little light on the subject—and getting nailed by an enemy bolt just as the damned thing ignited. Whoever fired that shot had to have been aiming in the dark.

But then, that would be no trick for a cat, would it?

Baird peered around his pillar, trying to show as little of himself as possible. The trick was not to look at the light, but to keep your eyes in motion, looking for any movement.

God, here they come!

Three blurred figures charged over the dying flare,

firing as they came. Almost before Baird had a chance to react, they were darting for the shelter of other pillars.

But one of them was moving a bit slowly. Baird's blast buffeted him to the floor, where at least four other shots caught him. Shorting circuits outlined the figure as it thrashed for a couple of moments, like a broken wind-up toy.

Yeah! Baird silently mouthed the word.

His attention was so caught by the dying hulk on the floor, he never noticed the gold-armored figure coming at him from the far side of his pillar.

Quarles backpedaled down the ramp, trying to keep his boots from scuffing on the stone pavement. Tamayo had done that, and Tamayo had gotten roasted.

The marine didn't know how many of his squad mates still survived. He and Morrisey had goofy goggles, which had helped. But not enough, damn it! Once the cats were in among them, the defense had quickly degenerated into a deadly form of blindman's bluff.

Quarles had been part of the patrol that had found the two trashed Abydans on the pyramid's outer portico. The physical evidence he'd seen there argued that the cats were strong enough to kill a man without any fancy armor. Their augmented strength made hand-to-hand an exercise in suicide.

And how did you beat an enemy that moved like something on a fast-forward videotape?

Quarles had begun the fight up near the archway from the Entrance Hall. He'd been in constant retreat ever since.

He ghosted around a pillar, checking his back trail, then the way ahead.

A little father, and he'd be in the anteroom with the big copper disk. Had to remember that. Didn't want to make any noise—

Seemingly faster than thought, an armored figure suddenly appeared before him. Quarles had been carrying his blast-rifle not quite at half port across his chest. A big, gold-gauntleted paw caught the weapon in mid-barrel and rammed it against Quarles's chest.

An agonized bellow burst out of him. His eyes squinted behind their goggles.

He never saw the finishing blow arcing toward his neck.

When Halloran and Weber heard the scream coming from almost outside the door, they knew they couldn't just stand there.

The lieutenant hurled himself out of the chamber, rolling low, while Weber covered him. Both had the last of the precious night goggles, so they were able to see the broken figure lying beyond the beaten-copper disk. They approached carefully, as if they were proceeding into mined territory.

"It's Quarles," the lieutenant said.

He caught movement on the inclined passage above him and nearly triggered his weapon before he realized the figure also wore goofy goggles.

"Morrisey?" whispered.

But the marine was looking beyond him. "Oh, my God!"

Halloran turned to see two unnaturally swift forms vanishing into the StarGate chamber.

They pounded in pursuit, but one of the figures stayed in the doorway, blocking their entrance with a virtual lash of blaster-bolts.

As for what the other one was doing, they could only imagine from the dull *boom* of the shotgun and the screams of the technicians.

Eerie luminescence welled from the chamber, even against the lurid bolts flashing from their weapons. A clear, crystalline chime seemed to ring out over the crashing discharges.

"They're running the StarGate!" Halloran shouted.

Completely desperate, he pulled a Rambo, charging and firing. It should have gotten him incinerated. Instead, a lucky shot sent the door guard staggering back.

Then Morrisey and Weber were on his heels.

The unearthly illumination faded even as Halloran leapt into chamber. The StarGate itself was dark, the golden chevrons that marked out the coordinate constellations moving randomly.

A huge, catlike creature stumbled from behind the

computer workstation that controlled the gateway. Its right arm hung useless. But the left arm worked, and so did the blast-lance clasped in the left hand. The invader managed to trigger two shots into the computer before the bolts from the three marines brought him down.

The sudden silence seemed unnatural. Here were the three technicians, who'd died where they fought. There was the dead cat who'd guarded the door and scrambled the system.

But the other cat, the other invader, was gone.

And thanks to the dead alien at their feet, they didn't even have a clue as to where their enemy had gone.

The big, balding marine looked down at Sha'uri in perplexity. "Ma'am," he said, "the colonel gave us our orders. We're supposed to guard this entrance. . . ."

"The colonel is now deciding whether to open up on a crowd of innocent hostages with his machine guns in order to stop two cats from getting by. I think we'd have a better chance of saving those people if we got up close and personal with those damned things."

She was getting nowhere, she saw. Switching to Abydan, Sha'uri said to the four blast-lancers, "Did you have a mother or father, a sweetheart, or a child who went out with the beaters for the hunt? They may be prisoners now, being used as shields to get past the camp so the cats can attack the StarGate."

Faces went pale as the men took in this news. "Wh-what can we do?" one asked.

"We can stop them," Sha'uri rapped out. "Moving in the middle of a mob like that, those monsters can't see everything that goes on around them. If we approached carefully, we could join the group, wend our way close—"

She reached forward to grab one man's blast-lance. "We know that these can lay the devils low."

"Take it, then." The warrior suddenly released his weapon.

Sha'uri stared at him in shock.

"I left behind all whom I loved on Abydos," the man said. "And I will not risk my life for strangers."

She nodded curtly. "Very well, then. Are the rest of you with me?"

The bald marine didn't understand what was being said, but he quickly rang in with an objection as the others cheered. "Ma'am, you can't just take these men and go."

"I'm the sister of Skaara, their commander," she replied. "Take it up with him."

She split her tiny force just as the groups of hostages separated. With only one man left behind for backup, she marched round the camp, half-crouched, keeping the gold-quartz weapon in her hand as low as possible.

The vanguard of the slowly moving mob of prisoners had almost come even with the berm surrounding the camp. Sha'uri could see the barrels of the machine guns placed at the corners swiveling to cover them.

She darted forward, hand to her lips as she glared at the frightened faces before her. Then came a nightmare jostling match as she forced her way against the tide.

There! She saw a flash of gold and tried to bring her blast-lance to bear. It was impossible in the press. How could the cat . . . ?

She received her answer as the militiaman who'd accompanied her gave a wild cry and charged.

He must have seen someone he knew, Sha'uri thought.

The flash of a blast-lance discharge erupted—and Sha'uri could see that it didn't come from her compatriot.

The cat-alien simply fired through the crowd. Though intervening bodies corrupted the bolt, it was enough to send the militiaman reeling back, dead on his feet.

Screaming panic exploded around Sha'uri. She was buffeted by people frantically attempting to escape while she tried to bring her blast-lance around, to find some trace of the alien to aim for.

A flash of gleaming gold was the only warning Sha'uri received.

The cat used his blast-lance as if it were a mere wooden staff, smashing it with numbing force against the weapon in her hands. The length of golden quartz was torn from her grasp. Then her legs were scythed out from beneath her by another blow.

The armored alien seemed much larger when seen from close up. Or maybe it was her point of view, lying on the ground.

They stood together in a quickly growing circle of emptiness as the other prisoners dashed away, taking advantage of their captor's present preoccupation.

A sniper on the wall would have an excellent shot at this fellow right now, Sha'uri thought as the cat brought around his blast lance to aim the simple, unadorned tip at her.

In fact, that's my only hope of surviving. . . .

CHAPTER 18
RESCUE OPERATIONS

Sha'uri knew how it felt to be on the receiving end of a blast-bolt. The muscles of her midsection tensed at the memory of the bolt she had taken from the blast-lance of a Horus guard. Only Ra's incredible technology had saved her—a glowing sarcophagus had literally brought her back from the far side of death's door.

But Ra's wonder box had been lost with the destruction of his flying palace. She'd lost Daniel, too—he'd been the one who'd braved Ra's wrath, placing her in the sarcophagus for revival.

She stared at the muzzle of the blast-lance aimed at her head, the last thing she expected to see. Then the weapon wavered, and the absolute *last* thing Sha'uri expected to see crowded into her vision—Daniel Jackson, a smear of dirt down his face, a wild look in his eyes, and a pistol in his hand.

He stood over her, and she could see that the seat of his pants and the backs of his legs were filthy. He must have slid down the outside of the earthen berm

surrounding the base camp to arrive at just this
second.

Daniel had no memory of how he'd gotten here.
One moment he'd been on top of the wall behind
one of the machine guns, wondering where his estranged wife had gotten to. Then he'd seen her fighting with one of the cats—and losing. Now he was
confronting the alien with a grossly inadequate
weapon in his hand.

It didn't matter. The pistol was all he had, so that's
what he would use. He thrust it in the big cat's face
and fired.

The trigger pull on this gun was smoother than
the other military pistols Daniel had used, and each
shot seemed to have more of a kick.

That was because the weapon O'Neil had given
him was not a 9mm Beretta. Daniel was firing one
of only five hundred pistols made solely for the marines—a specially modified Colt automatic, re-
nowned as a man-stopper since 1911. It threw a
bullet with twice the mass of the pistols Daniel was
familiar with.

Daniel had eight shots before the magazine ran
empty, and he put them all in the cat-figure's face. His
antagonist almost turned a somersault as the bullets
impacted. Although the armor denied penetration,
the cat was nonetheless battered savagely—knocked
down, effectively deaf, dumb, and blind—not to

mention nearly having had his neck broken by the force of the blows.

Sha'uri scrambled to her feet, snatched up her blast-lance, and delivered the coup de grace—two bolts to the head.

Then she glared at Daniel. "What were you thinking of?" she demanded in a harsh, gasping voice. "You could have gotten killed!"

He shook his head, as if he were coming out of a trance. "Guess it happened without my thinking," he admitted. Then he stood a little straighter. "But if I'd died, it would have been in a good cause."

"Oh, really?" Sha'uri inquired acidly. "And what if those bullets ricocheting off our golden friend there had hit you—or me?"

Daniel blinked. Oh, yes. He had a vague memory of something screaming past his ear while he fired to put the big cat down. "I had to—" He began fumbling for words. "I didn't—"

Then he noticed that Sha'uri was smiling.

For a second it was like old times again.

Jack O'Neil arrived, torn between fury at the civilians and relief at their survival. "That was the goddamnedest stunt *either* of you has ever pulled," he accused. "It's a wonder the two of you are still around to grin like idiots over it."

Sha'uri's smile faltered. "The others—?"

"Your two volunteers managed to put down our other playmate without losses," O'Neil said. "And I think the situation is stabilizing. The rest of our energy-weapons people are finally turning up."

They made their way back inside the camp through an entrance clogged with civilians. Where people had found lost loved ones, there were happy tears. But wails arose in the distance as new casualties were mourned.

"We've got to get these people all inside," the colonel said in a harassed voice. "Dammit, this is just a battle we've won, not the war."

The arrival of the reinforcements allowed Skaara to stand down from his machine gun. He, Kasuf, Sha'uri, and others of their followers managed to chivvy the civilians back into safety.

And just in time, too. Radio operators from the battle line in the hills reported that the cats up there had abruptly broken off their guerrilla war. They'd penetrated the perimeter and were apparently headed straight for the camp.

Six cats appeared in the clearing, to face the dug-in troops in the camp. O'Neil stood with his binoculars, observing the advancing enemy. So few, he thought. But they spent the day leading my riflemen around by the nose. If the Earth's military men ever found out how that armor worked, conventional armies might become an endangered species.

Either the cats were out of tricks . . . or they were out of time. Four of the aliens charged through the clearing in a frontal assault on the berm, while the remaining two tried to bypass the defenses, heading for the StarGate pyramid.

None of them got by.

Armor-piercing .50-caliber rounds were more than sufficient to put down even an armored cat. And a barrage of blast-bolts finished them off once they were down.

The running fight with the two flankers was a bit dicier, but in the end, numbers and weapons equality gave victory to the humans.

O'Neil was frankly suspicious. The adversaries who had repeatedly bloodied his nose had been defeated too damned easily.

The colonel kept remembering yet another of Murphy's laws of battle: The attack that's going well is probably heading into an ambush.

He just didn't see what advantage the enemy received from throwing troops away. True, there might be more cats out there. In frustrating point of fact, the humans still had no idea of how many adversaries they faced.

But O'Neil was positive there couldn't be very many more. He had two confirmed kills when the energy-weapons boys got out into the hills. Sha'uri's sortie accounted for two more. Six had died in this last hopeless exchange. Then there were the three cats who'd ambushed his attempt to reinforce the StarGate guards. . . .

That yielded a grand total of lucky thirteen, if the bushwhackers hadn't joined the last attack. The ominous radio silence from the pyramid suggested that the ambushers were instead busy elsewhere.

Thirteen, and they got this far, O'Neil thought. With a couple more they could have cut right through us to the StarGate.

A more disturbing thought occurred to him. They still might have. Repeated radio calls to Halloran still went unanswered.

"Basilone Actual, this is Eagle Six." The radio operator tried again to raise the lieutenant. He waited for a moment, then shook his head. "No response, sir."

"I'll need a squad of volunteers," O'Neil said. "We've got to find out what the situation is over there." He glanced at the radio man. "In the absence of further attacks, we might as well pull our rifles in. Tell Fuentes I expect him to make every effort to find the missing and wounded—which reminds me . . ." He picked up one of the maps to make sure he got the location correct. "We've got to get a retrieval team to this hill. Feretti is waiting for us."

Lieutenant Phil Halloran looked like hell. He stank of sweat, and his uniform was scorched where he'd caught the edge of a blast-bolt. He hadn't even noticed it in the heat of battle. The young man was pale-faced and seemed almost in shock as the adrenaline charge he'd ridden through the fighting drained away.

Worst of all was the bitter taste of defeat.

O'Neil's expeditionary force had found the three surviving guards in the StarGate chamber, ready to engage intruders coming in to use the portal—or emerging from it.

The contorted, still forms the colonel had encountered along the passageways told the whole grim story. Only the three technicians within the chamber had been laid out. The dead cat had been tossed outside, into the anteroom.

After checking that the rest of his command couldn't be helped, Halloran had forted up as best he could. The look on the lieutenant's face showed that he thought his best hadn't been very good.

"I wouldn't have believed that the enemy was capable of what they did," Halloran said for at least the fifth time.

O'Neil had to agree. But then, the cats had shown themselves capable of some very nasty surprises in his short acquaintance with them. He was especially impressed by the mountain-climbing act that had gotten the attackers inside. Lucky that Tamayo had survived long enough to pass the story along. They'd have to come up with some way to counter that in future.

But before he could contemplate tomorrow's battles, there were the exigencies of the present to be dealt with.

"What's the status of the StarGate?" he asked.

"Operational," Halloran responded. "But with the

computer system down, we can't operate the automatic settings mechanisms."

The colonel shrugged. "We can set it by hand," he said mildly enough. "We've done it before."

His voice became more official. "I've got a list of urgent needs—supplies, especially medical. Requests for personnel, including medics. A requisition for more energy weapons."

He looked at the three technicians who'd died because their weapons had been inadequate to stop the intruders and shook his head.

Then he produced several sheets of computer printout and began writing on the bottom of the last page.

"Plus, I've got a report that ought to make General West a very unhappy man."

Brillant sunshine poured through the window of General W. O. West's office and across his desk. It was the perfect day for enjoying the view from his new plum Pentagon office. But the general stared out at the green Virginia countryside as if he were surveying the ash pits of hell.

Greater powers than he were conferring over the implications of Jack O'Neil's reports.

The first had been jarring enough—that there were intelligent aliens on Ballas, and that they were armed and hostile.

One of the powers-that-be had exclaimed, "What

the hell is it with this gizmo? You go through, throw a rock, and hit an alien?"

O'Neil's conjectures that the aliens were not native to Ballas had created a further uproar. The generals and admirals had a hard enough time assimilating the notion of one interstellar empire. At least that one had been familiar, based on a known society— even if it did have to be decoded by Daniel Jackson. But in the final analysis, their motives and decisions were at least understandable. The possibility of mutually comprehensible dialogue existed.

These big cats, though . . . who knew what they wanted, or why they were on the planet in the first place? Maybe they needed a world-sized litter box. . . .

The general pulled himself away from these fanciful thoughts. O'Neil's second communication, his after-action report, was sobering stuff.

Barely a dozen of these armored cats had driven the equivalent of a rifle battalion from a series of eminently defensible positions. While the Abydan militia wasn't up to the professional level of the marines, West knew them to be tough and tenacious fighting men. These were the guys who'd marched out with only hand weapons to fight under the very shadow of the *Boat of a Million Years.*

It took something very special to make them run away.

On the scale of routed opponents, a rough calculation would seem to indicate that one cat was equal to about ten of Ra's Horus guards. And there was no way of estimating how many of these cats were prowling the universe.

Losses had been surprisingly light, except for the guards at the StarGate. But in view of the publicity they were sure to get, losses of any kind would be a nightmarish political football. This would not, could not, be a strictly military matter. Congress and the President would have to get involved. West shuddered at the thought of Robert E. Ashby poking his bulbous nose into the Ballas affair—or worse, throwing his considerable political weight around.

West sighed, lowering his face into his hands and massaging his features. Once upon a time Jack O'Neil had been his ace agent—a proven troubleshooter, with the emphasis on *shooter*. But somehow O'Neil had changed into a man who was always *finding* trouble, in places where his superiors would least expect to see it.

And by contagion, West was getting that reputation, too. That was why he wasn't in the meeting now in progress, deciding what responses were most feasible and palatable.

It was grimly ironic. The Fates must be laughing. Faced with the end of his career, West had saved the world because he didn't give a shit about political consequences. He just did what had to be done, getting weapons into orbit, fighting Earth's first space battle. But his very success had resuscitated his career. Now the general was forced to trim his sails to the winds of prevailing opinion in order to continue that career. And that meant acknowledging one of the bravest men he'd ever known as a political liability.

The decisions in this matter were all out of West's control, but he knew there was trouble on the way. The brass upstairs had vetoed all the requests O'Neil had sent in along with his report.

A bad sign, the general thought, his face still in his hands. A very bad sign indeed.

It was nearly dark by the time Sheb marched his aching legs through the base camp's entrance. He'd wanted to get out in this world, but he hadn't expected to see so much of it today.

The rifle company he had joined in such a free-and-easy way had come through the hills pretty much intact—except for Hemaka. Sheb's friend and old comrade had been wounded just as the devil cats had pulled away.

In a gruesome way, that was lucky. If Hemaka had been hit during the unit's frequent, scrambling retreats, he'd probably have been left behind. Instead, Sheb had convinced some of the men to put together an improvised litter.

He'd also served as stretcher bearer, gritting his teeth against the groans that burst from Hemaka's lips whenever they had to carry him over rough country.

The camp streets were full, and there seemed to

be almost a carnival atmosphere. Families were anxiously waiting for fathers to come home from the wars, and people who'd been separated during the hunt were still searching for one another. There were also a few militia captains—Skaara's trusted men—working to bring some order out of chaos.

"Wounded man?" one of the traffic directors asked as Sheb and one of his comrades carried Hemaka in.

Sheb managed an exhausted nod.

"Over in the Urt-men's quarter, the empty tents, Sha'uri has set up a hospital. Or if you want you can bring him to his family."

As far as Sheb knew, Hemaka had no people on Ballas. His family had refused to leave their home in Nagada.

"Hospital, I think," he said to the generous one who had helped him this far.

They arrived to find bright lights, clean beds, and many, many wounded, some being tended by family, others by female volunteers.

As he turned Hemaka over, Sheb saw a familiar face. "Tamit!" he said in surprise.

The woman, face glowing with perspiration and hair frazzled from the bucket of steaming water she was carrying, looked up. "Sheb."

"I didn't know you did this work," he said.

"Thonufer wouldn't have allowed it," Tamit agreed.

Sheb caught the delicate past tense in her voice. "What happened?"

"The company marched off to help guard the gateway, and was ambushed instead." Tamit deposited her load and sighed deeply.

"I'm sorry," Sheb said.

"You look hungry," she replied, gesturing beyond the tents. "They've been heating food over there. Come."

They sat, and ate, and talked of recent events. When Sha'uri had asked for volunteers, the widow Tamit had decided to respond

Sheb himself no longer had a family. His wife and two children had perished in an udajeet raid right at the beginning of the rebellion.

"It is good to talk," he said, sharing the caramels from his MRE.

Tamit nodded. "Yes," she said. "It is good."

The summons came when any reasonable person would be thinking of packing up and getting out of the office. General West rose from his desk, straightened his uniform, and set off for the third floor.

The third floor, E-ring, of the Pentagon is the U.S. military's version of Valhalla, home of the heroes. More specifically, it was home of the power—the offices of the Secretary of Defense, the Joint Chiefs of Staff, and their assorted flunkies.

One such was General J. Caesar Dixon. He was the son of a military family with a long lineage—there was a Julius Caesar Dixon who'd served as a brigadier in the Civil War—and J. Caesar Dixon IV, although he left off the Roman numerals, had risen the highest of his family. He'd shown himself to be a phenomenal staff officer, able to work the bureaucracy, or, as he called it, "the business side of the Army." He was an expediter, needed on any staff. Whatever his superiors wanted, his superiors got.

And in return the people who thought that fighting was the business of any military had christened J. Caesar Dixon "Cheeser Dixon" or just plain "cheese dick"—military slang for anyone who curried favor with the brass.

If Cheeser had been put in to ride herd on the Ballas mess, the politicians—both in and out of uniform—had well and truly screwed things up, West thought grimly.

"General," Dixon said cordially enough, indicating a seat. His tone was that of a man passing along a bit of business before stopping off at the officers club for a few drinks. "I understand you're tasked with the logistical side of StarGate operations. How long would it take to evacuate Ballas?"

West struggled not to show surprise at such a rational response. If these cats wanted Ballas, let 'em have it. Jackson had rescued plenty of other StarGate coordinates out of the computers aboard the *Boat of a Million Years*. There were lots of worlds out there, even for the Abydans.

"The original expedition had been organized by civilians and complicated by the amount of time necessary to assemble the colonists," West replied. "Depending on transport of personal effects, we could probably convey the colonists in hours rather than days."

Cheeser Dixon shook his head. "You don't understand, General. I mean U.S. personnel." He paused for a second. "Only," he added, underscoring his meaning.

West beheld the fine, racist hand of Robert E. Ashby. "Sir," he said, "the Abydans have fought and suffered—"

"Yes," Dixon cut him off, "and they asked for their own world, and they got one, which they are now responsible for." He frowned. "*Our* responsibility is to this planet, and to the government and people of America, which is on this planet. Colonel O'Neil's encounter with this unknown and hostile race has put his troops in harm's way—and exposed our people and our world to danger as well. We do not want a war with these cat-people."

The staff general grimaced at how silly that last phrase sounded, but continued. "We don't know where they come from, they don't know where we come from—and we want to keep it that way."

"Just close the door on the problem," West said, carefully neutral. "Leaving the Abydans out in the cold."

"We think we can protect the Abydans—as well as insuring that no one can link Earth and Ballas," Dixon responded. "It merely requires removing the door—something, I understand, a good number of Ballas colonists would welcome."

He went to his desk and picked up some papers. "Here are the authorizations for the necessary materials. You will draft orders for Colonel O'Neil and arrange passage of the special ordnance."

Dixon paused for a second, giving West a measuring glance. "All of this must be accomplished ASAP." He smiled a politician's smile. "So I'll just leave you to it."

Seconds later, West was standing outside the man's door.

"Cheese dick," he muttered in disgust.

Then West started off down the hallway. There was work to do. First and foremost, he had to see how much, if any, latitude could be squeezed out of these orders.

CHAPTER 19
ALWAYS LEARNING

It was full dark by the time the rescue party reached Hidey-hole Hill, the ridge where Feretti and his team had encountered the buried city, and the first wave of cat attacks.

Word had gone out on the Green grapevine that Feretti and his people had been jumped because they'd stumbled across some kind of underground base for the Pussies. While rescuing a wounded comrade was a tradition deeply ingrained in all marines, these men were not exactly eager to stick their heads in the cat's mouth to do it.

Starlight was not enough to let the men find a path, so they were forced to use flashlights. This did not make the marines happy. Any enemies out there in the dark could easily trace the light to its source, vaporizing both the flash and the person wielding it.

More important, the rescue team had been dispatched from the nearest unit, which meant these were riflemen. If they did bump into a Pussie in the dark, they wouldn't be able to handle him, her, or it.

"Should be the next ridge," Hank Young told the team leader, Corporal Ames.

The corporal nodded, keeping his eyes at about knee level and constantly moving, trying to pick up the barest hint of movement that might presage an attack. Four riflemen, two stretcher bearers—and a lot of darkness. Feretti had better have stayed alive to make this pickup worthwhile.

They crept forward, finding the gentle slope. Ames spread them out so that any enemy couldn't get them in one burst.

Then one of the young geniuses tried to undo the corporal's good work by shining his flash right up into the mouth of the cave. Ames's mouth compressed into a tight, furious line. "Strangle that light," he grunted.

The flash went out.

Ames didn't mind if fools got themselves killed. "Darwin in motion," his first sergeant had called it. The problem was, fools usually didn't seal just their own fates. There were five other people in this little expedition, and he was responsible for them all.

The night was broken by the distinctive sound of a rifle round being chambered. His people had come ready to party. That sound was coming from up the slope.

Ames signaled his people to get down. "Lieutenant Feretti," he called, "I hope to God that's you."

The voice that answered sounded more like an old,

unoiled hinge. "Whoever you are, I hope to God you're human."

Following the sound up the hillside, Ames found the lieutenant lying in the mouth of the cave. "How are you doing, sir?"

"I hurt like hell, and I'm dry as Abydos," Feretti replied. "When they blew me away, one of the things they got was my canteen."

Ames got out his own and fed the lieutenant a little water.

Feretti sighed gratefully. "I was going in and out for a while there. Thought maybe you were only in my head."

"Any cats come by, sir?"

"None that I saw," Feretti replied. "How big a crew did you bring? There's stuff inside here—"

"We brought enough to collect you, sir, and that's all." The corporal brought up the stretcher bearers, who tried to transfer Feretti as gently as possible, but still brought an anguished grunt from him.

"Let's head on out," Ames said.

That's enough, he thought. We're in, and we're out. If the colonel wants anything else up here, he should send people who could fight for it if necessary.

Hapi was not living up to the sound of his name as he showed Daniel around the fields the morning after the Battle of Ballas. The farmer had been up in the hills for the abortive cat hut, and hadn't gotten back to the base camp before dark, after all the shouting—and shooting—was over.

That was probably just as well. If he'd seen what was happening to all his work, he'd have probably been up on the berm taking pot shots at both foes and friends alike.

Cropland is laid out for maximum yield, not for fugitives to run through, hostages to stumble across, and enemies to charge. The three stands of grain—wheat, rye, and barley—were not living up to their names. The shoots had all been trampled flat. Both the squash and the beans looked to be total losses. Some of the other plantings might survive. The cabbages, for instance, were almost untouched.

But man does not live by sauerkraut alone.

"We can try replanting." Hapi raised his bowed shoulders in a shrug, then tilted his head back, squinting as his dark eyes searched the sky. "But I do not know the moods of this world."

Daniel felt another stab of useless irritation at the rush to settle here. By monitoring sunrises and sunsets, timing them by Earthly hours, the colonists knew that the days were getting longer. But how far were they into spring? How long was the growing season?

The answers might mean the difference between at least some self-sufficiency and another year's dependence on military rations warehouses. Assuming, he thought glumly, that the cats didn't come back with reinforcements.

After listening to Hapi's long litany of complaints, Daniel promised to get him some more help. "How about the kids?" he suggested. "The young ones might show more interest in something besides mining."

Hapi nodded at the suggestion. "And they are ripe to be taught."

I hope so, Daniel thought as he moved off to the next crisis. Barring a miracle—like the ancient aliens leaving behind a self-explanatory widget factory—farming will be just about all the next couple of generations will know on this planet.

Jack O'Neil was also busy with an inspection. He wanted a good look at the damaged StarGate pyramid, rather than the sketchy look he'd gotten while leading the relief force over the previous evening. Lieutenant Halloran had been given two squads—twenty-eight men—to improve the defenses. That meant almost all the blast-rifles on Ballas, and a couple of M16s as well. Halloran had also asked for one of the heavy machine guns, which O'Neil thought was carrying the worry over remaining cat guerrillas a bit too far, but he'd approved the requisition.

Now he'd get to see how they'd been put to work.

Despite the strong orange light pouring through the tall slit of a doorway, the Entrance Hall was a shadowy place without artificial illumination. The colonel needed a flashlight to see the scrapes and chips in the walls created by blast-bolts and the shrapnel-like flying shards from the destruction of the generator. The stark, uncompromising geometry of the room was shattered where the machine had once stood, the wall and floor showing what looked like the largest bullet pock of all time.

O'Neil noticed the defenses in the room had changed, too. The light, easily removed barricade that had blocked passage deeper into the ground had become considerably more solid, flanked by a pair of sandbag bunkers that put protective roofs over the men covering the doorway.

"Must get hot in there," he commented, peering through the firing slit.

"Be a lot hotter outside when we need 'em, sir," the corporal in charge replied.

The man looked as if he'd gotten some of the sand from the bags into his eyes. O'Neil suddenly realized that the men must have been working all night on the defenses.

Two large piles of wood stood on either side of the entrance slit. "Expecting a barbecue?" O'Neil asked.

"Illumination for night fighting, sir." The corporal pointed to bundles of dry grass at the base of the woodpiles. "It's wrapped around clumps of C-4. One blast-bolt, and they ignite a bonfire.."

O'Neil nodded in approval. Flames wouldn't stop an armored enemy, but it would throw more light on them than a flashlight. And it wouldn't allow intruders to target the lights—or the people holding them.

All in all, a much sturdier defense. The colonel frowned, however. "Where's the big .50-cal?"

The enlisted men looked among themselves, but no one answered. "Um, inside, sir."

O'Neil passed the strongpoint, his frown deepening. What the hell good was a weapon that hosed high-velocity bullets *inside* a structure? Rounds would be bouncing off the walls, as much a danger to the defenders as to any invaders. Even set up at the end of the long, sloping passageway . . .

The heavy weapon was not where O'Neil expected to see it, though there were plenty of other changes. More sandbags had been filled and emplaced, creating little fortlets between the vaulting pillars. The colonel noted that these were positioned to enfilade anyone going down or coming *up* the long incline.

O'Neil also saw that the spaces between the pillars—alternate routes for infiltrators—were now choked with obstructions. Halloran had set his few thermite and white phosphorus grenades in there as booby traps. He probably wished for more, but none would be available until supplies arrived.

Which brought the colonel to his other reason for visiting the StarGate, and the worry that was beginning to create a gnawing pain in the pit of his stomach. O'Neil intended to dispatch a message that should burn the ass of the logistics officer at Creek Mountain. Did they think he was just shuffling paper on this side of the gateway?

If they didn't send the reinforcements he'd asked

for, they could at least expedite the materials for tending the wounded and mounting a decent defense.

When a colonel marks a requisition URGENT, he by-God expects results.

If they don't occur, that means either a screw-up of monumental proportions . . . or problems being generated from higher up the military food chain.

The people back in Colorado should be used to dealing with crises and crash supply programs by now. Since nothing at all had arrived, that suggested that the suits back in Washington had convened to discuss Policy, with a capital P. And that meant all bets were off. O'Neil had *no* idea how the Pentagon and the civilian government would react to the situation here.

He tapped the pocket of his BDUs, where paper crackled. Maybe he should rewrite the message he'd intended to send though.

No. He could second-guess himself to death on this. Better to hold to the plan he'd made.

The colonel continued to inspect the elaborate defenses. No wonder the men looked tired. Unfortunately, when the C.O. gets religion, the whole outfit had to pray, he thought, his smile tight and ironic.

He reached the quiescent jump-off point for the short-range matter transmitters. The space was too small for a machine gun, which was just as well.

There wasn't one there.

The colonel suddenly halted, running through a

quick count of the troops he'd seen. Halloran had twenty-eight men at his disposal, and he'd used all of them up in the defenses outside the next room.

What the hell was the lieutenant up to?

O'Neil got several answers when he stepped into the chamber of the StarGate. Halloran sat behind yet another sandbag breastwork, manning the big .50-caliber machine gun. The weapon's muzzle pointed straight at the center of the StarGate torus. Since there was a solid stone wall just a couple of yards beyond that focus point, Halloran had to be betting that his bursts would keep going down the magic tunnel of the Puke Chute and come out on the other side. Otherwise, bouncing bullets would quickly turn the chamber into a pretty good impersonation of a meat grinder.

Halloran himself looked like a washed-out copy of the stiff, eager, mint-edition lieutenant O'Neil had met for the Ballas expedition briefings. If the men of the guard detail were tired, Halloran had worn himself to the bone. His face was pale, with dark circles surrounding the eyes.

But his eyes themselves were terribly alive, burning with anger and determination. Sitting at the machine gun, he'd have made an excellent model for a statue entitled, "They Shall Not Pass."

Then O'Neil noticed the switch beside the heavy weapon—and the blocks of C-4 in the corners of the room.

"What the hell is this?" he demanded. "The Mahu Memorial StarGate Bomb?"

"Sir." The lieutenant's voice sounded a little rusty as he spoke, and his eyes were still focused on the StarGate. "I was charged with preventing seizure of this facility, either by exterior forces or by assault through the StarGate itself. Experience has shone two types of incursions through the gateway—small-group infiltrators, or massive wave assaults supported by regimental or brigade-size units."

He patted the receiver of the machine gun. "This should be sufficient to deal with an infiltration group, while endangering only the operator of the weapon. In the case of a large-scale onslaught . . ." He hesitated for a second, probably aware that O'Neil himself had always been on the receiving end of the worst of those. "No defense we have used has been sufficient to stop the attackers from seizing control of the StarGate—neither on Abydos nor even on Earth."

O'Neil had to nod. "When Hathor's Horus guards came through, they did manage to gain control of the missile silo. Even though our people were able to drive them back through the gate again."

"The goal, then, is to deny the enemy the use of the StarGate at the moment when it looks as if he will gain control." Halloran licked his lips. "The quantity of C-4 is enough to bring down the roof in here, hopefully without causing destruction outside. It would destroy any enemy assets inside, while also rendering the StarGate useless for their purposes."

O'Neil nodded again, his face grim. Flesh, blood, and even armor didn't do too well when forced to coexist with matter blocking the StarGate's focus. He had seen pictures of what had happened to the advance guard Ra had attempted to send after the rebels buried the StarGate in ancient Egypt.

They hadn't been pretty.

"I understand your reasoning," the colonel said mildly enough. "In the short run, you'd deny the objective, while in the long run, we'd be able to recover it." He shook his head. "Given the number of able-bodied workers available, that might take years. And while you might be able to find people willing to take the risks of ricocheting bullets, you'll have a harder time finding volunteers to man that suicide switch. That's something you can't order people to do—trust me."

"Sir," Halloran responded, "it's only a temporary expedient—until reinforcements arrive, or—"

His words were interrupted by a mellow, bell-like note. The StarGate was beginning to cycle.

Corporal James Parnell was a short, wiry man whose specialty was communications. Usually that meant radio. Most recently, however, he'd been cursed as part of the comm team at the Creek Mountain facility. That meant acting as a messenger through the StarGate.

Transit was like taking the world's most dreaded amusement-park ride stoned on acid, while at the same time being tackled by the NFL's most brutal linebackers. Not for nothing was this particular thoroughfare colloquially called the Puke Chute.

Practice—too much practice—had taught Parnell to land on the other side with only a slight drunken stagger. But this arrival was enough to induce a heart attack.

His feet hit the ground, the dispatch bag slung over his shoulder slapping against his hip. Parnell jolted back from the impact, weaved slightly, righted himself . . . and realized he was staring into the muzzle of a machine gun.

That little black hole was only a half inch in diameter, but to Parnell it looked like a yawning manhole.

"Jesus Christ Almighty!" he swore. "Turn that thing away!"

Then he saw the set face on the gunner, and the worried gleam in Colonel O'Neil's face as he reached forward.

At the last moment, the gunner—Lieutenant Halloran—deflected the weapon. The lieutenant let go a long sigh. "I almost triggered it," he said numbly.

"I can understand why," O'Neil looked at Parnell. "We weren't expecting contact until 12:45, or a convoy of trucks bringing supplies." He made the last sound like an accusation.

"Sir, Colonel Diedriksen's compliments—orders arrived for you to be delivered ASAP." Parnell presented the case.

O'Neil opened it, unsealed the flimsies inside, and began reading. He said nothing.

But if his face had been grim before, it seemed carved from stone now.

Parnell was glad *he* had nothing to do with issuing those orders, whatever they might be.

. . . concurrent with withdrawal of all U.S. personnel and assets, emplacement of suitable demolitions devices to seal the nuclear charge within the StarGate chamber must be accomplished. When the nuclear ordnance is ignited, demolition of the StarGate will entail no more damage than an underground nuclear test. . . .

The words blurred before Jack O'Neil's eyes.

So this was the response of the geniuses in the puzzle palace. Pull out our boys and our toys, setting a few timers before we go. The first blast would bring down the roof of every chamber and passage in the pyramid, while the second, nuclear charge would vaporize that worrisome torus of golden quartz, hopefully not destroying the colony in its base camp a mile away.

Once again the powers-that-be were hoping to slam the door on that dark and dangerous universe out there. And if their actions endangered a few thousand Abydans, so be it.

The colonel shook his head. "Looks like you're going to have company on the trip back, Corporal," he said. "I'm afraid I have to query these orders."

Parnell kept his face carefully blank as he saluted. "Yes, sir."

O'Neil pulled out the nasty message he'd been about to send and started writing on the back of it. In case his arguments didn't work, he'd have to start the ball rolling on this proposed pullout. That meant drafting orders for Fuentes back at the base camp.

He'd have to get Halloran to send one of his men with the message, when he finally got it finished. Not that the StarGate would be opening up anytime soon. The cats' last stand had made sure of that, destroying the machinery that made the torus so easy to handle. Did Parnell realize that? he wondered.

"It will take a little while," O'Neil explained to the messenger. "The coordinates will have to be set by hand—"

He broke off as a detail called in by Halloran only had to make minute adjustments. Apparently, the appropriate astrological signs were only slightly out of the alignment necessary to make the chevrons lock on.

As the funnel of energy swirled out of the activated gateway, O'Neil turned to Halloran. "Was the StarGate always left half cooked like that?" he demanded.

The lieutenant's eyes flickered in the weird light show being broadcast by the gate. "Sir . . . I—I don't know."

CHAPTER 20
"I STAY"

O'Neil came rocketing out of the Earthside StarGate almost on Parnell's heels. He almost went into a forward roll, stopped himself, avoided crashing into the messenger, and finally got his bearings.

The colonel looked about the converted missile silo and saw that another round of redecoration had occurred during his absence.

Gone was any trace of the festive air that had prevailed during the first Ballas expedition, or the colonists' send-off. The face that Earth turned to the StarGate now was fierce, resolute . . . and armed to the teeth.

Haloran would be jealous of their fortifications, O'Neil thought, taking in the elaborate breastworks sheltering the better part of a rifle company.

Amend that, he chided himself. Those aren't fuddy-duddy M16s. These guys are armed with the newest variety of blast-rifle.

Ahead of him, O'Neil heard Parnell vent a great sigh of relief to be home.

If the little man had been upset to face the big Browning machine gun on Ballas, he'd go wild if he really knew what was aimed at him here, the colonel thought.

Part of the renovation-fortification at Creek Mountain had meant the end of the conference room overlooking the silo. The heavy Plexiglas window was gone. And in that open space he saw the heavy snouts of two mini-guns poking out to cover the StarGate from second-story height. The electric gatlings didn't throw a slug as heavy as the .50-caliber round. But those six barrels could fire at a rate of 6,000 rounds per minute as opposed to the big fifty's 550 r.p.m.

Getting hosed with enough bullets like that would transfer sufficient kinetic energy to damage even an armored man-sized, cat-shaped enemy.

O'Neil decided not to tell his companion about what those suckers could do to an unarmored target. Instead, he presented himself to the officer of the guard and requested a secure telephone line.

General West must have anticipated his call almost to the minute. He picked up the line instead of his female dragon.

When O'Neil tried, in the most polite ways he could manage, to disagree with what had come through the StarGate, the general cut him off. "Colonel," he said, sounding almost tired. "Those are your orders. You can't even demand that they be put in writing. They're *already* in writing."

"And very well written they are, sir," O'Neil said wryly. Reading them again, and listening to West, he realized two things. The general was only transmitting orders he personally despised, and he had done his best to keep them worded with sufficient vagueness to offer O'Neil as much maneuvering room as possible.

Even so, the colonel's hands would be tied once the nuclear charge arrived.

"In any event, sir, these orders were drafted in ignorance of certain critical data."

"And what might that be, Colonel?" The general's voice sounded as if he was getting interested in spite of himself.

O'Neil described how he'd found the StarGate before he'd just set off for Earth. "We can't be sure it was the same way when the cats attacked—all the technicians were killed in the final assault. But you can see the implication."

"If the settings for Earth were there, just slightly off—the enemy would know where we come from." The weariness had abruptly vanished from General West's voice. "This bears further investigation, Colonel. Talk to the technicians at Creek Mountain, and relay your findings to me." The general hesitated. "After that, I'm afraid you'll have to return to Ballas and carry out your orders. I can't rescind them."

"Understood, sir," O'Neil replied. "But if the political situation changes, I'd like to make a suggestion regarding the most ready reinforcements—the Special Operations Capable Marine Expeditionary Unit now training at Pendleton."

"The unit incorporating Major Kawalsky and the Space Marines." The colonel could almost hear West nodding on the other end of the line. "I don't know that they'd be able to take most of their air assets—"

"But man for man, I think that MEU would be the best equipped to handle the cats."

"Your recommendation will be taken under advisement, Colonel," General West promised. "Now talk to those technicians."

"Wrench" Stillson, the noncom in charge of the present shift of technicians, looked a little anxious when the colonel asked to talk to him.

"Sir, I got no idea why the materiel you requested hasn't come through," the sergeant said. "But if they told you it was because of problems with the Chute here, they were lying."

O'Neil shook his head at the pervasiveness of the marine grapevine, and explained what he was looking for.

Stillson shrugged. "I know some guys were doing it from the day we were on Abydos. With only one destination to dial up, why not leave the setting a red cun—er, just a fraction out of alignment." The man actually blushed at his vulgar slip.

"When big brass is going through, or the press is around, they'd go the whole nine yards, make it as dramatic as hell. Otherwise, quick and easy."

"It doesn't sound as though that's the way you do things, Sergeant," O'Neil said.

"Screwing around like that is fine if you've only got one destination," Stillson said. "But sooner or later we're gonna have people on a lot of planets. I'm no expert on what's inside the StarGates, but I'm a damned good mechanic. I want to see what wear and tear happens to the stuff we added—the motors and stuff for swinging those rings around. Better to know what goes wrong now than to end up with downtime in a situation where we can't afford it."

O'Neil nodded. "I almost wish we had you on our side of the gate, Sergeant."

Then again, he thought, maybe I should be glad we didn't. That particular carelessness may be the only reason we don't abandon Ballas.

"Cheeser" Dixon did not want to hear anything that General West had to say. He was conveniently—inconveniently—unavailable whenever his subordinate tried to contact him. But West had battled in the bureaucratic trenches before. He prepared a memorandum for record, with copies to several pertinent members of the Joint Chiefs' support staff. He also called whatever contacts he had upstairs.

It was called going over a superior officer's head, and it usually had repercussions that at best would be considered deleterious to one's career.

Oddly enough, West felt somehow better when he finished his preparations. Maybe he'd end up with the reputation of being a loose cannon in his old age. But at least now he felt as though he were firing in the right direction.

The order to present himself at General Dixon's office came with gratifying speed after the memorandum was released. Apparently, Cheese Dick could always fit in a little time to castigate an officer who intrigued against him.

Dixon's jowls were as red as turkey wattles as he confronted West, a demonstration of one of his famous rages—aimed only at those further down the line from Dixon's position.

"You dare to buck along this—this bovine scatology—on your own hook, circumventing the chain of command . . ."

"Sir, I attempted to contact you, stating on all occasions that it was urgent. You were not available—"

"Don't try to quote regulations at me! You are in deep kimchi here. Why you thought broadcasting your little quibbles—"

"Not so little, sir. I'm suggesting that the enemy on Ballas has acquired the StarGate coordinates for Earth."

Stated so baldly, it had the effect of a glass of cold water in Dixon's face. "What do you mean?"

West explained the custom of presetting the StarGate just slightly out of alignment, and how widespread it was among the tech community.

"But—but those idiots! To leave such sensitive information—"

"Up to this moment, it wasn't sensitive, sir. Our enemies in Ra's empire have always known the coordinate setup for Earth." West leaned forward. "So you see, sir, the situation has changed from the assumptions you'd initially made. We don't know where the cats came from, but they *might* know where we come from. We can't be sure, since the Ballas technicians died in the cat attack, and the Star-Gate has been operated since then. But it might be preferable to offer the enemy two potential battlefields instead of leaving Earth as the only target."

Jack O'Neil hoped that West would be able to pitch the bombshell he'd handed him where it would do the most good. In the meantime, however, he had orders to follow, and an evacuation to arrange, even if he hoped it would be canceled.

Rumint—rumor intelligence—had to be flying among the marines, but he was not going to show the orders—and reveal the Joint Chiefs as a bunch of horses' asses—unless he had no other alternative.

If the evacuation didn't come to pass, let the men think it was only a test.

He sat in his office as the preparations went on, waiting, hoping, *praying* for word that the orders had been rescinded.

"Sir!" The radio operator broke into his thoughts. "Report from Basilone Actual." That was Halloran and his guard command. "They've received something through the StarGate, and they think you should get over there ASAP."

O'Neil recognized the crate as soon as he arrived in the StarGate chamber. Both he and West had hoped for a little maneuvering room, waiting for the "nuclear demolition device" to arrive. But apparently, some genius had opened the vault right away.

No more putting off the unpalatable moment. They were expected to be moving out as soon as the improbable-looking weapon inside that big box was set up.

With a sigh O'Neil turned to Halloran, giving the orders for the standard demolition charges to be laid.

He himself would take care of the nuke.

But first he had a question that needed to be answered.

"Guess I can't complain," Feretti said to Daniel, a grin crossing his usually dour face like a lightning flash—there and gone again. "I'm the only one in this joint with a blond nurse."

Laughing, Daniel scraped up another spoonful of gruel. "Yeah. Too bad it's a male nurse, though."

Feretti's good humor abruptly disappeared. "They're pulling us out of here, you know." His voice lowered. "The rest of the jarheads, they think it's some kind of efficiency test, or that the colonel is just trying to keep the edge on them after that scrap with the cats." He shook his head. "But you and I know the colonel. He doesn't play those games. If he's got people cleaning up contingencies for an evacuation, it's because somebody told him to evacuate."

"Nobody's mentioned anything to me, or Sha'uri"—Daniel glanced over to where she was working in the improvised hospital—"or to Kasuf."

"This thing has got political written all over it," Feretti said. "People in Washington are worried enough that Ra's empire is pissed with us. They don't need trouble with a bunch of cats."

He stirred painfully on the cot. "If they leave here, though, they're also going to take a pass on the stuff I found under the hill. So it's going to be up to you to get it. You've got the degree in that ancient stuff. They have no idea what they're leaving behind! There's a whole floor full of technology lying there. And the pictures on the walls, they're incredible! I think you could learn a lot about the old guys who built the place—about the cats, too."

In spite of himself, the archaeologist in Daniel Jackson stirred at these words. The chance to understand the race that had spawned Ra, who in turn had planted civilization on Earth . . .

"Tell me about them," he said.

"I saw—"

Feretti suddenly broke off, looking beyond Daniel's shoulder. "Colonel!"

Jack O'Neil stepped into the tent full of wounded, smiling down at the patient. "At ease, Feretti."

"What's the real story on this evacuation, sir?"

The colonel glanced from Feretti to Daniel. "Guess there was no hope of trying to fool *you*, Lieutenant. Even flat on your back, you see more than most of the people around here."

He sighed. "Yes, we've been ordered to pull out. I've been fighting it, and so has General West. But events have forced our hand."

O'Neil leaned closer, making his voice very soft. "I've also been ordered to destroy the StarGate."

"And cut us off permanently." Daniel barely whispered the words. What Imiseba had tried, and the cats inadvertently had stopped, would come to pass anyway—*because* of the cats.

His head was spinning at the irony.

"There's a certain amount of weasel wording in my orders," O'Neil went on. "I'm supposed to evacuate all U.S. personnel and 'assets.' "

"What's that supposed to mean?" Daniel asked bitterly. "Your rations?"

The colonel shook his head. "I'm leaving all our food and as much useful material as I can." His smile was bitter. "What are they going to do? Knock points off my next evaluation?"

But O'Neil's eyes were grim. He knew how bad the winter could get if the colony didn't get a crop in.

Daniel could only nod in thanks.

"That's not the reason I had to talk to you, though," the colonel went on. "That 'assets' line was put in on purpose, I think, by the fine hand of General West. If the local commander had a creative bent . . . it could be stretched to include you, Jackson."

"I think that would be the first time you ever considered me an asset, Colonel," Daniel quipped. But he was just moving his mouth to cover the sudden roil of emotion running through him.

Things were quiet now, but the troubles of the last few months showed that many—if not most—of the Abydans considered him an outsider. Keeping on here would mean he'd be the lone Urt-man, the one to be blamed, the extra mouth to feed.

And, a cold voice in the back of his head advised him, a target for a knife in the back from Imiseba and his pals.

Or he could go back home .

Unbidden, the image of the sparsely furnished Washington apartment where he'd squatted came to his mind's eye, his seedy digs over the service station out in California . . .

"I hate to press you, Professor," O'Neil said. "But I need an answer quickly. "Is it 'I go,' or 'I stay'?"

Daniel glanced toward Sha'uri at the other end of the tent and found there wasn't a need to debate at all.

"I stay," he said simply.

"We all stay," a familiar voice said from behind them.

Jackson, O'Neil, and Feretti all stared at the man

who'd joined them—another alumnus of the first venture on Abydos.

Kawalsky had a deep tan, a big grin, and a major's oak leaves on his woodland BDUs.

"Just came through the StarGate, with new orders for you, Colonel, and to report as the advance guard for the 371st SOC MEU. They're chopping us from Pendleton to Creek Mountain, and we should be coming through shortly. We're here to fight your cats for you."

He hesitated for a moment. "I told Lieutenant Halloran to put aside that box I found by the StarGate when I came through. If it's what I think it is, I don't want it to affect the morale of my men as they come through."

O'Neil rose from beside Feretti's cot. "Then welcome to B.T.O."

"What the hell is that?" Daniel wanted to know.

"Ballas theater of operations." O'Neil turned to Kawalsky. "Let's liaise, Major. We're going to have to find someplace to put you and the rest of . . . your men."

The command tent was already hopping by the time they got there, thanks to radio messages from the StarGate pyramid. Personnel and supplies were already coming through.

"Send a message that fuel and food should be given highest priority. We've got no gas pumps here—so everything mechanized will be dependent on the fuel that comes over with it. As for the extra rations .. well, they'll be going to the people who live here. We're going to need the fields they're trying to plant for a motor pool and landing area for any choppers that will be coming in."

He glanced at Kawalsky. "How many of those do you expect?"

"Eleven for sure—eight Cobra gunships and three Huey command and control choppers," Kawalsky replied. "We know they can fit through the StarGate. Our big transports—the Super Stallions—can't. As for the smaller transports—the Sea Knights—they can wait for a second wave. Colonel Gunther, our commander, wants to get the fighting end of the unit through first."

The major gave a grim smile. "He figures we won't be going too far to look for a fight. It'll all be happening around the StarGate."

"What kind of strength can we expect?" O'Neil asked.

"You've heard about the air component. On the ground we've got a reinforced battalion landing team—about 1,200 officers and men. One armored platoon—four Abrams tanks—a battery of six 155mm howitzers, a light-armored recon platoon. Four of the light-armored vehicles have had their cannon replaced with the light artillery revision of the blast-rifle. And one of the leg rifle companies—the Experimental Energy-Weapon Command—is my headache.

One hundred fifty bad guys armed with blast-rifles, who call themselves the Space Marines."

The next hours became chaotic as O'Neil's command switched from preparing to pull out to hosting reinforcements more than ten times their number. The two commanders met, and O'Neil had to admit that Colonel Gunther was at least trying to be gracious for a man routed out of normal operations and forced into an emergency deployment of a kind never before executed—or even planned for.

O'Neil had gotten his wish for reinforcements. He just hoped the line of command wouldn't end up too tangled, and trip them all up.

At least General West's logistical arrangements, the prepositioning of fuel, food, and ammunition close to the StarGate, had paid off. The lieutenant colonel in charge of the 371st's service support group found himself with a larger ad hoc command than he'd ever had before.

Now was the time for diplomacy. O'Neil introduced Colonel Gunther to the Abydan leadership—Kasuf and Skaara, Sha'uri and Daniel.

"The government has made a commitment," Gunther said.

"Yeah, to fight as much as possible in somebody else's backyard," Daniel said.

That earned him a hard look from the MEU commander.

"I'm not knocking you or your troops, Colonel,"

Daniel apologized. "I'm glad to see them—considering the alternatives. And God knows, given the land-to-people ratio around here, we probably have lots of room for a good fight. The problem is, it's going to be damned hard to plant a colony with a war going on all around us."

"Point taken, Professor," Gunther replied. "That's why I've been authorized to offer transport for the Abydan—rather, the Ballas inhabitants—back to Earth as soon as my full command has transited."

Sounds as though West succeeded in shaming the powers that be into acting like human beings, O'Neil thought in surprise.

"You'll have at least a day to prepare," Gunther went on. "We're still expecting the second wave for my command, additional air-transport capacity, and more of the logistical tail—"

His explanation was lost as the command post's radio section suddenly went mad with incoming calls.

O'Neill didn't need to hear the reports, however. The snarl of riflery, the hammer of automatic weapons—but worst of all, the crash of blast-bolts coming from the StarGate pyramid told him all he had to know.

The window of opportunity to bring in supplies or bring out noncombatants had closed.

Whatever happened now, they were in for the duration.

* * *

STARGATE: RECONNAISSANCE

Earth's StarGate facility at Creek Mountain was even a greater madhouse than it had been for the last eight hours. A new shift was supposed to be taking the floor, but the present workers were being held on as well—orders from on high.

The source of those orders, General W.O. West, paced the silo floor—or perhaps the better description would be "stalked." Ever since his arrival—as a single passenger on an unscheduled jet—he had been directing a baleful eye at anyone unfortunate enough to be guilty of delaying the flood of men and materiel heading for Ballas.

West was by no means a logistics officer. But he'd spent his entire career coming up with answers— often unorthodox—for problems. And the current situation spelled problem with a capital P.

Rather than disassembling the helicopters in the airpower component of the 371st SCO MEU, he'd had one of the elevators servicing the silo removed and replaced with a winch. The Cobra gunships had been jackassed through. Now he was already at work on the second wave of reinforcements—the lighter air-transport units for the 371st, additional fuel, supplies, and ammunition.

West had a pessimistic intuition that his people on Ballas would need lots and lots of ammunition.

The first Sea Knight helicopter was actually on the silo floor, its woodland camouflage paint job looking completely foreign in this world of concrete and high technology.

The rotors on the big Bullfrog chopper sitting on the lintel of the Gate were folded together, a typical marine trick to save as much room as possible aboard aircraft carriers. West was most appreciative. That capability had made it considerably easier to get the copter to the StarGate.

But the Bullfrog wasn't going *through* the StarGate. West stormed over to the operating console to see what the hold-up was about.

The newly arrived technician in charge merely shrugged. "We've got the coordinates lined up, the chevrons are on, and power's being drawn," he reported. "We're just not making the connection." The young man grinned. "If this were a phone, I'd say we were getting a busy signal."

The people who'd already seen the general's earlier ramrodding tried to duck for cover, but the expected explosion never came.

General West merely went pale, and his eyes seemed to darken. He glanced off to the periphery of the silo, where truck exhaust filled the air with fumes—loads of supplies, possibly vital, the delivery of which seemingly had been overtaken by events.

"Then say a prayer for our people on Ballas," the general finally said. "If it's busy here, it means they're a hell of a lot busier over there."

He went in search of a secure phone, and contacted J. Caesar Dixon in Washington. "We've lost communication with our troops on Ballas. Which either means the StarGate is down, or hostile forces are in possession."

On the other end of the line, Dixon's voice began to gibber. "But those people were sent out as a deterrent—we didn't anticipate—"

West's worst suspicions were verified. "Sir, if those men were simply sent to show the flag, it wasn't simply the wrong message to send to these aliens, but an incomprehensible one. They don't know what Americans, or humans in general, stand for. All they really know is that when they attacked the humans on Ballas, the humans shot back."

He was sincerely glad that besides the flags in the expeditionary unit's hands, there were also weapons. Often enough in history, trained soldiers and their weapons had created foreign policy. The closed StarGate reduced the micro-managers in Washington to the status of their forebears two centuries ago.

Whatever the results, by the time we hear about them, it's a fait accompli, West thought.

From the gobbling noises over the phone, Dixon hadn't been able to think about the situation at all.

"General," West finally said, "we can't reinforce our people on Dallas, and we certainly can't recall them. All we can do is hope that they're acting as something more than speed bumps for an alien invasion."

"This is a disaster," Dixon cried. "I'm not sure we have the political will—"

West had heard those words often enough—always in bad circumstances. Wars abandoned because of unpopularity—and more important, people who had fought and suffered beside American forces left to their own devices. It was the roll call of the twentieth century—get a bloody nose and try appeasement.

"Then we'd better find the political will," West replied. "The StarGate and Daniel Jackson's coordinates gave the human race the greatest opportunity since speech. But if we don't protect the people we send out, we concede all those potential benefits to the cats."

He took a deep breath. "And we on Earth may as well start practicing the arts of proper submission, because soon enough the cats will be after us, too. Get that across to the Chiefs, the President, and the Congress. When we faced Hathor, we were fighting a dangerous tyrant, but one that was at least following human tendencies. With these aliens—" West broke off. "Do you have a cat, General?"

"My daughter has one," Dixon replied.

"Have you ever seen a cat play with a wounded bird?"

Draft of a proposed resolution presented to an emergency joint session of the Congress of the United States:

Whereas units of an unknown, nonhuman entity or government have terminated communications between Earth and the humans presently on the planet Ballas, creating a serious threat to peaceful relations;

Whereas this blockade is part of a deliberate and

systematic campaign of surveillance and aggression by armed units of the abovementioned alien entity against civilian colonists and military units rendering assistance;

Whereas the United States is assisting the former people of Abydos to establish a new home, and has no territorial, military, or political ambitions on this planet, but only wishes that the Abydan people be left alone to work out their own destinies: Now, therefore, be it

Resolved by the Senate and House of Representatives of the United States of America in Congress assembled, That the Congress approves and supports the determination of the President, as Commander-in-Chief, to take all measures necessary to repel any armed attack against forces of the United States and to prevent further aggression against the civilian colonists.

SECTION TWO. The United States regards as vital to its national interest, to the interests of the people of Earth, and for the other worlds where humans live, to maintain the peace and freedom of those humans currently established on the world of Ballas. Consonant with the Constitution of the United States and the Charter of the United Nations, and in recognition of the obligations incurred by the sufferings of the Abydan people, the United States is prepared, as the President determines, to take all necessary steps, including the use of armed force, to assist the humans on Ballas to protect their freedom.

SECTION 3: This resolution shall expire when the

President shall determine that the peace and security of the planet Ballas is reasonably assured by appropriate protocol or treaty, except that it may be terminated earlier by concurrent resolution of the Congress.

General West crumpled the fax copy of the passed resolution in his hands. "And may God have mercy on us all," he muttered, staring at the now dormant StarGate. "Come home safe, boys."